# MONSTROSITY

## TIM CURRAN

SEVERED PRESS
HOBART TASMANIA

# MONSTROSITY

1

Frank tried to hang on as long as possible, but when the walls started caving-in and coils of that white, blubbery foulness seeped through like pale fingers of wood rot, he knew they had to leave. He got the kids out to the barn and sat them down as he listened to the house—the house he had built fifteen years before—being reduced to kindling as what was beneath pushed itself up into the moonlight.

He sat Jasmine and Jerrod on hay bales and looked into their dark, wet eyes. "Things are happening tonight," he said. "I wish I could explain it to you in a way that would make sense, but what's happening here is happening everywhere."

"It's like an earthquake," Jasmine said, either a statement or a question and maybe both.

"No," Jerrod said. "It's the stories people told. Things down under the ground. Things rising up." He looked at Frank accusingly. "The ones you said weren't true."

And he had said that, hadn't he? Every time they came from school or a sleepover with crazy tales of monsters and horrors in the night, he always told them it was all make-believe, fantasy. And now, faced with the reality of it, he had to wonder if he'd done that so maybe he'd believe it himself.

*Janet would have wanted it that way. Just keep that in mind.*

Yes, he was only doing what a good parent would do. The things a man thought his wife would want. He could do no more.

"We're going to have to go out there again," he told them.

Their faces were grim and set at the idea. They reminded him of the cold stone faces of cemetery angels. Childhood had been scrubbed free. There was a terrible age in their eyes and around their mouths.

"But if that stuff starts coming out of the ground…what will we do?" Jasmine said.

"You let me handle that," he told them.

Jerrod folded his arms. "Dad knows what he's doing. Quit complaining."

There were tears in Jasmine's eyes. "But I'm scared."

Frank brushed his calloused hand against her face. "It's okay to be scared. I'm scared, too. Being scared will keep us safe."

He only wished he could believe it.

2

It took some doing, but he got them outside and into the field. The corn had long been harvested, and the field was flat and ugly, furrowed and set with broken corn stalks. The moonlight was dull yellow like dirty chrome, the mist bone-thin as it played through the apple orchard in the distance. It made the trees look like craggy hands breaking the mold of graves.

Frank waited there, his heart thumping in his chest, his children clutched to him.

*You will not get them. I won't let you. You better know that.*

Behind them, the rest of the farmhouse fell. He would not let the children look back and see it. He only looked himself because he needed to say good-bye to all that he had known. In the surreal glow of the moon, he saw things like creeping vines or maybe Jack's beanstalk push up through the wreckage, opening cups and buds like night-blooming orchids.

The children shivered to either side of him. He held them all that much tighter, whispering to them that he would let nothing happen to them. Did they believe it? He hoped so. He had never meant anything so much in his life. He told them to wait in the shadows of the little hollow while he scouted ahead. He had the blue-steel .45 in his fist. Whatever was out there, they had better goddamn well know that he knew how to use it.

Maybe he had waited too long, thinking it would pass.

If he had pulled out two days ago, he could have taken the truck and been over the state line into Michigan or even Minnesota or Illinois, to one of the camps the National Guard ran. People said you could be safe at those places. But Frank doubted it. He doubted there was safety anywhere. The world had gone stark, raving mad. Besides, it was no easy thing to give up the land you had worked and sweated for. In the dark soil ran his own blood.

So he had waited, hoping it would all pass.

But it had only gotten worse, and now they were in a real fix. The farmhouse was destroyed, the truck tumbled into some deep, dark hole far below.

Enough of that. The children. They were all that mattered now. He had to get them somewhere safe even if he didn't know where that was.

In the distance, he knew, was Shinneman's farm.

That's where they would go. Carl's truck might still be there. Yes. That's how they would escape—line of sight. First to Shinneman's, then to whatever was beyond.

He gathered up the kids. "Now," he said. "Follow me."

3

They moved carefully in the darkness. Frank led them forward, picking his way through meadows. Cold stars looked down from above. The night was so silent it was as if it were holding its breath. It was like a hunted animal, he figured, one that dares make no sound in case something might hear it. Crazy thinking on a crazy night. He tried to suppress it in his mind because he could not come apart at the seams, he could not lose his way now. The children were counting on him, and he was counting on himself to get them to safety.

He only hoped he was doing the right thing.

All his life, he had second-guessed himself and doubted himself. Physically, he was a big man, square-shouldered, well-muscled, tanned and callused from a life spent in the sun, raising crops and mending fences, tending livestock and working on machinery. But mentally, he always worried. Worried that the potatoes or corn, soybeans or rye wouldn't come in. Worried that he'd lose the farm that had been in his family line for five generations of Bowmans. That he would let his family down. That he would make some fool mistake and they would pay for it.

*You're smarter than you give yourself credit for,* Janet said many times as his face creased with doubt. *You're good and you'll take care of us. I know you will. Now hold me and let me smell the outdoors on you.*

Even now, on this night, that made him smile. His old Carhartt jacket smelled the way she liked it—faintly of gasoline and diesel fuel, hydraulic grease and hay, good black Wisconsin soil and a hint of manure. It was a real, honest smell she had told him more than once, and he had believed her.

*Trust in myself,* he thought then as they crossed a field of straw-yellow grasses. *I must trust in myself and my instincts.*

By his figuring, Carl Shinneman's farm was about three miles by road. But if they cut through the boonies, they could easily cut a mile off of that.

They walked on for another twenty minutes and then he spotted the river. When Jasmine and Jerrod commented on it, he shushed them immediately. Quiet was so very important now. They followed the river until they reached an old footbridge that Frank knew his family had put up many, many years ago. It had spanned the Cane River for at least eighty years and probably closer to a hundred. It had been washed away in spring floods, fallen under its own weight once, and burned up in a freak lightning strike another time. But always, a Bowman rebuilt it.

"Okay," he said to the kids. "Wait here. I'll cross and make sure it's okay."

Jasmine shook her head. "No, no, Papa! Don't leave us alone."

Frank went down on one knee before her, brushing the tousled dark hair from her face. "I have to, Duck. I want to make sure it's safe. You'll be fine with Jerrod. I'll only be gone two minutes."

She didn't like it, but she knew better than to argue. Janet had taught her that. You didn't argue with adults…at least, not so they'd hear.

He kissed her soft cheek and felt something in his heart go loose like warm butter. That girl. That darn girl. She had him wrapped around her finger and she knew it.

"Go ahead, Dad," Jerrod said. "I got this."

Frank smiled, set his knapsack down, and stepped through the bushes to the footbridge, his heart beginning to pound.

4

He moved slowly over the bridge and saw there was no danger, but knew that at any moment the worst could happen. The river was running clear, bubbling and foaming amongst the rocks. Farther down, he knew, past the bend were good trout pools created by deadfalls and stranded logs. He used to fish them with his old man. Sunday summer afternoons well-spent. The bridge reminded him of Janet. It made him ache inside for her. The first time they had made love was in the meadow below. Under the moonlight, the air smelling of clover and honeysuckle, he had taken her in his arms and laid her down in the grass with only the chirping crickets as witnesses.

*Enough*, he told himself.

Now was not the time.

He crossed the bridge quickly and studied the footpath beyond that cut through a stand of wild blackberry bushes and into the forest. He didn't like leaving the kids, but he had to be sure it was safe ahead. They were his cargo and they were precious. He moved down the path amongst the blackberry bushes, thorns scraping against the sleeves of his coat.

He stopped.

He listened.

There was no sound. Not a night bird crying out in the woods or even a frog or an insect. There was something terribly disturbing about that. He followed the path until he was through the stand of bushes and the field ended at the woods. He squatted there, waiting. After a minute or two, he moved closer to the tree line. Still no sounds. He searched the footpath until he found a stone. He tossed it out amongst the trees. It bounced off a tree trunk and skidded into the loam. Nothing. The noise stirred up nothing.

He jogged back to the bridge and across it, and for one moment, a nameless panic sent white needles into his belly because he didn't see the kids. Then Jerrod and Jasmine came out from behind a bush. Jerrod had hidden them while he was away. Good thinking.

"It's all right," he said. "Let's go."

## 5

As they crossed the bridge, Jasmine tugged at his sleeve. "Papa? Are the fish sleeping right now?"

"Yes," he told her. "They're sleeping."

He got them into the blackberry bushes where they had to walk single-file because of the thorns. Jasmine said something to Jerrod and he wisely shushed her. Then they were in the field, following the path through the trees.

"Dad, look," Jerrod said.

In the moonlight, Frank saw what looked like a great jagged crack in the earth that had to be a dozen feet across. It cut through the woods and disappeared in the darkness. Whatever had opened it up, it took out dozens of trees, collapsing them into a jackstraw deadfall. The moonlight showed him glistening white globs at the edges of the crack like infected pus seeping from a wound. He knew what left it. The foulness had oozed from the earth, leaving bits of itself behind, bits of tissue.

"Come on," he said.

The kids didn't ask questions, and he was glad of that because he did not feel like lying to them. As they moved deeper into the forest, amongst the hemlock, oak, and jackpine, he saw something in the rays of moonlight that struggled between the branches. It looked like snow. Snow falling. But it was too early for that yet, even this far north.

"Wait here," he told Jerrod.

He followed the path in the dimness, amongst the spoking black shadows, the dips and hollows and rocky outcroppings. He brushed against a low scrub pine, and its branches broke apart as if they were made of glass. He didn't like it. The beams of moonlight were strongest just ahead. He stopped near to them, and he could feel the flakes falling down on him. Not snow, of course, but something more like cigarette ash. A down of it fell over him. He pulled the flashlight from his pocket and scanned the beam about. Yes, there were nearly two inches of ash on the ground. The beam was filled with spinning gray flakes. The trees around him looked odd, weathered, and leaning. Skeletal even.

"Something awful happened here," he said under his breath.

He stepped over to what looked to be a very common beech tree. He played the light over it. Its bark was split open in places, cracked deeply as if it had been worried by woodpeckers and bark beetles for many, many seasons, only it appeared as if the inner bark and sapwood were dark. There were no leaves on the tree. He tapped it with the barrel of the flashlight, and the bark crumbled and fell to the ground. He did it again and more desiccated bark

6

fell free. He put his hand on it. The tree was old, dead, and dry. Its limbs snapped free with hardly any exertion. He gave it a kick and limbs fell from high above, some of them quite large, just missing him. He pushed it and it fell right over, crashing into other trees, all of them shattering and breaking apart, a cloud of gray flakes rising into the air before settling down.

He checked the other trees.

They were all cracked open like desert soil. Bark and limbs went to a gritty gray powder in his hands. Using his knife, he tried to peel the bark and get at the living tissue beneath. But it was dried out and dark, too. Even the ground shrubs and bushes were dead. The entire forest was like that. Whatever had passed here, it had sucked the life out of everything. The flakes falling in the moonlight beams were bits of the forest. It was scaling away like dead skin.

## 6

He went back and got the kids and led them through the flaking forest before he could change his mind. They could hear the mummified trees cracking apart and dropping limbs, pitching right over deeper in the woods. Even the grasses and loam underfoot had gone dry and crackly. In a few days or a week, the forest would be a rubble pile of bones, an ossuary of dry, pitted things.

Frank's greatest fear was that there would be no end to the gray zone of death, but gradually, it petered out and he felt a great relief. The idea that the deadness was consuming the living earth inch by inch was more than a little terrifying. But finally, they were free. They followed a hillside out of the graveyard forest and stood there in the moonlight, brushing the gray flakes from each other.

"It's only about twenty minutes to the farm now," he told the kids.

"My feet are dying," Jasmine said.

Frank scooped her up and let her ride on his shoulders. That made her happy, and if she was happy, he was happy. Jerrod just shook his head and muttered, *"Girls."*

*Yes, girls,* Frank thought, smiling.

But the smile did not last because in the distance there was a droning choir like hundreds and hundreds of locusts. The sound grew louder and louder until it was like the distant roaring of a jet engine, and then it faded and there was a rumbling that shook the earth and then nothing.

"Papa...what was that?" Jasmine asked and he could feel her shivering on his shoulders.

"I don't know. But I plan on giving it a wide berth."

More determined than ever to get them to safety, he moved on down the footpath, feeling danger pushing in at them out of the night.

## 7

They walked on, and Frank kept them clutched tightly to him like precious jewels. They were what his life was about and he couldn't lose them. Whatever else happened—and he suspected many things would—he could not lose them. Whenever he began to feel glum or depressed about abandoning Bowman land that had been worked by so many generations of hands, sweated and toiled over, he told himself that land was just land and dirt was just dirt. His real, irreplaceable treasures walked at his side (or rode on his shoulders).

## 8

It was hard to know these days what was right and what was wrong, what was truth and what was fiction. Instinct and common sense were more important now than ever. For so many years, movies and TV shows had warned of invasions from outside. Whether that was Martians or communists or terror cells, it didn't really matter: it always came from beyond. So when the real invasion came from below, nobody was prepared, and mainly because they found it hard to believe.

And you couldn't really blame them.

The first hints that something exceedingly strange was going on appeared on the Internet and in the tabloids. But since everyone knew those particular sources were 90% bullshit, they ignored it all. They laughed at tales of immense, monstrous things traversing the night and the grainy photos of the huge prints they left behind.

When images of the creatures themselves appeared, they were usually taken with IR lenses (like your average ghost-hunting show) at abstract angles so that they could have been trees or water towers...or Godzilla and Rodan for that matter.

By the time the legitimate press started paying attention, things were quickly escalating out of control. That's when the authorities got involved. Frank could remember high, randy tales of entire villages being emptied in the Midwest and New England and towns being completely destroyed down south and out west. But despite all the fuss in the media, he and the other farmers in the Cane River basin paid very little attention, and when they did, they didn't take any of it seriously. At least, not on the surface. Down deep in the welling darkness of their souls, maybe it was a different matter. *Giant monsters. Jesus H. Christ, of all the ridiculous, fool, half-baked, comic book bullshit.* Those were Frank's exact words and they mirrored the general consensus.

Then one day, Bobby Welch called and said something was after his sheep. He wouldn't say what it was exactly, only that he needed help badly. He needed men with guns in their hands that would help him fight for his herd. Frank showed with a dozen others, everyone from Carl Shinneman and his boys to Doug Pelsap down the road and the Van Deusan brothers. Even George Beagle came, and for once, he was sober. By the time they got there, Bobby was ranting and raving, saying how the sheriff was treating him like some little old lady that was afraid of the dark.

And those gathered wondered if that wasn't too far from the truth.

Then they heard a cry split open the warm summer air.

It was like nothing anyone had ever heard before.

It sounded (as Reg Van Deusan said later) like about a dozen wildcats getting the hides peeled off them at the same time.

The group of men, posse if you like, jumped in the box of Bobby's pickup, taking a rough and bouncing trip out to the north pasture near Frenchman's Pond where his flock was feeding on the summer-rich sweetgrass. Or should have been...except, something was feeding on *them.* What that was, was really hard to say because it seemed to be many things and nothing particular at the same time.

Doug Pelsap, always itching for a good fight, crept through the grass like a buffalo hunter (even though—as he claimed later—he was so scared that it felt like his ass was trying to crawl up his spine). He got within range and put three hollow-tip rounds from his 30-06 into the beast, which it completely ignored. Being that it was somewhat larger than your average bull elephant, it wasn't too surprising.

"My goddamn flock!" Bobby was shrieking. "Look what it did to my goddamn flock!"

It was an atrocity, that was for sure.

Bobby had fifty head out in the north pasture and the majority of them had been torn in half like paper dollies...crushed, beheaded, and in several instances, driven head-first into the ground like locust poles. The beast was lounging among them, fat and overfed, reminding the posse of a chubby boy that had emptied out a box of sweets and was taking his time unwrapping them one by one.

"We better get gone before it notices us," Carl Shinneman suggested.

But no one was moving.

They just stood there, watching the creature as it ate. It was an awful sight. Apparently, it didn't care for the woolly hides of the sheep because it peeled them like taffy in wax paper before it stuffed them into its mouth. The sound of it feeding was appalling—chewing and sucking, crunching and gnawing.

"We gotta kill it!" Bobby told them. "You boys got guns! Use 'em already!"

"Like hell," George Beagle said. "Doug already tried. We piss that thing off, it'll roll right over us."

With that, he retreated along with the Van Deusan brothers.

"Awww! Come on! That's my livelihood out there!" Bobby cried.

They all felt for him because they'd all been on the brink of financial disaster more than once. That was the reality of farming, hand to mouth, strictly hand to mouth. But as George Beagle had pointed out, Doug Pelsap had already pumped three slugs into it, and all the creature did was shudder as if it had a bad case of gas. And even if you were suicidal enough to do some shooting, what were you supposed to aim *at?* Was that bobbing sphere at the top with the crest of spikes really a head? Were those spurred limbs arms? Was that shivering central mass actually a body? And if so, where might its heart be and did it have only one? What about those snakelike tendrils coiling in the grass? Were they tails of a sort or something more along the lines of the tentacles of a deep-sea squid? Nobody really knew and nobody honestly wanted to.

"Damn cockatrice," Bobby muttered as if maybe he'd seen one before.

Nobody knew what a cockatrice was, but when Frank Googled it later, he discovered it was a sort of mythical dragon with the head of a rooster. What they saw in the north pasture was certainly no cockatrice. Before he got the hell out of Dodge, Reg Van Deusan mused that it looked like something from the late, late show or maybe from *Creature Features* when he was a kid. There was logic in the latter because what they saw that day was a little of *Yog, Monster from Space* and *The Green Slime,* and a whole lot of *The Blob* and *The Monster That Challenged the World.*

So despite Bobby's vehement protests, they withdrew.

An hour later, they had the sheriff out there. One look at what was inhabiting the north pasture and he got on the horn with the National Guard. They came equipped with a Javelin anti-tank missile. A split second after they fired it, the beast was spread for 300 yards in six different directions.

After that little episode, people started taking things very seriously. The authorities, and particularly Colonel Mathis of the Guard, began talking tough about the Cane River farmers abandoning their spreads before it was too late. Which pretty much showed what he knew about Wisconsin farmers and their lands. Prying them from their ancestral soil was like trying to pluck your thumb free of your hand: it could be done, of course, but not without a lot of bleeding and hurting.

Bottom line was that Frank and the others did not want to leave.

Frank had built his farmhouse on his father's lands and those lands had been Bowman land stretching right back to his great-great grandfather. This is where Janet and he had raised the kids (or got a good start on them). This is where she'd lived and died. It was the only home that Jerrod and Jasmine had ever really known.

And it was the only place that Frank ever *wanted* to know. Besides, just where were they supposed to go? It was happening everywhere, and one place was just as good as another.

Maybe had he not been so stubborn, he could have gotten the kids somewhere safer like one of the Guard camps, but it wasn't easy to abandon his lands.

*I put them in danger, Janet,* he thought then as he moved the children down the footpath into the night. *Forgive me, darling, but I was never as smart as you thought.*

And maybe he wasn't.

Maybe in this life he wasn't a lot of things he should have been. But one thing was for sure: he was going to make amends for that. He was going to get the kids somewhere safe.

Or die trying.

## 9

Not too far from Carl Shinneman's, he began to get a real bad feeling. Whatever it was, it was down deep in his guts where he couldn't shrug it off. It sent icy chilblains into his chest until it felt like he could barely breathe. What it was telling him was that there was danger near, something dark and possibly malefic that was putting them all at risk.

Beyond that, he couldn't get much of a sense of it. Only that whatever form it was taking, they were getting closer and closer to its black beating heart.

They hiked along for a few more minutes, and by then, the bad feeling had become full-blown anxiety. It filled his stomach with a feathery-edged heat that continued to build until he was nearly breathless with a sense of impending doom.

He made the kids stop.

He led them off into the woods and settled them at the base of a big oak.

"Wait here," he said. "Something's up ahead and I have to see what it is."

This time, Jasmine did not argue.

In the past ten minutes or so, she had gone very quiet, as had Jerrod. Something which was uncharacteristic, particularly for her.

Frank firmly believed that they were feeling it, too. Whatever had crawled inside him had now crawled inside them as well.

"I won't be long," he told them, digging the flashlight out of the knapsack.

He was glad he couldn't see their eyes. He imagined they'd be glassy with fear and doubt, possibly even disappointment in him. He didn't look back. He took off at a good clip, feeling his heart thudding in his chest at the idea that he might never see them again.

*Enough,* he thought. *Quit thinking like that.*

## 10

He let his instinct lead him.

He followed the path up a grassy hill, hesitating there like a hunted animal, then continued down through a copse of trees. He emerged from them and paused again. The breeze must have shifted for he became aware of a particularly nauseating stench that he should have smelled long before—an acrid, foul effluvium of burning hair and steaming fat. It was an odor that any farmer would know, he realized, especially one that had had to burn the remains of contaminated livestock. He'd had to do it more than once and it wasn't an odor that you ever really forgot.

"That smell," he said under his breath without realizing he had done so. "God, that smell."

Part of him told him to ignore it, but another part—the human and caring part—would not allow that. He needed to get the kids somewhere safe, but first he had to know. He was certain that it was important.

He found a little clearing and could smell the awful charred stink blowing out at him like the breath of a cannibal. It made his belly cringe as if it were a startled animal. Tense with worry and apprehension, he jogged out there, pausing in the tall, coarse grass. There was no way to be quiet. The grass was dry and it crunched under his boots like straw. If anyone was around, they would know exactly where he was.

Screw it.

He had to find out.

He moved out of the wild grass and saw a gray and splintered tumbledown shack in the moonlight. A good sneeze could have knocked it down. It and the farm beyond, Frank knew, had once belonged to a man named McGee, Chester McGee, but he had been dead many years now, the spread abandoned (but apparently not as abandoned as it should have been). Around the other side, he saw what he somehow knew he must see, and seeing it, was sickened to his core.

*It can't be. It just can't be.*

He clicked on the light. He saw a leaning post with a crossbar nailed to it, the sort of thing you'd bracket a scarecrow to. It was blackened and smoldering as was what was fixed to it with what looked like fence wire. It was small, very small, cremated right down to the skeleton. That the remains belonged to a child, he did not doubt any more than he doubted that it had been offered as some sort of sacrifice.

What other explanation could there possibly be?

He had heard some wild tales from other farmers, things about cults and crazies, but nothing like this. Had people really fallen this far? Had they become this savage and superstitious, this downright fucking medieval in their beliefs? Did they honestly believe that an offering—a *burnt* offering at that—could somehow stem what gripped the world?

He didn't know.

And, dear God, he didn't *want* to know.

## 11

When Frank got back, he told them there was nothing to worry about. He sensed that they did not believe him any more than he believed himself. They were young, yes, but they certainly weren't stupid.

They could have been to Carl Shinneman's farm in a matter of minutes, but he wasn't about to walk the children past the clearing where the remains were still smoldering. He cut off the main path to a secondary deer trail which cut even deeper into the woods along a stream that sidled up within a stone's throw of a frog pond that had been known as Buzzard's Wash when he was a kid. It was more of a small lake that sat in a boggy hollow that filled up each spring with snow meltwater. A muddy, mucky area where dead trees rose from the black waters like posts, it looked much like a prehistoric swamp in the summertime with buzzards perching themselves on stumps. It was the home of bullfrogs and muskrats, cranes and water snakes, as well as some truly monstrous snapping turtles. And mosquitoes. Huge swarms of them patrolled the pond in buzzing, bloodthirsty clouds.

It was, as Frank's mother had often said, a place best left alone.

Frank led on and they came within fifty feet of it. That was plenty close enough. Jasmine remarked on the volume of noise coming from its weed-choked runs. Frank explained that ponds were very active places at night. It was true…but they weren't like this. The peepers and tree frogs were singing with a shrill, almost rhythmic noise that sounded nearly human in tone. The whippoorwills were shrieking with unearthly cries, the bullfrogs croaking at deafening levels. Listening, he heard a great splash that made him draw in a sharp breath. He couldn't say exactly what it was, but it sounded like something about the size of a Holstein calf had jumped into the water.

"Wow!" Jasmine said. "Must be some reeeeeeaaaal big frogs in there!"

Frank laughed, but moved them along that much faster.

*Goddamn nature is going crazy,* he thought.

No, more than crazy—absolutely fucking deranged. After countless years of man dumping his industrial runoff, radioactive byproducts, medical refuse, and toxic waste into landfills, rivers, streams, and the deepest depths of the oceans, nature, weary, diseased, and violated, had returned the favor. The crust of the Earth cracked open like the skin of a leper and what oozed out in white, pulsing globs was something along the lines of a hyper-enriched, mega-nutritive, teratogenic nightmare food. A food that was alive, animate, and aggressive. A food whose cloying honeyed sweetness and blood-smelling richness drew in living things, whether prey or predator, and when they couldn't get to it, it got to *them,* seeping into barns and pens and zoos, hijacking their biochemistry, creating a gluttonous addiction, forcing them to eat it until they were stuffed with it, engorged and infected. Then it began to change them, evolving them, creating hybrid lifeforms, hideous aberrations, and entirely new species of extreme grotesqueness, both plant and animal and sometimes freakish distortions that were both and neither.

Nobody knew exactly what it was.

Nobody knew exactly why it was.

And nobody knew exactly the sort of organic womb it had crept from far, far below.

All they knew was that it was here. A white, creeping horror like a living congealed fat that contaminated any living thing it touched. So far, it had shown no interest in man, but there was a deadly certainty that this was only temporary. For now, though, it was no longer nature that was under siege and on its last legs, but the human race.

The Food, as it was known, was relentless and ever-hungry for genetic material to exploit.

"How much farther?" Jasmine asked.

"Not far now."

Frank had steered them well away from the main path (and what was still burning in the clearing) and it was time to bring them back around. They topped a rise and he could easily see the moonlit countryside before them. The moon looked huge, the fields silvered. Carl Shinneman's farmhouse was just visible in the distance. But between them and it, there was something else, something inexplicable.

Jasmine tugged Frank's hand. "Is that a river, Papa?"

It sure looked like one, but there were no rivers in this direction, he knew. Nothing but a few minor creeks. What he saw was a luminous white ribbon draped over the countryside like an immense snake. He couldn't say exactly how long it was, but it must have been big, real big.

"That sure as heck ain't no river," Jerrod said.

"What then?" Jasmine wanted to know. "A monster?"

It was, under ordinary circumstances, a childlike leap of logic, but now with the way things were, it wasn't so far off the mark. Frank opened his mouth to tell her not to worry, but the words never made it to his lips because that white ribbon—which he was near-certain had to be several hundred feet long—began to move, coiling and writhing obscenely like an earthworm in direct sunlight. The foremost third of it rose up and up, twisting against the sky in some revolting peristaltic dance. It made a high-pitched noise rather like a steam whistle and then squirmed slowly out of sight.

"I'm scared," Jasmine said.

Jerrod sighed. "Of what? It's a hundred miles from here."

"Your brother's right," Frank said. "It's a long, long way from here."

He led them down the rise and off the deer trail. They connected up with the main path soon enough. Ten minutes later, they saw the shadowy bulk of Shinneman's barn. The farmhouse was just beyond.

"We're here," he said.

## 12

The kids were excited because he had told them this is where they would find a vehicle that would get them somewhere safe, but now he wasn't so sure. The farm looked very dark and he did not like that. Carl Shinneman was a wily old cuss, and he might have been keeping the lights off so as not to attract the attention of things in the night, but Frank was not convinced.

In fact, he was feeling more than a little apprehensive as he studied the shadowy farmhouse.

"All right, guys," he said. "Here's how it works. You wait here while I scope things out. If it's all right, I'll come and get you."

"Oh, Papa," Jasmine said in frustration. "I don't like you going away and leaving us."

He laughed. "It'll only be for five or ten minutes, I swear."

Jasmine sighed.

"Just go, Dad," Jerrod told him. "I'll break out the beef jerky."

"Oh, jerky!" Jasmine said with delight.

Jerrod shook his head as he dug in the knapsack. "Kids," he said.

Frank suppressed a smile and went off with the flashlight and .45, refusing to look back.

## 13

He cut across the yard, hiding behind a large ornate bird feeder that was filled with wet leaves. It was one of the decorative touches that Ellen, Carl's wife, had made so the spread looked more like a home than a working farm. She had died eight years before and Carl, broken up inside, had let the feeder go to hell as he had let the wild roses, raspberry bushes, and tulips likewise go to seed, as if his inattention to these things might draw her back to set things right.

Staring at the farmhouse in the moonlight, Frank didn't see anything that immediately concerned him. He decided against going up on the porch to knock on the front door. This was farm country. Friends didn't use the front door; that was for strangers. Friends used the back door because back doors on farmhouses invariably led right into the kitchen where the coffee was brewing in winter and the ice tea was to be had come summer. And it was at the kitchen table that things were hashed out.

Besides, Carl was well into his seventies and notoriously cranky. If he caught someone lurking around the front porch, he might shoot first and ask questions later. The last thing Frank needed was a load of birdshot in the belly.

So he circled around back, every waiting shadow potentially something that might open up and bite him in half. The moonlight was patchy streaming through the branches of the big elms, but there was enough of it so that he saw something which made his breath hitch in his lungs: the entire back of the farmhouse was staved-in.

Frank felt everything inside him sink at once.

He felt dizzy. He felt hopeless. But there was no time for that. He crept closer to the wreckage, clicking on the flashlight. The beam showed him what he already suspected—there was no way in from the back. It was just a pile of wreckage…beams and joists, a shattered outer wall and broken glass, the collapsed back porch looking as if a giant had stepped on it (which might have been true, he realized).

A voice in his head muttered: *Get out of here before what did this comes back.*

That was great advice, but Frank knew he couldn't follow it. Not without ascertaining whether Carl was alive or dead. If there was any chance he might be among the living, then Frank had to look for him. After all, Carl had taken a shine to Janet and him. A friend of Frank's dad, he was always there when they needed something. Frank wasn't about to abandon him now.

He walked around the side of the house.

He found an open window and called, "Carl? Are you in there? It's Frank Bowman."

There was no reply, only an odd sort of tinkling sound like grains of sand falling. That was peculiar. Frank put the .45 on safety and wedged it into the back of his pants, then pulled himself through the window. He landed silently on the floor, praying the house wouldn't come down on top of him. He clicked on his flashlight and got the gun in his hand. He knew the power was out so he didn't bother searching for a switch. He knew the house well. He had spent a lot of time there as an adult and even as a kid. Guiding himself with the flashlight, he stepped out of Ellen's old sewing room, noticing with a twinge of regret that nothing had been changed. Carl had left it as it was, as if maybe she might return to it one day. It made Frank think of Janet and how long she had been gone now. The years were like arrows, he decided. Each one punching in that much deeper until you bled to death.

Out in the hallway, he moved towards the kitchen because it had been Carl's favorite room. He loved to sit in there and read paperback westerns after a long day in the fields while Ellen baked bread and made soups and stews on the old potbelly stove that had belonged to his mother and his mother's mother. Even after Ellen was gone, he still sat in there, surrounded by ghosts, couched in yellow memory.

Frank got within a few feet of where the house was collapsed. "Carl?" he called out. "Are you in there?"

If he was caught in that mess, he was probably dead, but Frank's conscience would not allow him to simply turn away. He went back down the hallway. There was that powdery tinkling sound again like the ceiling of a cave slowly flaking away. He traced it to the front of the house, to the room that Ellen had called the parlor with some humor and Carl had simply referred to as the living room.

Frank saw right away what was making the sound.

Whatever had caved-in the back of the house was the same thing that had destroyed the forest. The parlor was likewise ossified and slowly crumbling apart. He pressed the shaft of the flashlight to the wall and it broke apart. The furniture, the lamps, even the carpet underfoot was dry and cracking.

And that included the figure in the easy chair.

"Oh, Carl," Frank said.

He was split open like termite-ravaged deadwood, slowly going to powder. The most disturbing thing was that he had died lounging in his favorite chair, as if whatever had come into the house had gotten him while he was sleeping or had been so silent that he never heard it coming. Judging from the condition of the kitchen, that seemed pretty unlikely.

Frank wasted no more time.

He found the keys to the truck hanging on the peg in the entry and went out the front way, the floor underfoot seeming to give unpleasantly with each step. Then a quick dash out to the barn. There was the truck, a Dodge Ram pickup. Perfect. He jumped behind the wheel and turned it over. It started right away. For a moment there, he was afraid it wouldn't, that his life was about to play out like some bad horror movie. But he should have known better. Carl was a real stickler for machinery, as most farmers were. His engines were always finely tuned.

Okay.

He drove out of the barn, headlights splashing across the fields and two shadows came running to meet him. He pulled to a stop and the door opened. Jerrod helped Jasmine get up into the cab because it was high. Then, looking cautiously over his shoulder, he tossed in the knapsack and jumped in himself.

"All right," Frank said. "Let's get gone."


14

By his figuring, it would take them a good ninety minutes to make it to the National Guard camp down in Juneau County. That was, if their luck held. It was hard to say what they might run into.

From what he had been hearing, there were a lot of wrecks and abandoned vehicles on the county trunks. Out on Route 7, word had it, it was even worse. So bad that they were using big front-end loaders to push the wrecks onto the shoulders so the traffic could keep moving…something which seemed unbelievable.

For twenty minutes, he drove with the window open, scooping the fresh night air into the cab and feeling for the first time in many hours that they might really have a chance. The moon looked silver over the forests encroaching from either side of the road. He could smell hay and manure, dark soil and green growth, honeysuckle and Evening Primrose, the crisp smell of pines.

And also something else. Something verdant and foul and unnatural.

Jasmine drifted off slowly, talking the entire time. When she hadn't said anything for five minutes, Frank knew she was asleep. She was snug against him and he had his arm around her. He kept his eyes on the road, refusing to sit and stare at her as he often did as she slept, wanting to kiss the top of her head. Jerrod was awake. He was studying the countryside rolling by. There were things on his mind, but he was a typical boy and he would not speak of them. In his silence and unwillingness to express his emotions, Frank could already see the man he was going to be. A man much like himself, good or bad.

As Frank mused, he became aware of an odor sweeping into the cab that was neither sweet nor fresh and certainly not becoming. It smelled, he thought, rather like green decay and moist death. The stench of drainage ditches filled with stagnant water and black sucking mud or compost heaps at high summer. It grew so strong that he quickly rolled up the window.

"What the heck is it, Dad?" Jerrod asked.

But Frank could only shake his head. "I don't know. Something dead."

Jasmine came awake. "It's getting cold," she said sleepily.

He wrapped his coat around her and she snuggled in again. Her very nearness and fragility made him feel the depths of aching sorrow he would know if anything happened to her. He tightened his arm around her, gave in, and kissed her head.

Jerrod said, "Dad, look!"

He brought his eyes up in time to see something struggling across the road. *Crawling,* he supposed, would have been a better word for what he was seeing. It moved over the pavement and slid into the ditch on the other side. He couldn't be sure what it had been. It almost looked like a collection of large oily green Hefty bags struggling over the road.

"What was it?" Jasmine asked.

"A porcupine or something," Frank told her, the lie coming almost too easily.

He could feel Jerrod's eyes on him. *A porcupine? Really?* But, of course, he didn't say anything. He didn't need to. If that thing had been a porcupine, it had not bred on this world.

## 15

About half an hour later when they were scarcely twenty minutes from Route 7, he noticed that the fuel gauge had dipped down to quarter of a tank. That wasn't good. It meant they'd have to stop for gas. There was a convenience store just down the road. Chances were, it was closed up. But there would be gas there, and as an old farm hand who knew his way around machinery, he would get some one way or another.

Still, the idea of stopping disturbed him. It created an entirely new set of problems. It meant putting them all at additional risk and he did not like that idea at all. His mind looped through all the terrible things that could happen to the kids and succeeded in creating one mother of a tension headache. Stress, so much damn stress.

The kids were quiet.

Jasmine was still sleeping, feeling completely safe snuggled up against him, no doubts in her mind that her father could handle this. That was faith. That was real faith. Not the barmy they taught in churches and Sunday schools, but the real thing. The sort of faith only love could inspire. It made Frank feel equal parts invincible and impotent.

Jerrod was still watching out his window.

He'd been through a lot, too, but he'd never speak of it. He'd spent far too much time around his father and the other farmers of Cane River. All of them old-school, working-class types, men of the soil who had little patience or respect for weakness or angst. Something which was not necessarily a good thing.

Frank kept driving, watching the countryside roll by: meadows and pasturelands, forests and hills and wooded hollows, now and again the finger of a silo pointing skyward in the moonlight. He had seen only three abandoned vehicles on the side of the road, two trucks and one minivan. The latter looking as if it had been crushed like a beer can. He tried not to think about what that might mean.

They kept going, seemingly chasing the moon across the sky. They were close to the convenience store now. It would be just around the next bend, within spitting distance of Route 7.

Jerrod suddenly sat up, leaning forward. "Dad…Dad, what the heck is that?"

Frank, his mind daydreaming, saw something just ahead blocking the road. He hit the brakes and slowed the Dodge to a crawl. It was huge, whatever it was. No, strike that, it was fucking *immense*, and it was moving. Whatever in the Christ it was, it was alive. It hesitated, then crossed the road on many scampering legs, disappearing into the night.

Frank knew he had a choice to make.

Either he turned them around and got them out of there, tried siphoning some gas at one of the farms, or he pushed forward. He decided on the latter. It was a chance, but it was the only logical thing to do. Whatever had been up there was gone.

"Dad?" Jerrod asked.

"I don't know, son. It's gone now. Let's be thankful about that."

Calm, reasonable, confident. It sounded good. Frank was almost impressed with himself. Then, as they passed the stretch of road where that mysterious thing crossed, a shape vaulted out at the Dodge. In those microseconds before impact, it occurred to Frank that whatever it was, it came rushing at them like a grasshopper leaping up onto a blade of grass. Then it hit. It rammed into the truck, and he heard Jasmine scream and Jerrod cry out as the wheel spun from his hands.

"PAPA! PAPA! PAPA!" he heard Jasmine shriek.

He'd had the truck tooling along at about forty miles an hour, which he figured was a good clip, yet slow enough to brake and avoid any wrecks. Whatever hit them knocked them hard enough to lift them off the pavement and swing them around an easy 125° where they came down with a screech of metal and a resounding explosion, which he knew was one of the tires blowing out. Then the truck nosed down into the ditch and moved no more.

16

Thank God they were all belted in.

Still, Frank was more than a little dazed, and he heard Jerrod asking if he was all right. He was a little sore from being bounced around and from the belt holding him like a vice, but other than that he was fine. Jasmine was sobbing.

He got out of his belt and got her out of hers. "Sshhh, baby, sshhh," he told her, stroking her hair. "You're okay. If anything hurts, just tell me."

"Dad," Jerrod whispered. "We better be quiet."

The windshield was spider-webbed with cracks, but out of the driver's side window, he could see something like a post…except that it was moving, vibrating slightly. It was a chitinous thing like the leg of a blue crab, but slender, smooth and shining. What he could see of it in the moonlight and the reflection of the truck's headlights, looked to be a sort of dull, dirty pink striated with black bands.

Jasmine started sobbing again, and it was Jerrod this time who told her to be quiet.

Frank brought his face as close to the window as he dared and saw a titanic shape about the size of a mobile home hovering over the truck.

Jesus.

Jasmine was quiet and Frank pressed a finger to his lips to keep her that way. The thing poised over them began making a wet sort of clicking sound and droplets of something struck the roof of the cab as if it was drooling.

The engine had conked out, but the headlights were still on. Did he shut them off or would that make matters worse?

They were in very bad trouble.

If it was powerful enough to knock the truck off the road, then it was powerful enough to crush it flat if it so desired. Even if it didn't do that, how long before it peeled the roof off like the lid of a sardine can and feasted on what was packed inside?

Something brushed against the roof with a slow sliding sort of sound like a tree limb. It was lifted free and then it came down again, striking the roof with such force it put a three-foot dent in it.

Jasmine was shaking and Frank held her to him, her face buried into his shoulder. Jerrod had slid in closer now, too, and he was shaking as well. Outside, that clicking came again, and the creature let out a resounding keening cry like a million locusts crying out simultaneously. The shrilling grew so loud it was nearly deafening, then it stopped, echoing off into the night.

The creature's leg lifted up and up like a cat holding its paw in the air indecisively. Frank could see that it was jointed, and judging by the fact that it was forward facing, it must have been the foreleg of some gigantic arthropod. As he sat there, watching it, his entire body greasy with cold sweat, he remembered from agricultural school that your average arthropod leg consisted of the coxa, where it was attached to the body, the trochanter, which was like the femoral ball which snugged into the hip socket of a human being, the femur, the tibia, the tarsus, and metatarsus. What he was seeing was the tarsus, and it was as big around as a porch pillar. The leg drew up a bit more, and he saw the metatarsus which tapered to a point so fine you could have threaded a needle with it.

Then the thing moved.

He expected the earth to shake (the way it might have in the Mesozoic as a thunder lizard plowed through a primordial forest), but it didn't. The stride of the creature was remarkably light. But that would stand to reason, because it was a predator and stealth would have been important. There was a slight padding sound as it moved off. The leg was gone and the air around them suddenly seemed lighter as if a great weight was not pushing the atmospheric envelope down upon them any longer.

*See?* a trembling voice in Frank's head said. *See? It's gone now and things are going to be all right.*

But that was too much to hope for.

The best option, he decided, was to play possum. Just wait here for another fifteen or twenty minutes, then peek outside. If it was nowhere in sight, then it was probably safe to strike out.

"I'm scared," Jasmine whispered.

Frank had to bite his tongue so he didn't confess that he was scared, too, completely petrified. "It'll be okay. We just have to be quiet for awhile," he told her.

The seconds ticked by, becoming minutes. With each passing one, he began to feel lighter, hope trickling back in. He would get these kids out of here. Nothing could stop him. Not if he used his head. Not if he used his very human capacity for reasoning, something that stupid brutish monster did not possess.

About the time he was ready to take a look outside, that keening cry came again and this time from right in front of the truck. It blasted at them with volume and a few pieces of glass fell from the windshield. Then the front of the truck was hit, and the truck itself slid four feet out of the ditch and rolled back down again. It happened again, then again, as if they were being butted by a rhino. There was that clicking sound once more and it was horrible. It made him think of dozens of sand crabs on a waterlogged corpse, their claws picking away at it.

The front of the truck was seized and lifted up three or four feet. The kids and he clung to one another as it was shaken and they were bounced around. A sheet of webbed glass fell from the windshield, and in the glare of the headlights, he saw the thing quite clearly. The sight of it struck him mute with horror. He clutched the kids to him, so they could not see it.

## 17

The creature was a low—that was debatable—streamlined insect, though he could not say with any certainty that it indeed *was* an insect. A sort of arthropod was as close as he could get. It was oddly skeletal like a walking stick, its body long and arched at the spine, as if there were up-thrusting bony plates just beneath the skin. It stood on four stout, yet slender legs, walking on the tips apparently, and was easily thirty feet in length. The real horror was its plated crocodilian-looking head that was set with a series of black, glassy eyeballs that reflected metallic blue in the headlights.

As Frank waited there with the kids, shriveling under his skin, he watched the creature prod the bumper of the Dodge with its snout. Jabbing it and darting back, jabbing it and darting back, each time making the truck bounce on its springs. It was obvious that it didn't quite know what to make of it.

*Maybe it'll leave,* Frank thought. *Oh dear God, just let it leave.*

But it wasn't leaving.

It waited there, illuminated by the headlights, curious but confused, holding one of its legs up in the air as if it was readying itself for combat at any moment. Frank wondered if the .45 would do him any good and decided that it would have been like trying to stop a train by throwing peas at it.

They waited.

It waited.

Finally, it made up its mind and lunged forward, the snout opening into four hook-like protrusions like separate jaws. They yawned wide, and he could see inside its slimy mouth and the gullet beyond. The jaws were like claws ready to clutch prey. It grabbed the front end of the truck, two of the jaws seizing it from below and two seizing the hood above. It shook the truck, and then drew its jaws back, nubby serrated teeth digging grooves in the metal. Then it seized it again, and this time with force, the hood crunching with metal fatigue and collapsing. The creature shook the truck, and Frank and the kids were thrown to the floorboards. Then the truck was dropped with a jarring impact.

There was silence for a few moments.

Frank pulled himself up carefully, looking out the missing windshield. The creature was gone. He started to breathe again. Far in the distance, he heard its keening cry.

"All right," he said. "We need to get out of here right now."

His door was banged in so they fled out the passenger side. Frank lifted Jasmine free while Jerrod grabbed the knapsack.

"Papa," she whimpered. "I think I peed my pants."

## 18

Ten minutes later, they were on the road. Getting to the convenience store was more important than ever now. After their encounter with Claw-Face (as Frank had come to think of the creature), walking out in the open like this was unnerving. He couldn't decide if it was better to lead the kids down the center of the road where the moonlight was bright or stay to the shadows on the shoulder. Out in the open seemed to make them easy targets, but, on the other hand, who knew what might be lying in wait in the shadows?

"Where are we going now?" Jasmine asked.

"There's a store down the way. We need to get there," he told her. "We'll be safe there."

"Will we?" Jerrod said in that way kids have of not wanting to be heard but wanting to be heard all the same.

Frank felt his anger rise. "Yes, we will. Keep your mouth shut and your eyes open."

It was harsh, but sometimes you had to be harsh when kids got his age. They could be very selfish, very cruel, very apathetic to anything but their own needs and wants. Jerrod wasn't like that usually, but Frank was beginning to see it more and more. The last thing he needed was him scaring his sister any more than she already was. They needed to stand strong now, stand together.

As they walked side by side, the moonlight winked out and he could see a dark mass of clouds scudding overhead. Within minutes, the wind picked up, hissing through the trees and the air was noticeably colder. It had dropped easily ten degrees.

"A storm's coming, I think," he said.

"Boomers?" Jasmine asked. She did not like electrical storms with booming thunder.

"Maybe."

"It scares me," she admitted.

"Don't be a baby," Jerrod said.

"Enough of that," Frank warned him.

What amazed him was the resiliency of Jasmine. After what they had been through with Claw-Face, she should have been shaking and whimpering, but she wasn't. In fact, she was holding up admirably. Her greatest concerns were her boomers. They were scarier than the things they had seen and those worse things that they guessed were ever-present. Such is the gift of youth.

## 19

By the time they sighted the dark hulk of the convenience store and Frank could clearly see the darkened Shell sign high above on the post out front, a few raindrops began to fall. Without the moon, the night grew very dark. It was as if a shade had been pulled. By the time they reached the edge of the Shell parking lot, it was so black they were holding hands so they didn't lose one another. They literally could not see their hands in front of their faces. The wind was getting strong, and they could hear it whooshing through the forest, making signs creak outside the store. This was real night. This was real blackness. The blackness of nature without electric lights. The darkness their ancestors had known as they huddled around peat fires in their European hovels in the dead of night.

Though Frank did not like the idea of turning on the flashlight, thinking it might draw unwanted attention, he did so because it was like trying to navigate through a mineshaft. He clicked on the light and there was a row of gas pumps right before them. They looked utilitarian and somehow menacing with the shadows crawling over them, like the faces of automatons that had come to exterminate the human race.

He led them from one island to the next until they reached the store itself which was like a plate glass box. There were a few cords of cut firewood out front, a *USA Today* newspaper box, an ice dispenser, and an empty rack which might have held bottles of windshield wiper fluid once.

"It's so dark in there," Jasmine said.

"It's dark out here, too," Jerrod reminded her as if she needed reminding.

Frank approached the double glass doors. The lower panel of the one on the left had been broken. He had no idea what they might find inside. But as the rain began to fall, he didn't really see that they had a choice. Down on his knees, he went in first, crawling carefully through the broken glass on the other side. He helped the kids inside. They were out of the rain. That was something.

Since they had nothing better to do, they searched around. The majority of the store was untouched. Someone, apparently, had ransacked the beer coolers, but that was about it. The snack foods were untouched, but with the power out, the broasted chicken and hot dogs in the steamer had gone bad. There was plenty of bottled water, warm soda, and all the candy, chips, and beef jerky one could hope for. They also found lots of batteries, more flashlights, and even a couple battery-powered lanterns. Once they lit them up, it didn't seem so bad in the store. While the kids indulged themselves on pretzels and Hostess pies, Frank scavenged about for anything they could use, peering out the plate glass windows into the rain. There was a pickup truck parked around the side and that was intriguing.

He wondered who it belonged to.

He wondered if it was drivable.

He wondered if there was any gas in it.

The rain started sweeping through the missing panel in the door, so, with Jerrod's help, he pushed a floor freezer filled with melted ice cream in front of it. The lightning started flashing not long afterwards, and Jasmine predictably became nervous. She'd been that way since she was a baby. No amount of reassuring from Janet and him on the harmlessness of boomers would convince her that there wasn't something very nefarious about them.

By lantern light, Frank held her while Jerrod became terribly impatient and bored with it all.

"It'll blow over," Frank said. "It always does."

As they waited, listening to the falling rain and the wind blowing, the occasion peal of thunder, he became certain he was hearing something else just beneath it. Maybe it was the wind, but he wasn't convinced. There was something. *Something.* He sat there for the longest time, thinking and listening, ears attuned but not so the kids would notice. He didn't want that. Not yet.

Once he had Jasmine more or less settled, he went over to the windows and studied the flooded parking lot in the sporadic lightning flashes. There wasn't much to see. Now and again, he thought he caught sight of a darting sort of movement at the very periphery of the lot. But as much as he focused during each strobing flash, he couldn't be sure. The only thing he *was* sure of was that his nerves were bent and that his own reflection in the glass looked like it belonged to a haggard, gaunt man twice his age.

"Is there something out there?" Jerrod finally asked him.

"No, just watching the storm. Waiting for it to let up so I can get a look at that truck out there."

It seemed reasonable; at least, Jerrod seemed to buy it.

## 20

About five minutes later, when he was about to go back to the kids, Frank heard something very distinctly. In-between the thunder and the moan of the wind, he heard a fluttering, snapping kind of noise like a flag on a pole. It came and went. It could have been anything. Then, three minutes later, when he heard it again, and this time with great volume, he knew it was something specific, and whatever it was, it seemed to be concentrated in the general area around the store. It came again, and this time, it sounded like a thousand bed sheets flapping on a thousand windy October clotheslines.

"Dad, what was that?" Jerrod asked.

*I wish to God I knew, son. But I got the worst feeling it's something bad, something very bad.*

"I don't know. It seems to come and go."

"Like the boomers?" Jasmine said.

"Oh, would you stop with the boomers," Jerrod sighed long and low.

"Something like that."

Frank waited there, the tension rising in him. Nothing this night—or in the past few weeks for that matter—gave him much hope. He always expected the worst and he was rarely disappointed. The flapping was intermittent. Sometimes, it sounded like it was right on top of them and sometimes way across the parking lot.

"Like birds," Jasmine said.

And that's what Frank did not like about it. *Like birds.* Yes, it was in his mind, but he hadn't really put it into words because sometimes admitting to things could be the worst medicine of all, like calling out the names of demons at tomb-mouths and daring them to show themselves. Sweating now, his nerves jangling ever so slightly, his jaw set and face grim, he got up and went over to the windows.

*All right, if you're out there, goddamn well show yourself.*

Which again, he believed was bad medicine, because he was offering a challenge. Something large and dark swooped past the window very quickly. He saw another dip over the bed of the pickup out there. *Here we go.* The kids were getting concerned now; he could see it etched into their faces. They were thinking they were about to step into something like their encounter with Claw-Face, and Frank had to agree.

He kept watching.

There was nothing for some time, but he knew they were out there, those veering amorphous shapes that seemed even blacker than the night itself. He had the worst feeling that they were not circling the store at random, but attracted to it by either the lantern lights that were burning or, and more likely, because they knew there was prey inside.

*Thump-thump-thud.*

"Over there!" Jerrod cried. "It was right there!"

Frank swung around, but he wasn't fast enough. Whatever it had been, it bumped against the glass and then flew off. Frank crossed the store quickly, pausing only to pull the .45 from the knapsack, and then he was over there, waiting for it to reappear.

"What did you see?" Frank asked.

"A shape...I don't know," Jerrod said. "A big black shape."

### 21

Jasmine took this opportunity to totally lose it, letting go with a high shrilling whine before subsiding into a fit of coughing, gagging, and whimpering. Jerrod went to her, but it was obvious he wasn't too happy about it.

Frank turned away from the glass for only a moment, but when he turned back, something flew off. He only caught the briefest glimpse of it...something leathery, black, and winged. It had been hovering there like a night insect, and he had the most unsettling feeling that it had been watching him. There was no way he could know that, of course, but the feeling ran deep.

*Thump-thump-thump-BANG!*

From over near the checkout counter this time. Jasmine wailed a little louder, and he turned in time to see a spider-webbing of cracks run through the glass. It had been hit hard. Now the thumping and bumping were coming from every direction, and he could see vague dark shapes bouncing off the windows. In the reflected glare from the lanterns, he could actually see the glass flex. It wouldn't keep these things out. That was for sure.

*THUD-THUD-THUD!*

It was a near-constant hammering and pounding and not just from the windows either; he could hear noises on the roof like something—many things, in fact—were walking around up there. Jasmine was having a full-blown fit by that point, and Jerrod could barely keep her under control as she writhed in his arms. There was no time for that, not now.

Frank charged over there, his face feeling hot. "KNOCK IT OFF!" he shouted at her. "RIGHT GODDAMN NOW!"

And, of course, felt instantly guilty when her little face seemed to shrivel, to sink into itself, her lower lip jutting out like a juicy wedge of fruit. Her face was beet-red, wet with tears, her dark hair pasted to it. In the back of his mind, he found it absolutely heartbreaking, but they could not afford theatrics at the moment. There was simply too much at stake.

He heard breakage, and the spider-webbed sheet of glass behind the checkout counter exploded in. Rain came with it, along with a sodden breeze that peeled flyers off the counter and overturned a cardboard Slim Jim display. For the briefest moment, Frank saw a shining black wing…or something like a wing.

He didn't wait for confirmation as to what it was connected to—he fired.

He put two rounds into the black shape, and it made a low sort of squealing sound like a guinea pig that had been stepped on. One thing was for sure: it understood pain. That was comforting in its own way. He rushed over to the counter, and though he saw things pass, but could not get a good look at them. There was something very frustrating about that. It wasn't that he really *wanted* to see them, but seeing them would give him a frame of reference and he very much needed that.

He went over to the other side of the store.

He had the flashlight in his hand this time and he directed it out into the darkness. He saw raindrops in the beam of light, a ghostly refracted image of himself…and then something came veering out of the darkness with incredible velocity. It came so quick that

Frank nearly went over in his shock. He tried to track it with the light, but it was far too fast.

Then something landed on the roof of the parked pickup and he saw what it was. And, more importantly, what it wasn't.

## 22

He put the light right on it, or as much of the light as there was after shining through the window and rain. But in the darkness, it captured one of the flying things sure enough, exposed it in enough detail to raise the hairs along the nape of his neck. At first, as it perched there on the cab roof, he thought it was a manta ray because that's what it looked like: one of those manta rays you saw on nature documentaries, standing there fluttering its wings.

But, of course, it was no manta ray.

Manta rays were marine animals and this thing…God only knew what it was. It was shaped like a kite, a near-perfect quadrilateral. Four feet tall and just over three in width, its flesh was an oily midnight black that glistened with rain. It stood there on stubby feet, hooked talons like those of a barn owl gripping the cab roof. He couldn't say that it had a face exactly, but up near the top, there was a sort of triangular swelling with a puckered protrusion that looked a little too much like the mouth of an old woman without her teeth in. It was sunken in a V-shaped line so that it looked like it was grinning.

Frank recorded all that in the five seconds he watched the thing. Then it just seemed to rise like a hot air balloon, whipping suddenly off into the night, but not so fast that he did not see that it had a tail—a whipping, barbed tail, sinuous and jet, that wagged from side to side as it rose into the storm—and, as it dipped forward to glide, two shining eyes like ball bearings.

He backed away from the glass, not sure what to think or what to really do about any of this.

Then—

*THUD!*

Jasmine screamed and Jerrod let out a cry he tried to pull back at the last moment. One of the things had landed on the glass and several others were circling just behind it like moths around a streetlight.

Frank took two or three drunken steps back, overturning a rack of Doritos, then fumbling through them, crunching bags of Nacho Cheese and Cool Ranch under his boots. What was clinging to the glass was pretty much what he had seen on the cab of the truck, with one major difference—the puckered mouth had opened like a suction cup and was attached to the glass. He had the worst feeling that if that sucker hooked onto you, it would never let go. The idea made something like the wings of blackbirds flutter in his belly.

The creature itself was like a little umbrella supported by a framework of what apparently were collapsible ribs, from the ends of which grew swollen, greasy-looking tentacles like pond leeches.

Now others crowded the glass.

More and more pressing in all the time until it was buried in their winged, pulsating bodies that up close like that seemed to be covered in a fine series of hairs like cilia. He kept seeing weird flashes of bluish light coming from them, and he couldn't begin to know what that meant. The glass was beginning to bulge from the weight of the creatures, and he knew damn well that it would shatter at any moment.

He had to get the kids out of there.

A backroom.

A cellar.

*Anywhere.*

It was at that moment that the worse-case scenario was realized in full nightmarish splendor: one of the windows near the door came apart in an explosion of shards and one, then two of the things were flying about almost drunkenly, banging off the ceiling tiles overhead and overturning displays. The second one tried to fly right through one of the windows—revealing the level of its intelligence—and collided with its own blurry image, bouncing free and smashing a canoe-shaped Leinenkugel's display to the floor. It crawled about, trying to free itself from the crumpled cardboard display. It looked like a stingray stranded on a beach, flapping its wings—or fins—trying to get some traction, a night-black thing that looked like it was made of oily neoprene rubber. It made no sound in its struggles. Now and again, its coiling, barbed tail would strike the floor and there'd be a brief flash of blue light…and a very noticeable sharp reek of ozone.

Both Jasmine and Jerrod wanted a closer look, but Frank waved them back. "GET DOWN!" he shouted. "GET DOWN TO THE FLOOR!"

## 23

The other kite was circling overhead, obviously confused. It smashed into displays, overturned jars of pickled sausages on the counters, and flew over the tops of aisles, scattering an assortment of chips and boxed movie candy about. Every now and again, its serpentine tail would lash out and strike something—a box of cereal, a bag of marshmallows—and there would be a sort of lashing, cracking sound as of a bullwhip followed by a brief fusillade of crackling blue light.

Frank wasn't sure what it meant exactly, but in the back of his mind an idea was forming, engendered by a twin-pack of Bounty paper towels that took a direct hit and fell to the floor smoldering as if it had taken a sudden, devastating electrical charge.

As the kite on the floor wiggled its way free of the Leinenkugel's display, finding its feet and standing unsteadily as if it might topple over at any moment, the other one dove in at Frank and he barely got out of its way. He ducked and its tail lashed out where his head had been a moment before.

There was no choice then.

He fired at it, missed, and put two rounds in the one on the floor which made that same sort of rat-like squealing as the other one he had shot. It flopped forward, and an inky sort of blood spread out on the floor beneath it. It convulsed two or three times, then vomited out a gush of something that looked either like half-digested spaghetti or a fluid ball of intestinal worms.

The other one started swooping like mad as if it knew what he had done or had felt the death throes of its comrade. As it circled about, its tail slashing with menacing intent, it made a trilling noise that was instantly answered by the others outside. Without further ado, a half-dozen of them flew in, followed by twice that many.

Frank fired a few blind shots in their direction and grabbed up the kids, leading them towards the back of the building and the storeroom. They were almost there when one of the plate glass doors of the milk case swung open and a hand reached out, seizing Jasmine's wrist.

## 24

Jasmine cried out, and Frank brought the .45 to bear, expecting the worst. What he saw was a large woman with a black eye and a purple bruise on her cheek.

"In here, you dummies!" she snapped. "Hurry!"

She looked edgy and intense, but it was the best offer they'd had all night so he let her hoist Jasmine in and then he pushed Jerrod in after her.

Two of the kites dove at him and he ducked under them, firing another shot in their direction. As he climbed in, another one came at him, and he reflexively struck out at it, feeling his hand brush the frilly edge of its wing which felt oddly soft like a rotten plum.

Then the cooler door was closed.

"C'mon, back here," the woman said, indicating a small room just behind the coolers where the milk was evidently stored and shelved when there was milk.

"That was a close one," she said, blabbering on non-stop about how she had watched them from the coolers for some time but, things being the way they were, she had not revealed herself.

"Couldn't...not until I knew what your deal was. Lots of weirdos out there. They come in every stripe."

Jerrod kept his distance from her, and Jasmine still hadn't made up her mind, clinging close to Frank. They all sat on milk crates as the woman introduced herself as Candy McCullough, and once they knew each other's names, she told them of the strange chain of events that brought her to hide out in a milk cooler.

"My old man's dead," she told them. "Two months out of the joint and one of them things out there got him just down the road. We were on his '74 Ironhead burning pavement down Illinois way to his brother's place outside Springfield. Pickle—that was my old man—blew a tire because his idea of maintenance on that ride was putting more air in when the tread was worn. We hiked it back here and Pickle started helping himself to that warm beer out there, and when he drinks, he gets mean. Soon enough, we had ourselves a first class punch-up going and that's when those things showed, just about sundown. Pickle was out there, he was out there pissing and—"

A thumping sound from out in the store cut her off and Frank was thankful. He had no idea where she was going to go with that, and with the kids around, he really didn't want to know.

The kites were on a real tear out there, mashing and bashing, shattering windows and generally just crashing into things. They'd already taken out one of the lanterns, and it probably wouldn't be long before the other followed suit.

"Are they attracted to the light?" he asked her.

"Can't say. Maybe, maybe not. When I heard you guys coming, I climbed in here, figuring I'd be safe. So far, it's worked."

There was more noise out in the store. "Why won't they go away?" Jasmine asked.

"They will, hon," Candy told her. "Like any other animal, they'll get bored sooner or later and take off. We just have to wait it out."

*Well put,* Frank thought.

It was exactly what Janet would have told her and what he would have wanted to tell her himself if he didn't have such a poor grasp of words in times of trouble.

Candy lit a cigarette, and if nothing else, it lit up the coolers and the room behind them a bit. That was a good thing because the darkness (and what might be in it) was beginning to get a bit worrisome to them all.

Jerrod, who rarely missed the opportunity to say the wrong thing at the wrong time, said, "You shouldn't smoke. It's bad for you. It can kill you."

"That's right," Candy said, nodding her head as she took a drag. "Smoking's bad, real bad. Make sure you never do it."

"I won't."

"Good for you."

"But why do you?"

Candy chuckled. "Who knows? I've spent my life making poor choices and, trust me, tobacco is the very least of my demons. But why? I don't know. My guess is that my head is empty."

Jasmine giggled. "It's not empty; you got a brain it!"

"Don't be too sure of that, my little monkey." Candy slapped her leg. "You know what? When I was little I had long pretty hair just like you. It might be hard to imagine now, but I did. I had two older brothers. They used to punch me all the time. Does your brother punch you?"

"He better not!" Jasmine said.

Jerrod groaned.

Candy laughed. "Well, mine did. You know what else?"

"What?"

"They called me Skunk."

"That's a bad name…was it because you smelled?"

"No, no. I'll tell you why it was. We had a tire swing in the backyard. It was hooked with a chain to a tree limb. I used to watch those guys turn the tire around and around until the chain was twisted real tight. Then they'd jump on and the tire would swing 'round and 'round real fast. Well, I just had to do it, too. So one day when they were gone, guess what I did? I turned the tire 'round and 'round until the chain was twisted tight and I went for a ride…only I didn't notice that my ponytail was caught in the chain."

"Did it hurt?"

"Yeah, it hurt. It tore my ponytail right off along with about four inches of hair on my head. I had a bald stripe. That's why they called me skunk."

Jasmine was laughing, warming up to Candy to the point that she had abandoned Frank to go sit by her.

"Where are you brothers now?"

Candy butted her cigarette. "Oh…they died a long time ago. They got in a car accident."

Frank was starting to warm up to Candy himself. There was something endearing and honest about her. On the surface, she was tough and hard-looking, but underneath, he had a feeling she was something else entirely.

Jerrod said, "It's quiet out there now."

"Let's give it a little while," Frank told him.

Jasmine wanted to hear more stories of Candy's childhood misadventures, and Candy was only too happy to dig into her nearly endless supply of them. She launched into another one about breaking her collarbone when she took her brother's bike down a rough tract known as Suicide Hill.

"You ever break your collarbone?" She put the question to Jerrod this time because he hadn't exactly thawed.

"No."

"Well, let me tell you what it feels like…"

## 25

They decided the best thing to do was to bunk down in the cooler for the night. The floor was concrete which wasn't too comfortable, so Candy slipped out into the store—the single lantern was still burning but getting dim—and came back with not only the lantern but several waterproof plastic tarps. It wasn't the softest bed in the world, but it was something. The kids bunked down using their jackets as pillows which was about the best they were going to get under the circumstances.

Frank knew that Jerrod didn't care for it.

He figured he shouldn't have to go to bed with his little sister who was just a kid in his book. Regardless, he fell asleep quite quickly.

Which left Frank with Candy. He had the jitters and sleep was beyond him. They sat in silence for some time near the door which was as far from the sleeping children as they could get.

"What are your plans?" she asked him.

He found it hard to speak of them as if admitting them out loud might put a jinx to it all. Which only showed that his thinking was beginning to fray around the edges like a lot of other people. The horror inflicted on the world from The Food was beginning to infect his rational mind. He did not like that. "Nothing definitive," he told her. "The first thing is to make it to the National Guard camp down in Juneau County. Supposedly, it's a sort of safe area. Lots of people there. Food, water, housing, medical."

She nodded. "Yeah, I heard about it. Most states have some. Secure Zones, they call 'em."

They were transitional areas where the Guard helped families and individuals, got them on their feet again before moving them to some of the larger, better secured areas out west. For some reason, The Food was not causing as much trouble out there. Not yet.

"Place you're talking about is Volk Field," Candy said. "It's an Air National Guard base. I know it. My ex was in the Guard. I been there a few times."

"How about you?"

Candy shrugged and lit a cigarette. "Who knows? With Pickle…with him gone, well, guess I'm going to have to come up with something else."

"You're welcome to join us," Frank said before he could stop himself.

*Are you out of your mind?* the voice of paranoia scolded him. *You know nothing about this woman. Jesus, look at her—some kind of biker woman. Full of tattoos and bad habits. Jasmine is captivated by her. In a week, she'll be dropping f-bombs and threatening her brother.*

But he knew that was bullshit. Just parental concern and anxiety being rechanneled into suspicion. Sure, Candy was rough around the edges, but his gut instinct told him she was probably all right.

"I might take you up on that," she said with some hesitation as if she could sense his thoughts.

They had the lantern turned down so as not to bother the kids. But they were exhausted; they could have slept under a spotlight. Frank noticed that Candy had the logo of the punk band Pennywise tattooed on the back of her left hand. They were one of his favorites in high school. He made note of it for a future conversation.

## 26

"We were in Cleveland for awhile," she told him. "It was fucking insane there. Everything's broken down. Even the cops and the Army aren't bothering with it. One day, it rained *black.* It was weird, man. Real weird. Like ink coming out of the sky. People said it had something to do with The Food. I don't know. Weird shit."

She said that at night they could hear something real big walking through the city and everyone was terrified.

"Not just big, Frank, but fucking *giant*. I heard some of those stories, but I didn't believe any of it. Most of it was from the news and the internet. But the news is all opinion these days and the internet is ninety percent bullshit. So I didn't buy any of it. *Was I wrong.*" She sighed and pulled off her cigarette. "At night, that thing would walk around the city and you could hear it. In the morning, you'd see buildings knocked down and huge prints in the ground the size of a house. I shit you not."

"What was it?"

"Fucking Godzilla? I don't know. Whatever it was, it never made any sounds. It didn't roar or anything. At least Godzilla roars to let you know he's coming." She shivered. "That was the scary part—how quiet it was."

Frank had heard his share of tall tales, too, but he'd rejected most of them. At least, he'd tried to. But after he saw that thing eating Bobby Welch's sheep in the pasture, it got harder and harder to disbelief any of it. The world was fucked up and the monsters had come. That was it in a nutshell. An ugly, dark nutshell—the monsters had come.

Candy stared at him for a long time before speaking. "It's not my place to tell you what to do and all. But those kids of yours...God, they're adorable...and they're in danger, you know? There's stories out there about cults sacrificing kids. Maybe it's not true. I don't know."

Frank swallowed. He'd seen that little smoldering skeleton bracketed to the post. That was only a few hours ago and not too far from where he now sat. He didn't think he'd ever get the image of it out of his mind much as he tried. He could tell himself, as Candy had, that such things could not be...but he would never convince himself that there weren't some very, very bad, fucked-up people out there with ash pits for brains.

"It's just very dangerous for them is all I'm saying," Candy went on. "When we were in Cleveland, kids were getting snatched after dark. Some thought it was the things in the night, but I heard that wasn't it at all. Probably nothing to it, but you should just be aware of how dangerous it is for them out there."

Frank said, "Let's not talk about. I got enough to worry me."

"Sure, sure," she said. "But maybe I'll come along with you. Might be a good idea. I can help you safeguard the little ones. I can be very resourceful. I'll make your enemies mine and God help any of those pukes out there if I do that."

## 27

After a sodium-rich breakfast of Spam and Chef Boyardee Beef Ravioli (which Frank ate cold and found surprisingly appetizing), he gathered the kids together while Candy looted around out in the store.

"Candy's going to be coming with us," he announced.

"Oh, good!" Jasmine said.

Her enthusiasm, however, did not touch Jerrod who simply nodded. His lips were drawn tight, and it was obvious he was not pleased.

"It'll be good to have her with," Jasmine said. "At least I won't be stuck with all boys."

"That's what I was thinking," Frank said.

Jerrod still had no comment.

Frank cleared his throat. "Jerrod? C'mon, say it."

"I don't want her with. I don't like her."

"Why?"

"I don't know. I just don't."

"C'mon, there must be some reason."

He turned away. "What's the difference? You didn't ask my opinion anyway."

"I'm asking it now."

"She shouldn't be around Jasmine. Not with the way she talks."

"She talks just fine!" Jasmine said.

That wasn't it and Frank knew it. Jerrod was a good brother to his little sister, but brothers were still brothers. His dislike of Candy had nothing to do with her colorful language. There was something else.

"Tell me what it is," Frank said.

"What's the difference?"

"Oh, he's being a baby!" Jasmine said.

"You be quiet," Frank told her. "C'mon, Jerrod. We're in this together. Tell me what's bothering you, pal."

"She's…she's not like mom."

So that was it. "No, she's not. Nobody ever will be. She's just traveling with us to the Guard camp. That's it. She's not going to be my girlfriend or anything. She's just a friend. Somebody that can help us with things. That's all."

Jerrod softened a bit. "Okay, we'll see how it works out."

With that, he went out into the store to join her. Jasmine tagged after her.

"You shouldn't be a baby," Jasmine said.

"Shut up, you little wart."

"I am not a wart!" Jasmine stated as if to dispel any rumors of the same.

Frank sighed, wishing, as he did every day, that Janet was still here. She would have known exactly how to handle this. The best he could do was bumble through it. He was no good with people's emotions, let alone his own.

"Are you coming or what?" Jasmine called.

"Yes, yes," Frank said, mentally preparing himself to handle yet another day.

## 28

The first bad news of the day was that the pickup parked around the side had no keys in it. They spent another thirty minutes searching the store, but they found nothing. Candy said she could probably hotwire it, but with no keys, the steering wheel would still be locked so it wouldn't do them much good.

They struck out on foot.

Frank didn't like it, and he could easily sense the unease of the others. He seriously hoped that the kites and old Claw-Face were strictly nocturnal denizens of this very screwed-up new world of theirs.

They trudged on, up the road. Jerrod was silent as stone and Jasmine, on the other hand, wouldn't stop talking, wouldn't stop asking Candy questions. They walked side-by-side holding hands. Having a woman with them was good for her. She had been too long in the company of boys and men. Candy was very good with her. They were fast friends. Maybe in Jasmine she saw the innocence of her own youth before it became sullied and stained by poor choices and a world that forced girls into women long before they were ready. Regardless, Jerrod didn't like it. His dislike of Candy was obvious. He had withdrawn almost completely into himself, and whenever Frank asked him a question, he would reply with a curt "yes" or "no" when he was feeling chatty and just a shrug of his shoulders when he wasn't.

Frank knew he had to take the boy aside and have a long heart-to-heart with him away from the highly attuned ears of his sister, but there was no time for it. They had to move. They needed to put miles between themselves and the convenience store. This is what he kept telling himself because he dreaded talks like that, knowing down deep he was emotionally blunted. His words always seemed ineffective, bungling, and forced as if he was reading from a script, regurgitating every poorly written soppy sentiment from every movie he'd ever seen.

Things like that had come so easy to Janet. The things she said were real and natural. He sighed inwardly. This business being Dad *and* Mom was tough.

Route 7 wasn't far now. It would have been a short little trip in a car, but on foot, it was a real hike. The road wound up and down through the hills, twisting and turning as if it was trying to reach back into itself.

About fifteen minutes into it, they saw something coming over the crest of a hill just ahead of them. Frank got them to the side of the road and he got his gun out. Just in time, as it turned out, to see that the something was a guy on a bicycle. Using the downward slope of the hill, he came racing in their direction—a man in a business suit with a tie and bowler hat on, rushing forward as if he was late for a meeting. As he passed, he tipped his hat to them and disappeared around the last bend.

Jerrod was trying to maintain his stony exterior, but he allowed himself a laugh.

"Well, now I've seen it all," Frank said.

"Yeah," Candy agreed. "Who'd have thunk we'd run into Don Draper out here in the toolies?"

"Is he going to work?" Jasmine asked.

"He's going somewhere," Candy said. "Maybe crazy."

## 29

They plodded on.

After a time, they stopped speaking, even Jasmine's near-constant monologue dried up—*I'm getting tired of climbing hills because when you climb one hill you have to climb another and don't your legs get sore until you want to fall down and you think, I'll never get up and nobody can make me, but then you do it again and how many hills do you think you can climb in one day and what are we going to have for lunch?* Frank had noticed it, of course, and he wondered if they were feeling dread like he was. He kept trying to catch Candy's eye to see if she would telegraph him some sense of what she was feeling, but she only watched the road, gripping Jasmine's hand. He had the most gratifying sense that it would have taken an army to make her ever let go.

Jerrod was walking ahead of them.

Not far, maybe twenty feet, close enough that if something happened, Frank could be there within seconds. He wondered if the boy was doing it out of a sense of adventure or just to be away from them. Maybe it was a little of both.

Frank watched him moving up a steep grade, which marked the last of the hills. Once they got to the top, they would see the valley below and Route 7 which would take them where they needed to go. Jerrod led and they followed. When he got to the top, he stopped, looking back over his shoulder.

"Dad, this doesn't look good," he said.

Frank hurried to get up there, ignoring the questions that Jasmine asked in a wild flurry. He stood by his son on the apex of the hill and felt something tighten in his stomach. He felt suddenly woozy, his guts weak and fluttery as they had been once when he was twelve and had a particularly nasty bout of the stomach flu.

His eyes followed the road as its serpentine length moved through fields and thickets down into the valley. Less than a half a mile in the distance, it was simply gone. There was a jagged scar-shaped cleft in the earth, and from it, he could clearly see, was a bubbling white emulsion oozing out like blood from a gaping wound. It was not blood, of course, but The Food: a gaping wellspring of it. But this was not the Manna of the Israelites falling from heaven, but a far different sort of nourishment that had seeped up from hell.

"What are we going to do, Dad?"

"Go around it," Frank said. "Way around it. We don't have a choice."

The cleft was maybe half a mile in length, probably no more than ten or twenty feet across. The white material had spread out from it in gobby strings like snot. The vegetation around the cleft was feeding on it, he knew. It was lush and tropical green, bushy and rising in bifurcated stalks that looked unpleasantly animated. He saw a jungle of purple and blue flowers that looked vibrant and almost juicy with life. They looked very much like the horns of old Victrolas. He couldn't be sure, but he almost thought they seemed to be pulsating. The trees—hemlock, oak, and maple—leaned like posts, their leaves wilted and brown.

The thing that scared him the most was that he heard a sort of low trumpeting noise down there that he was certain was the plants communicating with one another.

He and Jerrod went back down the hill to Candy and Jasmine.

"Slight change of plans," he announced.

## 30

They trudged for hours through green forest and yellow fields. Finally, they chose a hilltop and rested. They were tired, and they sat for about ten minutes without even speaking. Frank was just glad the kids weren't asking questions because he wasn't much in the mood for inventing some ridiculously optimistic forecast to keep their spirits buoyant. Lying about such things was getting harder and harder. Yet, at the same time, their silence concerned him.

The day was warm as it edged into afternoon. They ate Spam and crackers, drank water from bottles, and watched Monarch butterflies and cabbage moths winging about in the sunshine. It seemed to be a perfectly ordinary day. It was hard to believe that the world, the world they all knew so well, had become an alien nightmare.

Candy, sensing perhaps that Frank was in a blue mood, engaged Jasmine by directing her attention to bees flitting about brilliant stands of wildflowers. It was the perfect distraction and Jasmine loved it, fully admitting that sometimes she wished she was a bee because she loved honey.

Frank finally pulled out of himself, mentally figuring on how far out of their way they'd have to go to avoid the cleft. It was only about a half a mile long by his figuring, but he knew that the wildlife directly around such places tended to be frightening so it was best to give them a wide berth. They had already gone about three miles out of their way, but that was the only way they could safely circle around the cleft and what it contained. Three miles didn't sound bad, but when you were trailblazing through thickets and woodlands clogged with undergrowth, it was no easy bit.

"What's our plan?" Jerrod finally asked. "Or is it none of my business?"

He was getting a real mouth on him. Frank didn't like that. "Why wouldn't it be your business?"

Jerrod shrugged. His mouth had that tight look it used to get when he was a toddler and was about to cry. "You make decisions without asking me."

"Like what?"

"Like inviting her."

Candy. Back to that again. "I've already explained that, and I don't see why I should explain it again. She's traveling with us."

Jerrod nodded, his mouth still tight.

"And if we meet other people who are alone and I think we can trust, we'll invite them along, too," Frank went on, making his position clear. "Or should we leave them to die out here because it might upset you?"

"Do whatever you want."

"Son—"

It was no good. He'd turned away from him and completely shut him off. If this had been the old days before the madness of The Food, Frank would have barked at him about turning his back on him.

Candy and Jasmine came back over and Jerrod, of course, ignored them.

"We were watching bees," Jasmine announced.

"Were you?"

"Yes!"

He smiled. She was his light. As she went and sat down, he looked over at Jerrod brooding ten feet away and the smile faded. That boy. Dammit. He had read once that a parent will often have a favorite amongst his or her children, one that they will give more adoration and attention. Was it that way with him? Was he too attached to Jasmine? After Janet died, he made a point of giving them equal amounts of himself, but had he failed at that somehow? Was that what this was about? Was Jerrod feeling marginalized somehow?

Feeling guilty, he went over to him.

"Son," he said, "I know this is all tough…but if you need to talk, I'm here. I'll listen. You know that."

Jerrod would not even look at him. "What's there to talk about?"

## 31

By late afternoon, they had successfully circled around the cleft, giving it a very wide margin. By Frank's figuring, in an hour they would sight the road. Then they could get moving again and be done with this goddamned pathfinding. Enough was enough. It was starting to feel like they were in a maze going in circles or in one of those dreams where you need to run but your feet are concrete blocks.

As they came to the top of another hill, Candy told everyone to stop. Frank saw right away what the reason was. Down below, following a dry river cut, there were seven or eight men with rifles whose barrels glinted in the sunlight. Frank's first thought was, *so what?* Then he started thinking about some of the crazies out there, the cults and religious freaks he'd heard about. That brought to mind the little skeleton he'd found smoldering.

Maybe those men were trying to escape. Maybe they were hunting down some bad people or something that wasn't a person at all. Then again, maybe their intentions weren't quite so noble.

"Who are they?" Jerrod asked.

"I don't know. But these days, it's best to avoid people and particularly when they're armed."

"Could be part of a militia or something," Candy said. "I've heard there's a few around. They kill and rob, ask questions later if you know what I mean."

"I'm scared," Jasmine said. "I don't like this."

"It's okay," Candy told her.

But it wasn't. None of this was okay and particularly when you lived in a world where you not only had to fear monsters that crawled and crept but monsters that walked on two legs.

Jasmine began to sob and Candy immediately held her, pressing her face into her denim jacket to muffle the sound. They did not want to attract the attention of the militiamen—if that's what they were—down there. They had rifles. Frank had a .45. The outcome was obvious.

When Jasmine calmed down about five minutes later, she wanted Frank to hold her which he did. Gladly. The armed band was nowhere in sight by then. Long gone hopefully.

"Why do they want to kill us?"

"Nobody said they were going to kill us."

"Candy said."

"She didn't mean it like that."

"Oh."

"Just that it could be dangerous. People are afraid now, baby. Just like we are. They might hear us coming and start shooting, thinking we're an animal or something."

"Oh."

Candy reached out a hand and stroked her hair. "It's just my big mouth," she said. "I shouldn't have said any of it that way."

"No, you shouldn't have," Jerrod said, quick to leap on her.

"Jerrod," Frank said.

The boy turned away, and Frank thought about how it was getting that he knew the back of the boy's head better than his face.

"No, he's right," Candy said, impervious to the criticism. "Sometimes I just open my big mouth when I should keep it closed. Don't mind me."

She acted like it was all her fault and maybe it was, but Jerrod didn't need to smart off like that. Frank was going to have to have a long talk with him, the verbal equivalent of a trip to the woodshed. One of the things he was going to drive home was that Candy was not like his mother. She had lived a rough life and probably survived things that would have broken others. She was tough. She wasn't somebody to fool with. In fact, he would say, *son, if you want to keep your teeth in your mouth, I'd step easy around her.*

## 32

Frank was more unnerved by the armed men than he let himself admit. He made his little group stay put for another twenty minutes. Candy knew exactly what he was doing, and she read his apprehension clearly. Jerrod did, too. But he was miffed about something, probably Candy, maybe many other things as well. He made a big show of being bored. Stretching his legs and tapping his fingers and sighing a lot.

Finally, he said, "So are we just going to sit here all day?"

"We're conserving our energy," Frank told him. "We have a long walk ahead of us. And once we start, there's not going to be any time to rest. So enjoy it."

Jerrod smirked at the idea.

*Go ahead,* Frank thought, *be difficult. Sooner or later, you're going to wish you hadn't acted like this. The time will come.*

But as much as he thought about screaming at him, he still felt hurt because he knew that down deep the boy was sad, very sad.

## 33

Thirty minutes later, they were walking, and the hilltop and what they had seen was far behind them. Still, Frank reminded everyone to keep their voices low. No sense attracting any unwanted attention. As he walked, he thought about the armed men. It hadn't occurred to him at the time, but the direction they were taking would lead them directly to the cleft. Had that been their purpose? Were they going to see it firsthand? Were they going down there to do some shooting?

No matter.

They kept walking, and other than Candy and Jasmine whispering to one another from time to time and doing a bit of giggling, it was quiet. *Too quiet,* as they said in the old movies,

Frank decided. He wasn't hearing any birds in the trees or animals scampering in the undergrowth. There were a few bugs winging about, but nothing else.

It was a bad omen as far as he was concerned.

When he had begun believing in omens he did not know. Only that he seemed to be actively seeking them now like an old woman searching for prophecy in tea leaves and the webs of spiders speckled with morning dew. Not that long ago, he would have laughed at the very idea. He did not laugh now. He was becoming oddly superstitious at his core, and he did not like the idea of that at all. He had never gone in for any of that. Hell, he had never even gone to church. Janet took the kids to Christmas Mass and what not, but that had been the extent of their involvement with the unseen.

*You're getting this way and half-believing in the unbelievable because you're feeling desperate and powerless,* he told himself. He supposed there was a ring of truth in that. It was probably why people had been superstitious in the first place. The world was huge and they were small. It was governed by forces that their uneducated minds could not grasp. They needed an edge against that and the one they found was a stalwart belief in prophecy, folk magic, divination, and spirits, signs and portents.

He told himself he would stop looking for signs.

They fought their way through a tangled thicket of third- and probably fourth-generation forest, a mutiny of saplings and scrub brush, pickers and thorns. When they finally emerged from the other side, they saw a dirt path, and laying dead center of it was a creature about the size of a good heifer. It was no cow, of course. In fact, it was hard to say exactly what it was or what it was trying to be. It had a stout, powerful form covered in broad green scales the size of poker chips, a jagged row of bony plates down its back, and appendages that were somewhere between fins and clawed fingers. And eyes. Two shining gray eyes that looked flat and dead, yet somehow more than a little menacing. It smelled foul, absolutely foul like black swamp mud.

Jasmine clutched Candy, and Candy reassured her that whatever it was, it was dead and it couldn't hurt her.

"Must have come from down there," Jerrod pointed out, staring down a weedy hillside that led to a swampy run of cattails and black pools of stagnant water.

The grasses and weeds had been pushed aside and the progress of something large and muddy could clearly be seen leading from the water below to the trail before them.

"Heck is it?" Candy said. "That a fish?"

"Maybe a lungfish," Jerrod said. "Some of them have gills and lungs. We learned about them in science."

Despite the stench of the thing, he was fascinated by it. Candy and Jasmine kept their distance. Jerrod didn't get too close, but Frank knew his fascination with anything unusual that hopped, crawled, or slithered. He was always catching frogs and bringing grass snakes into the house.

"Just keep away from it," Frank told him.

"It's yucky and it smells bad," Jasmine said.

Candy laughed at that. "Looks like a cross between a carp and a boar," she said.

Which is exactly what Frank himself was thinking. Its general body shape and stubby snout were very hog-like, but the scales and tail were those of a fish. And as for the fins, they looked like they were designed for swimming *and* crawling.

Then Jerrod, true to form, found a stick and poked the thing. One of its fins fluttered a bit but that was all.

"It's either dead or close to it," he said.

"All right, leave well enough alone. We need to get moving here," Frank said.

But Jerrod couldn't help himself. Since he'd already poked the thing and gotten away with it, he got in closer and poked it right in the snout. Frank's mouth opened to yell at him, but then the fish-thing moved. A sort of rolling muscular contraction moved through it, and it made a low croaking sound like a big daddy bullfrog. As Jerrod flung himself back and succeeded in tripping over his own feet, the creature's great flabby lips parted and ejected a stream of water that struck him right in the chest. He went down.

"Jerrod!" Frank said.

"I'm all right," he said.

It had been some sort of reflexive action, no harm done. But the image of Jerrod standing there, scowling, dripping wet, and smelling made the others start laughing. Something which he obviously didn't care much for.

"God," he said. "I really stink."

"Then quit poking things with sticks," Jasmine told him in a superior tone. "Sometimes they poke back."

## 34

After another hour of hard walking, they spotted a farm with apple orchards spread out for many acres in both directions. They also spotted a pickup truck parked in the drive before the house. Frank knew the spread. It belonged to Ray Trawley. Ray was a great guy and everyone loved him. His Red Delicious and Braeburn apples were locally famous for their sweetness and crisp bite, as well as for their size, all of which were the result of a well-guarded family secret. He had a huge contract with Mott's for their applesauce and probably pulled in more in a year than most of the locals did in ten.

"I say we invite ourselves to that truck down there," Candy suggested. "My feet are getting worn out."

But Frank wasn't quite so sure about that.

Now Ray was a wonderful person, but his wife was an entirely different matter. Her name was Madel, and she was from the Philippines. He had met her through one of those Asian dating sites. Many of the local boys had chuckled behind Ray's back about his mail-order bride, but when they saw her for the first time—a pretty, olive-skinned, leggy girl with lustrous black hair down the middle of her back—their jaws hung open. Sure, Ray was doing well, but he was like fifty...and he had a drop-dead gorgeous wife who was twenty-five? It wouldn't last. It just wouldn't last.

But it did.

Madel was entirely devoted to Ray, and she had a good mind for business and had turned Trawley Orchards from a lucrative enterprise into one with amazing profits. And Ray couldn't have been happier. He had the girl of his dreams and walked around with a big shit-eating grin on his face all the time. That was the upside of it all. The downside was that Madel was fiercely territorial and even predatory. The locals considered her to be mean as fresh cat piss, and it was no secret that she often greeted trespassers with a loaded shotgun.

Which is why Frank wasn't too crazy about going down there and helping himself to Ray's truck. If Ray was about, he would help them...but if they ran into Madel...

Not good.

"I know whose farm that is," Frank said.

"Yeah, it's the guy with the big orchards," Jerrod put in. "The one with the crazy wife."

Well, *there*, it was said.

Frank gave Candy a quick primer on what they were talking about, keeping a G-rating on his language with Jasmine there. Very often when Madel was discussed, expletives had a way of flying.

"Maybe we better just forget about it," Candy said. "We don't need to get on the wrong side of that Filipino cooze."

"Filipino *what?*" Jasmine asked.

"Nothing," Frank said, glaring at Candy. Her and that goddamn language. She was trying to keep it clean, he knew, but words still had a way of slipping out.

Jerrod was smiling at it.

Frank had a decision to make and one that wasn't very easy. He wasn't about to drag the kids down there, not until he knew things were safe and Madel wasn't trigger-happy as usual...but that meant going down there alone and leaving them with Candy. She seemed all right, but the idea worried him. They were all he had. The idea of losing them—

"I can sneak down there and take a look if you want," Candy volunteered.

But Frank knew that wouldn't work. "No, I'll do it. Madel doesn't know you. I might be able to talk sense to her, but she'd probably shoot you."

"I'll come," Jerrod said.

"No, you won't."

"But Dad..."

"You've never met her either. No, it'll be best if I do it. She probably won't shoot me."

"Probably?" Candy said.

"Oh, Papa," Jasmine said.

He reassured her that there really wasn't any danger and made his way down there. He took the gun and the flashlight. He looked back once and Candy was watching him. He thought, *don't you dare let me down, lady.*

## 35

He made it through the orchards intact, feeling the gun in his hand and wondering if he should have left it with Candy. If someone were to come, like crazies with guns, it would have given her something to defend them with. Yet, he just didn't like the idea of having her armed. Either way, he knew, he would still worry.

At the edge of the drive coming in, he paused. He felt like a soldier behind enemy lines. He waited there for a few moments getting a feel for things. The farmhouse—two stories of sturdy red brick with tall stacked chimneys—looked silent. No one was peeking from the windows. He saw no activity whatsoever or sign of the same. A weathervane atop the barn cupola creaked in the wind.

Frank waited there, knowing that this sneaking around business would only make Madel suspicious if she was watching, so, sucking in a deep breath, he stepped onto the dirt drive and walked casually towards the house. He felt dread in his bones.

Again, he hesitated. He didn't know what it was, not exactly, but it was almost as if something physical was locking him in place there on the drive. He swallowed. His body felt tense. His belly seemed to do a high dive off a narrow plank. He stepped off the drive and squatted there by a red air-blast sprayer that Ray used to keep the pests off his trees.

*Trust your instincts. Follow them.*

Yes, he knew how very important that was. But what was it? What was getting to him about that house? He couldn't be sure. Close as he was, he studied it in more detail. The windows all looked dark, sort of gray with indifference. There was no threat that he could detect, yet he was certain that one existed.

But he couldn't wait for it; he had to draw it out whether or not he liked the idea.

He reached the steps and wondered if he should call out, warn Madel and Ray that he had come calling.

He decided against it.

So he went right up the steps.

He knocked firmly on the door. Waited. Knocked again.

Swallowing, he tried the door. It was open. And as he turned the knob, preparing to let himself in, he wondered if Madel was really as crazy as she acted. If it wasn't all bluff and blow. Then again, since the coming of The Food, she might be that much crazier. Too late. He threw the door open.

The thing that stopped him was the smell.

It was like a solid wall of gassy, putrid spoilage that made him suck in a breath and wince as if he had been punched. It was like breaking the seal on a tomb, the mephitic, concentrated stench of death and decay blowing out at him, hitting him in a hot wave that made him clench inside. *God.* It was more than the smell of dead things though, he knew, but the stench of those things that came *after* death, the morbid growths and excrescences—mildew, mold, and grave moss.

*The keys,* he told himself. *Just get the keys.*

That was the thing. Trying to breathe through his mouth and wondering just what he might be breathing in, Frank moved through the house. Out of the foyer, he peered through a set of pine French doors that led into the living room. He'd never been in the house before, but it wasn't too hard to find the kitchen. He figured that's where the keys would be if they were anywhere.

What he found was destruction.

The cupboard doors were open, everything they held spilled onto the floor—dishes and glasses were shattered underfoot along with pots and pans, burst boxes of cereal, bags of sugar and flour. It was everywhere. The silver-faced refrigerator was much the same. It had been cleared out and many of the things it had held like cheese and milk and eggs and lunchmeat were on the floor, too, rotten now, stinking, crawling with flies and ants and several large black beetles.

Had some of the crazies come here to scavenge?

It seemed unlikely, because if they were looking for food, they had dumped most of it out. Frank spotted another cupboard door half open. He saw undisturbed cans of soup, pasta, and packages of noodles.

No, whoever had done this was not after food.

That was for sure.

Regardless, it wasn't his worry. He searched around for keys, but found nothing. There were no key hooks or corkboards, not so much as a candy dish with keys and pens and paper clips tossed into it.

He tried the drawers.

Silverware, kitchen gadgets, wooden spoons. Just the usual. No junk drawers of the sort most people have that hold everything from rubber bands to masking tape to takeout menus. Nothing.

Though he knew he didn't have the time, he would have to do a more intensive search. He needed those keys. He needed that truck out front. He checked the dining room, the downstairs bathroom, the bedrooms, closets. No keys. It meant he was going to have to go upstairs. And that was the last place he wanted to go because he was pretty certain that the awful smell was coming from up there.

*Just do it fast and it'll be done with,* he told himself as if speed was the answer. He knew it wasn't. Speed and carelessness walked hand-in-hand like recklessness and danger.

He went back towards the stairs, following their progression to the second floor with his eyes. That hot, rank stink blew down at him. It was nearly palpable. A demon that wanted to consume him.

### 36

He heard a thump.

It stopped him, made his hand tighten on the .45. He thought the noise came from the porch. He went back to the doorway and saw no one out there. But there was someone; he was sure of it. He could feel them very close to him. A chill played over his shoulders. He tried to wet his lips with a tongue that was straw-dry. The coat closet. It was the one place he hadn't looked and it was right there, three feet away.

*So check it.*

He didn't want to. The very idea disturbed him. Yet, he reached out and gripped the knob, certain he could hear a slow shifting from behind the door. The sound of someone drawing back or tensing themselves to spring. He turned the knob and began to pull the door open...and it was hit from the other side.

Frank stumbled back, nearly losing his balance, his arms pinwheeling. A shape rushed out at him. In that split second of discovery, he saw only the glaring whites of two crazy eyes and a scowling mouth wet with drool. Before he could even hope to bring the gun to bear, the shape was on him, stiff-arming him in the chest, and planting him on his ass just as quick.

"GET! GET! GET!" the voice cried. "WE ALL GOTTA GET! GOTTA GET! GET! GET!"

The shape ran off, and Frank knew it was Ray Trawley, but not the Ray Trawley he had known but one broken by fear and dementia.

"Ray!" he called. "It's me, Frank!"

But by then, Ray was already in the kitchen, stumbling and slipping through the debris in there, making a sort of sobbing and moaning sound.

Frank went after him.

He didn't want to. His first priority was his kids...but Ray...well, he couldn't abandon him, toss him aside like an empty can. He was messed up and he needed help.

Frank went after him.

He was still in the kitchen. He was on his hands and knees scrambling around in the wreckage, looting through the pots and pans and broken dishes as if he was seeking something. His face was white with flour, as were his arms. When Frank entered the room, his head turned quickly, eyes glaring in that clown-white face, mouth opening and closing as if he was gulping for air.

"Ray..." Frank began.

Ray looted around in the debris like a scavenging rodent. "You better get! You better get! They come at night, and you don't want to be here so you better get!"

"Ray," Frank said. "It's me. It's Frank Bowman. I want to help you."

59

That stopped him for a moment or two. He hesitated there, licking his lips, looking perfectly ridiculous. He looked at Frank as if he remembered him, then shook his head as if the memory was gone.

"Ray, listen to me. We need to get out of here. We need to get in your truck and get away from here. Down in Juneau County, the Air Guard has a camp set up. We can be safe there. I got my kids with me. We can all go together, but we need your truck. Where are the keys?"

"The keys?"

"Yes, the keys to your pickup truck."

Ray burst into laughter that was not remotely sane. It had the same intonation as the barking of a dog. He kept shaking his head, eyes full of tears even as he laughed. "Keys? Keys to the truck? Well, *she's* got 'em. She's got 'em up there. You go ask her! She was drinking from the well, but you go ask her!"

Frank knew there were things he could read into that, but he didn't have time for caution, for dark possibilities. He needed to make things happen, and he needed to make them happen now.

## 37

He turned away and left the kitchen. Back at the stairs, he steeled himself, then he began to climb up them. They creaked under his step. The only other sound was that of flies buzzing at the windows. A sound which grew louder and busier as he reached the landing, his stomach lodged uneasily in his throat. It was warm upstairs. Very warm. Damp, almost tropically humid. He noticed right away that there were streaks of black mold on the ceiling of the stairwell and running down the walls. That seemed more than a little strange because he'd heard that Madel was obsessively fastidious. Ray himself had told the boys down at Pillton's Feed that she wouldn't even let him in the house if his shoes were dirty.

Frank started down the hallway and it seemed impossibly long to him. The cream-colored stucco walls were covered with the black rot...only it was not just a discoloration now, but thick fungus-like growths that were moist and dripping. Frank figured if he poked one with the sharpened tip of a No. 2 pencil, sap would have squirted out like pus from an infected wound.

The stuff was getting thicker now, strung like cobwebs in the corners and the smell—that mucid, warm decomposition—was almost more than he could take. There were flies everywhere. They covered the window at the end of the hall in a buzzing dark blanket…flies upon flies upon flies. Were they feeding off the mold or was it something else? The majority of them ordinary blue bottles and meat flies, but some were big, very big, easily the size of rotund bumblebees, and he did not like that at all.

There was a door at the end and he knew without a doubt that's where Madel would be. The door was furry with the rot. There were flies all over it, and it was not his imagination now that many of them had bodies swollen to the size of large grapes. They lit in the air in churning black clouds. They flew past him, some bumping stupidly into his face and others settling in his hair. He waved them away, catching hold of one especially fat one between thumb and forefinger. As he held it before his widening eyes, its wings buzzed with a shrill sawing sort of sound, its beady eyes staring up at him, its proboscis tickling over the edge of his finger.

He tossed it with a cry.

The flies disturbed him, but he knew there were worse things and one of them was behind that door. As he got close to it, waving away swarming insects that bounced off his hands like marble-sized pellets of hail, he saw tracks outside the door, a flurry of them.

*Those aren't from feet,* he thought then. *No human feet could leave prints like that.*

Whatever left them, they were black with the rot, stained with it like India ink, smeared and absolutely abnormal. They were roughly the size of a child's footprints, maybe a toddler, but oddly oval, like the bottoms of stout chair legs or baseball bats. From the unmuddled ones, he could clearly see that each had three appendages protruding from it in a triangular arrangement. There were at least a dozen of them.

Trying to fight back the fear that expanded inside him like hot gas, Frank noticed that the multitude of tracks were not only before the door but all over the floor near the window. There were many of them on the walls and even on the ceiling, and the reality of that was nearly too much for him.

Whatever made them was behind the door.

He had the most appalling feeling that it was waiting for him. Maybe it had called itself Madel once, but now it was something else, something beyond imagination.

He knew he could've walked away at any time, but something was pushing him forward, and he had to wonder if it wasn't just plain old morbid curiosity. *But the keys. The keys.* Fuck the keys. Yes, he needed them, but he wasn't even sure he wanted them by that point. He was so desperate he was taking the word of a madman who was probably leading him into some kind of trap.

In the room behind the door, Frank could hear a low hissing noise that was not only perplexing but unnatural. It reminded him vaguely of a steam radiator he'd had in his room in college. At night, the pressure relief valve would piss out air with a steady hissing.

He didn't know what to make of it, but his instincts were telling him it wasn't good. That whatever was making such sounds was something he'd be better off not tangling with. Yet, he was curious—and he needed those damn keys—so he pressed his ear as close to the door as he dared without bringing it into contact with all that furry mold. The hissing was intermittent. He had to really concentrate to hear it because of the flies constantly buzzing around him.

Maybe if it hadn't been for that, he might have heard the stealthy footfalls that crept up behind him. By the time he did, it was too late. Something collided with his head and he hit the floor, numb, senseless, his eyes rolling in their sockets.

"I told you to get," Ray said.

He was standing over Frank with a torque wrench in his hand. Frank tried to speak, but all that came out was gibberish. His hand fumbled about for the gun, but it was gone. Just before he completely lost consciousness, Ray said, "You wanted to see her, now you can. I been bringing people to her for the past three weeks. She'll like you, you're big…and meaty."

Then Frank went out cold.

## 38

His dream was a nightmare.

In it, he tried to escape from an enclosing darkness, crawling on his belly down a passage that was barely large enough for him to fit through. He pushed himself forward, finding another passage and another, all of them barely the size of heating vents, it seemed. They became tighter and tighter, his sense of suffocation and claustrophobia increasing. Then the dream fragmented, and he was suspended in midair in a hammock, swinging slowly back and forth while a woman peered at him with the narrow face of a rat. She was speaking, only he could not understand her words. They were garbled, secret things, and he could not understand them. The only thing he knew for sure was that he could not move and that she kept getting closer and closer until he could see her yellow teeth and beady black eyes in some detail. And it was about then that a voice was activated in his head, saying: *You better wake up! If you know what's good for you, you better goddamn well wake up before it's too late! You're in a fix, a real fix, and you got two kids out there who need you—*

## 39

He came awake screaming...or at least, he thought he did. Damp with sweat, eyes bugging from his head, his mouth was open and an audible moaning came from his throat. He could barely swallow down his own fear. His mouth felt horribly dry, parched, ready to crack open.

The air was thick around him, a sweet and appalling stench of rot carried on it.

He was numb.

He couldn't seem to feel his legs, and he couldn't seem to feel his arms. It was as if he had been shot up with something. He could feel his body okay—his heart was pounding and his lungs were pulling in ragged breaths, sweat running down his face in cool beads. He could feel all that, yet, his limbs weren't responding. He began to wonder with rising fear if Ray had hit him hard enough to damage him permanently. Maybe the impact had fucked up his brain.

*No, no, no,* he thought. *This isn't acceptable. Jerrod...Jasmine...oh my God...I have to get to them.*

He blinked his eyes.

There was light but it seemed very hazy, as if it was being filtered through some kind of blinds. He could move his head back and forth and his body was responding, but his limbs were numb...*they're not numb, you idiot, they're tied down.* It was true. He was trussed up so tightly that the circulation was cut off to his arms and legs.

*What the hell is this about?*

Why the hell would Ray tie him up? But the answer to that was obvious: it was to restrain him while he met what was behind the door upstairs. That's what it was all about.

Frank licked his dry lips. Now things were coming into focus and making a certain amount of sense...even if that sense was of the most horrible variety.

He had to do something.

If only he could see decently. The light was yellowed, somewhat opaque, dim and filled with bobbing shadows. Gathering his strength and flexing his muscles, he began to feel some pins and needles in his arms and legs. That was good. That was a start. He began working them. And as he did, he began to swing back and forth like a pendulum. Just as in the dream, he was swinging side to side. He was tied up and hanging, bound like a suckling pig.

He did not like what that suggested.

He had to get control of this situation one way or another.

*Wait...what the hell was that?*

He listened again, but didn't hear it. At least, not for another few moments and then there it was again: *ticka-tick-tick.* It could have been perfectly innocent, but he didn't believe that for a moment. *Ticka-tick-tick,* it sounded. *Ticka-tick-tick.* There was something very awful about that, but he wouldn't let himself think what it might mean.

He waited, but he didn't hear it again.

The fear inside him was sharp and cutting, but he knew he couldn't let it take control of him. As awful as this was, he couldn't let himself panic. He had to think about the kids. He had to concentrate on getting to them, no matter what it took.

Okay.

He took inventory. He didn't have the gun; he knew that much. He had lost it in the hallway. So much for that. The good thing was, he was almost certain he could feel the bulge of his lock blade knife in the pocket of his Carhartt jacket. The problem would be getting to it. There was also a box of waterproof matches in his pants pocket. He could feel them there under his hand which meant that his hand was somehow strapped to his leg.

That's where he would start.

He kept trying to peer through the hazy light, but there wasn't enough of it to be sure of anything. All right, all right. He concentrated on his right hand. He didn't want to thrash too much because that would make him swing and the swinging gave him a terrible sense of vertigo. He flexed his hand and his wrist. Whatever he was tied with, it wasn't rope or twine. It was elastic like a bungee cord, but much finer. He kept moving his hand and wrist until it was stretched enough that his fingers were free. He wiggled them.

It was a start.

He kept at it, his hand nearly free of the loop that held it. The stuff was sticky. Whatever it was, it made the back of his hand itchy, as if he had been handling fiberglass insulation. There. His hand was free. He hooked his thumb into the pocket of his jeans and pulled his hand up, stretching the material even further. Just a little more and he would be able to reach into his pocket. He fought against the stuff and realized that in his exertions, his entire body was looser now. The feeling was coming back into his legs and, despite the throbbing bump on the back of his head, he was feeling stronger now.

*Hang tight, kids. Your old man's coming now, he's coming to—*
Something was happening.

He was beginning to swing again with a gentle side-to-side motion and he realized, now that his eyes had adapted themselves a little better to the murkiness, that it wasn't just him in motion but those bobbing, thick-bodied shadows all around him. All of it was connected to the same network that he was part of and all of it was in motion now, swinging and swaying, stirring up that gassy, cloying stink of decay that made bile come up the back of his throat.

He did not move at all now.

He was afraid to.

The network was in motion because there was someone in it with him, someone pulling at it or striding along it like a spider. Sweat ran down his face again. His spine felt greasy with it. Some instinctive need to scream scratched at the back of his throat. It took everything he had not to panic, because if he panicked, he knew, all was lost.

*The kids. Remember the kids. They're done without you.*

The idea of that didn't calm him so much as it steeled him, made him tense and ready for action. He heard that hissing sound again. It was just below him, and he could sense something moving down there, something large. Then the network stopped jiggling, and he distinctly heard a disgusting slobbering sound like someone trying to suck the pit out of a peach.

*Just wait.*

*Just keep it together.*

The sounds stopped and the network was no longer moving. He waited silently for ten minutes, maybe twenty. There was nothing save that *ticka-tick-tick* now and again. He moved his hand carefully, inching his fingers into his pocket. It took a little straining and twisting, but he found the box of matches and carefully slipped them out. It went well at first. Pressing the side of the little box against his leg, he slid the drawer open and plucked out several matches with his thumb and forefinger. Then he promptly dropped them. He tried again and again, losing control of them every time. His fingers were shaking and he couldn't get them to stop. He was afraid that what was below would come to investigate, and the idea of that was singularly the most terrible thing his mind could imagine.

*Just take it easy. You've got to take it easy.*

Which was exactly what he was trying to do when something brushed against the back of his left hand...something scuttling and hairy.

"*Guh,*" he said involuntarily. It just came out of him.

He breathed slowly, drawing air through his nose and releasing it from his mouth. He repeated that maybe a dozen times and began to feel calmer. And as he felt calmer, he felt stronger and more capable. *I can do this. I've got to do this.* He tried again, snagging three matches this time and fiddling with them until they were tight in the grasp of his fingers. Now the hard part. While holding the matches between his thumb and forefinger, he wedged the little box against his hip and held it in place with his other three fingers. To strike the matches, it was going to take dexterity. Real dexterity.

The first strike was too slow.

The second, he missed the strike zone.

The third, he nearly dropped the matches.

The fourth, he got a little spark.

*Okay, you've got the feel now.*

Sucking in a breath and letting it out through clenched teeth, he struck the match heads. There was a spark, a flash of light that seemed blinding, and the matches lit, all three of them blazing up and he saw exactly the nature of the place he was trapped in.

## 40

He wanted to scream.

He nearly did, but something stopped him at the last possible moment. It was not like the wind was sucked out of his lungs, but pulled in that much deeper and held there in a hot, expanding mass until his frayed nerves stopped jangling and his eyes stopped bulging and his lips stopped trembling. Then it was exhaled as a gentle susurration of air.

Biting down on his lower lip, Frank saw that he was in a web of sorts. A primeval terror in him assured him it was the lair of some monstrous spider, but his working, thinking, *rational* mind told him that *no,* this was not a spider's web (as much as his horror delighted in the very idea). He had been through agricultural college. He'd crammed on his fair share of entomology and this, along with his own experience in raising fruit trees, told him that this was no spider's web; it was a cocoon. It was a nest of intertwining silk sheaths like that of a tent caterpillar.

A cocoon this large…something must have spun it or gave birth to the things that did. And that was the terror that owned him and debilitated him, the fear that pierced his belly like a single gleaming fang.

But there was no time to curl up and sob; he had to do something. If he didn't give a damn about himself, then he had to care about the kids. The flame ate through the silk strands very easily and the burned stink of that was nauseating like singed hair. The matches were burning down and he couldn't allow that. He placed them between his teeth and fumbled out some others, lighting them even though it burned his lips. He held the flickering matches up.

*God.*

All around him were thick packets of silk about the size of pillows. They were semi-transparent, and he could see inching larval forms within them, dozens and dozens of them. He was webbed right in a mass of them. They dangled about him like party balloons. And scattered amongst them, he saw corpses. Mummies really, shriveled things that glared out at him with grinning death masks. They were webbed, too, nearly encapsulated in shrouds of silk from which blue-gray hands poked free and faces pushed out…faces with eyes eaten from sockets, lips peeled free, tongues gnawed down to the roots.

And over them crawled things like caterpillars.

Maybe they weren't caterpillars exactly, but some vermicular larvae that had to be two or three feet in length that inched forward on small suckering feet. They were greenish-yellow with swollen segments, bright yellow spine-like hairs rising from them.

As Frank watched, he could see they were eating the dead bodies and that skin-crawling *ticka-tick-tick* sound he had heard earlier was the sound of their chewing mouthparts. They inched over the corpses, selecting some delectable soft tissues, and then, arching their backs, they dug right in, sucking and biting, glutting themselves on carrion.

*That's why you were hung in here,* Frank thought then. *To die and rot. When you were rotten and soft, they would have devoured you.*

He was certain the corpse above him and to the left was that of George Beagle and the one next to it, was probably his wife, Rochelle.

Automatically, Frank plugged the burning matches into his mouth and lit four more, searing his lips again. He brought the flame to the strands of silk that locked his left hand to his leg and burned them away. The flames caught and traveled up a skein and ignited one of the pillow-shaped cocoon packets which promptly split open with a weird sizzling sort of sound.

Right away, larvae were dropping all around him.

One of them landed on his chest and appraised him with cold glassy green eyes that seemed to be filled with a flat deranged hatred. It made the *ticka-tick-tick* sound, and he realized that it wasn't because of what it was eating but simply the sound of its glistening mouthparts rubbing together like blades. A foul ooze of saliva hung from its mouth. As it arched its back, perhaps to bite him, he batted it aside.

It made a high keening noise and he knew that he had hurt it.

Now all the larvae were looking at him.

That keening sound had alerted them as the network continued to burn, putting out stinking, oily plumes of smoke. They all stared at him in the guttering light. *Ticka-tick-tick, ticka-tick-tick.* It came from everywhere now, rising in volume and urgency and what might have been anger: *TICKA-TICK-TICK, TICKA-TICK-TICK—*

Frank began to thrash violently as they descended and skittered down threads in his direction. Another landed on his chest and he reached out without thinking, grasping it, and crushing its bulging gelatinous body in his hand. It squealed like a newborn mouse, green juice squirting out between his fingers.

Now they were all keening with a sound of wrath and hate, moving faster in his direction, abandoning their tents and zeroing in on him. He knocked them aside and one of them peeled the flesh from the second knuckle of his pinkie as it brought its mouth to bear. Another got in his hair and still another wrapped its furry body over his neck. He ripped it free and smashed another with his fist while a stream of silk was ejected at his face.

By then, the network was not only burning but swinging rapidly back and forth, a keening, squeaking pandemonium of larvae dropping onto him and nipping at his face, trying to web his hands.

Then he had his knife out, slashing and cutting, creating a mist of blue-green blood. The blade was double-edged and razor-sharp. He cut one larva completely in half and it still moved—body sections crawling in different directions. Other larva tried to crawl up his pant legs and one dropped on his face, its suckering feet leaving welts as it converged on his eyes. He speared it with the knife. It squealed and thrashed as he tossed it aside, hacking at a squirming tangle of them that tried to bite through the tough material of his Carhartt.

And then the network collapsed.

### 41

Frank fell no more than four or five feet, he guessed, thudding into a hardwood floor, rolling over and smashing a swarm of the voracious larvae which exploded like water balloons filled with blood and tissue.

Still hacking, still cutting, he realized that he was in a room, the master bedroom, which was strewn with webs and silken chambers.

A dirty sort of illumination came down from above now that the webby cocoon was torn and burning and falling apart. It came from a skylight high above in the ten-foot ceiling. The room was filled with smoke and burning silk, the floor washed green with the blood of the caterpillars.

He stumbled away, slipping and sliding on the greasy mucilage underfoot, leapfrogging corpses and ducking away from shadowy, webby masses that seemed to come from every direction.

He found the door and threw himself out into the hallway, gasping for air. The burning stench wafted from the open doorway in oily, fuming clouds.

He saw the gun. It was right where he dropped it.

He kicked away several caterpillars and got to his knees, the gun in one hand and the knife in the other. Just in time to see Ray come charging at him full bore, his face twisted into an ugly, demented mask, the torque wrench raised high. *"YOU CAN'T! YOU CAN'T! YOU CAN'T DO THIS YOU DIRTY SONOFABITCH—"*

Frank brought up the gun and squeezed the trigger.

The last thing he wanted to do was shoot Ray Trawley who had always been a friend to him. But the Ray he knew was gone. This Ray was a monster. This Ray was a fucked-up deviant.

The bullet punched into Ray's chest and spun him around like a top. He hit the floor hard, trembling and gasping, a tangle of blood spraying from his mouth. Within seconds, he stopped moving.

*Dead,* Frank thought with despair. *Must have caught him right in the ticker.*

On his hands and knees, he crawled away from the doorway, six or seven feet to Ray's corpse. Despite what he had been put through—and the experience itself would fill his sleep with nightmares for years to come—he felt anguish. He felt hollow inside. He had killed another human being. Worse, he had killed a friend.

The hallway was filling with smoke now.

The bedroom and all it contained was blazing, and he could hear the pathetic keening of the caterpillars as they were roasted to death in there. The smell was horrendous. He saw two or three of the larva come scuttling out of the doorway, blistered and singed.

And then he heard a single strident noise cutting through the keening. It was a droning sound, but shrill and tortured with an almost human tone of misery and grief. It was an inhuman cry of mourning like a mother shrieking over the grave of her child.

Then something stumbled out of the room.

42

Frank, seized with terror, the gun shaking in his fist, watched as a contorted, grotesque form pulled itself from the burning bedroom in a swirling helix of smoke.

He looked at it and nearly lost it right there.

What he had been through was bad enough, but this...*but this...*

What he saw was beyond anything he could have imagined. It was bulging and hunched over, droning madly like a cicada.

It was Madel.

Madel reimagined as some mutant, noxious hybrid of human and sawfly. She no longer had hands, just chitinous-looking appendages that ended in hooks that she gripped the doorframe with, trying to pull herself free. Her body was pink and gray, striated with yellow bands, hunched and insectile and set with sharp spines that quivered. She stared at him with black compound eyes, her head cocked to one side as if in recognition, strands of shiny blue-black hair still hanging from her bifurcated, scabrous scalp. She had no nose. Both it and her mouth had been replaced by wiggling fine-haired palps and a long spongy-looking proboscis that wiggled in the air as if it were tasting it. Her thorax was plated, but still maintained an upthrust suggestion of mammaries. Her thorax below was swollen into some bloated, pulsating egg sac that was nearly transparent.

She stared at Frank, the proboscis licking the air frantically now. Green snotty juice hung from her mouthparts and palps. She, like the caterpillars, was broken and scorched, nearing death.

Frank just crouched there by Ray's corpse, trembling.

The Madel-thing let out a droning cry, and there was something terribly pitiful about it. For a moment, her eyes directed at his, it was almost as if her mind had touched his own, mated with it, shared what it was: a hot, crowded chamber of instinctual hate, predation, and insanity. Then it was gone.

Frank was no fool.

If she got to him, if she gasped him with her hooks, she'd render him right down to the bones, vomit acid on him, and suck up his remains with that horrible proboscis. She took two, then three meandering steps from the doorway, clearly hobbled, clearly injured, but her hate drove her forward, that droning cry cycling out of her along with gouts of that green saliva or bile or whatever in the Christ it was.

Frank did not hesitate.

He pumped two rounds into with the .45 and both found their mark, punching into the pulsating egg sac and sheering it open. Madel squealed as what seemed hundreds of kidney-shaped eggs evacuated in a slimy river of gushing birth fluid. She tottered and went down amongst the dying eggs of her children, making a few last piping noises, and then moving no more.

Something broke loose inside of Frank.

This was too much.

This was completely fucking insane.

He jumped to his feet and ran for the stairs, stumbling down the stairs, and not stopping until he was out in the grass, something between laughter and sobbing coming from his throat. His body convulsed with dry heaves, his mind whirling with dizziness.

There were things you could look upon that were meaningless and then there were those that would forever haunt you.

And as much as he wanted to lay there, shuddering with delirium, there was only one thought in his mind: *the kids, the kids, get to the kids.* And this is what got him to his feet and sent him running.

## 43

The shadows were growing long.

Frank did not know how long he had been in the house, how many hours he had been out cold, a prisoner of the cocoon. But it must have been many. It would be dark in thirty minutes or less.

Jesus.

It had all gone so wrong, all so completely wrong. He had wanted the truck so badly that he was willing to crawl on his belly through Hell to get it, and in the process, he had endangered the kids. He didn't care about that goddamn truck now. He ran, huffing and puffing, up into the tangled hills above Ray's spread, jogging through wild grasses that came up above his hips. He did not stop until he made the tree line, and it was there, drenched with sweat and nearly mindless with fear, that he went to his knees in the very spot where he had left Candy and the kids.

There was no doubt of it.

Here were the birch trees he'd marked their spot with. He could see the trampled-down grass where people had stood and sat, waiting, waiting, waiting.

*But you never came back. They pushed on.*

Shaking his head from side to side, Frank would not believe that. Yes, Jasmine might go if Candy told her it was what her father wanted, but there was no way Jerrod would. He would have stood his ground for days, if necessary. He was stubborn and he did not like Candy. There was no way he would have went with her or allowed her to take his little sister away.

*Unless there was danger,* he thought with a combination of hope and dread. *Those men with rifles, maybe they came back. Maybe Candy had to get the kids somewhere safe.*

That was reasonable.

That was possible.

But deep in his heart, his parental guilt still tortured him. It would not believe in anything so optimistic. Not now. Not with the way things were going. Not after the fact that he had left his children with a complete stranger.

*She played you for a fool, dumbass. Candy was waiting for a situation like this. She's one of those cult freaks that sacrifice kids and now she's got yours. She might have sold them to someone else by now. They might be—*

"No," he said loud enough that his voice frightened him in the stillness of the woods. "I won't accept that."

He stood, thinking, reasoning, knowing he could not allow himself to panic. If he panicked, he would make a bigger mess of things than they already were. The answer to this was in his head. He had to think it out.

But the parental guilt, the instinctive need to protect his young, blazed up inside him, hot and immediate. It had no patience with thinking things out; it wanted results, and it wanted them now.

Tossing common sense to the wind, he ran into the woods, screaming out their names, "JASMINE! JERROD! CAN YOU HEAR ME? WHERE ARE YOU?" His voice echoed through the stillness around him that was broken only by the hushed sound of the breeze through the tips of the trees around him. *"JASMINE? JERROD? CANDY! GODDAMMIT, YOU ANSWER ME!"*

But there was nothing.

A bird cried out in the distance, but nothing else.

Night was coming, the shadows that had whiled away the day under logs and in dark thickets and sheltered ditches, were crawling out now, gathering, thickening.

Frank ran wildly in all directions, stumbling over fallen rotting trees and jumping stumps, splashing through creeks and plowing through stands of scrub maples, sticks scratching his face and puckers caught in his pantlegs and hair.

He was in a fix.

A real fix.

And it came to him as he stood there, leaning against a pine tree, his boots caked with mud, his face cut and bleeding, his jacket splashed with caterpillar blood, that he had fucked up in more ways than one.

*The grass, you idiot! The grass!*

In his panic, he hadn't thought of it. Being a farmer and a guy who'd stalked bucks every November, it should have been the first thing that occurred to him but his anxiety had muddled his thinking mind.

The grass.

The grass was deep. He had left a trail through it going down to Ray's farm and coming back again. He had even seen the matted-down grass where Candy and the kids had waited. If he had used his head and calmed down, he would have been able to track them through the grass because they would have left a path right through it. At the very least, it would have shown him what direction they had gone in.

*Idiot.*

*Fucking idiot.*

But now it was getting dark and it would be full dark by the time he reached the hillside overlooking Ray's spread. But he had to get there. If nothing else, he had to get there.

## 44

It was raining.

By the time he found the hillside in the gloom, it was raining. Everything was gray with it as the sun disappeared behind the horizon, and there was nothing he could do but wait as nettles of fear opened in his belly.

He crouched under one of the birch trees, the biggest he could find and tried to keep dry. Getting drenched and sick now would not further his ends. From now on, he had to think, he had to use his mind. He could not let himself degenerate into some mindless animal or all was lost.

*They're okay.*

*They're going to be okay.*

*They have to be.*

He still had the waterproof matches. There was plenty of dry grass and weeds under the trees, lots of sticks sheltered in a deadfall just beyond where he sat. Yes, now he was thinking. A fire. If they were out there, huddled and freezing, they would see the light of his fire and know it was him. Or, at the very least, Candy might come closer to investigate.

Getting the fire going was easy enough, but keeping it going was quite another matter. Everything was damp and nothing wanted to burn. He had to monitor his blaze constantly, nurse it, feed it, but finally, he had a respectable fire going.

The night was dark, and the fire on the hilltop should have been visible for some distance despite the gray sheets of rain coming down. If anyone was out there, they were either afraid to approach him or they were keeping undercover with the storm.

He leaned against the tree, trying to keep awake, knowing that not only did he have to worry about any weirdos that might show but the bizarre animal life out there. Regardless, he was exhausted. His head kept slumping forward. The harder he fought to keep awake, the more his eyes closed. An hour into it, he went out. It was inevitable.

His sleep was hard and dreamless, the sleep of the physically and mentally exhausted. Maybe he would have slept all night like that and woke with a kinked neck and sore back, but a crashing brought him out of it.

He came awake in a panic, the gun immediately in his hand.

*What in the hell was that?* he queried himself.

But he didn't know. He was certain there had been a crashing sound out in the woods like a really big tree had fallen. Now, however, all was quite. He wondered if he had dreamed it, but he didn't believe it.

There had been something.

Something very loud.

He listened for a long time, but there was nothing. Once he thought he saw a bird, a huge nightmare bird wing past overhead, but he couldn't be sure. It was just too dark. Other than that, there was nothing. When the rain finally let up, the moon came out, and he could see a great distance into the valley below.

That was how he spotted the light out there, that lone light burning.

Then he knew exactly where he had to go.

## 45

It just showed where his mind was these days that he hadn't thought of it before. It was so glaringly obvious he felt like an idiot for not realizing it. At the far end of the valley was the farm of Bill and Bonnie Nordstrom whose son, Danny, was one of Jerrod's closest friends. It made perfect sense that when Frank hadn't returned from Ray Trawley's, that Jerrod would suggest they hike over to the Nordstroms. They were practically family to him.

## 46

Feeling elated, light, and brimming with hope, Frank abandoned his post at the tree, stretched to work the kinks out of his back, and started down the hillside, gun in hand. The fire was burning low and he just abandoned it. He supposed the responsible thing to do would have been to extinguish it, but it would never burn out of control on a wet night like this.

And maybe if it did, it might not be a bad thing.

*A good burning. That might be just the thing to drive The Food back where it came from.*

It was a miserable, wet hike down into the valley. A constant chill drizzle was in the air, the grasses sodden, water dripping from tree limbs. Twice he stopped, certain he could hear something behind him, something following, but it must have been his imagination.

*Don't be too sure about that,* he cautioned himself.

He was living now purely by instinct with a dash of rational thinking to even things out. He knew that animal instinct alone would not suffice any more than clear, reasonable thinking would. Combined, he figured they gave him an edge. So even though his thinking brain told him that what he heard was probably his own sounds coming back at him, his instinct was not so sure.

He paused only once as he crossed through Ray's orchards, grabbing himself a couple apples for later because he had not eaten in some time now. What he needed was some meat and vegetables, but the apples would keep his stomach occupied until he found some.

Twenty minutes later, he squatted in the wet grass and appraised the Nordstrom farmhouse. A light was burning in the window and the way it was guttering, it was either from candles or a fire. It wasn't the steady light of a lantern.

He knew he had to be careful.

It was night and showing up at someone's doorstep could conceivably be very dangerous. *And you don't know it is the Nordstroms, now do you?* Yes, in his excitement he hadn't thought of that. Bill and his family could have been long gone. Might be some kind of squatters living in there, maybe friendly, maybe not. It was happening a lot lately.

Throwing safety to the wind (and mainly because he didn't have the time or patience for it), Frank went up on the porch and knocked loudly. "BILL! BONNIE!" he called out. "IT'S ME! IT'S FRANK BOWMAN FROM DOWN THE WAY!"

Maybe he was being reckless, but he was still careful enough to step to the side of the door in case someone tried to shoot right through it.

But there was nothing.

He didn't like it. There was silence, and then there was silence. And this particular form of it was very much in the second category.

He rapped on the door again in a loud, insistent rhythm, and he could hear it echo through the house and, worse, echo out across the empty, rain-soaked lands behind him.

"THIS IS FRANK BOWMAN! I NEED HELP!" he shouted. "IS ANYONE IN THERE?"

That same silence remained unbroken. He had, of course, first thought that whoever was in there was huddled frightened in the dark, fearful of this sudden midnight visitor appearing on the threshold...but now he was almost certain there was no one inside. The knowledge of that, or imagined knowledge of the same, pretty much sucked the wind out of him.

"What now?" he said under his breath. "Oh, Jesus Christ, what now?"

But that was obvious.

There was only one thing to do and that was to go inside. At least he could warm himself in there and get the damnable chill out of his bones. That would be something.

So, gun in one hand, a curious tingling along his spine, he did just that.

## 47

It was empty in there as he thought.

He didn't need to walk room to room to know that; he could feel it. It was a certainty in his belly and in his brain. His instinct and reason had come to full agreement on this for once. Had someone been there, he was certain he would have felt them. The threat of a stranger would have perked up his ears and hardened his heart.

But there was nothing.

The house was empty.

Down the short hallway, he could see the flickering light that had drawn him down from the hills through wet fields and dripping thickets, the inescapable sense that he was being followed creeping along his backbone like swarming ants. Inside, the light flickered orange and yellow, it danced over the walls like witch-fire. Yet for all of that and the vague unease it made him feel, there was comfort to be had. There was nothing quite like an old Midwestern farmhouse with a fire blazing in her belly. It was probably his upbringing, but it always brought peace to him. Such places stood up proudly year after punishing year against blowing wind, baking summer, and freezing winter gales. They meant safety.

He walked into the living room.

The fire was dying down in the grate. Somebody had been here in the past few hours. He saw cups and plates set about. They had stopped long enough to get a fire going and to eat. When they had left, they didn't even bother locking the door. What did that mean? He just wasn't sure.

He could hear the rain out there beginning to fall again.

Feeling chilled, he fed a few logs into the flagstone hearth and the fire blazed up hotly again, hungry for fuel. It lit the room up and he saw that the plates were stained with yellow sauce. Macaroni-and-cheese, he figured.

Jasmine loved that stuff. There were always blue boxes of it in the pantry at home.

The memory of that brought a sharp, choking sensation into his throat. He wiped his eyes, settling into a rocking chair that he knew had been much loved by Bonnie Nordstrom. He stared into the fire, thinking, thinking. Candy and the kids had left without him. They must have had a good reason. The only thing that troubled him was Jerrod. He couldn't make himself believe that Jerrod would have abandoned him. He rather doubted even Candy could have kept him from going down to the Trawley farmhouse to investigate.

What then?

What then?

*It was Candy. She took them away. Or maybe someone else. They had to hide. To escape. If that's the case, then tomorrow they'll probably circle back to the Trawley spread. You'd best be there when they do. And if they never show?*

It was too much.

He took out one of the apples and cut it open with his knife. And cried out. There were squirming things in it, tunneling into the pulp. They were worms of some sort, segmented and evil-looking. One of them fell to the floor and he smashed it under his boot. He threw the apple into the fire where it sizzled and steamed. The other apples went with it.

It was troubling.

Frank had been around fruit crops his entire life. He knew the types of parasites that could get to them, but he'd never seen worms like that before. *That's because they didn't exist before. Not before The Food.* Jesus. Everything was going bad. He wondered how far the pestilence reached, how many counties it had absorbed and assimilated now. It made him think back to Ray. What had he said?

*She was drinking from the well...*

Madel drinking water contaminated by The Food. It had turned her into that thing and that very same water had gotten to the apples. From now on, Frank decided he would only eat and drink from sealed containers.

He found a battery lantern on the floor. There was still plenty of juice left in it. He used it to guide his way into the kitchen. Pots and pans were strewn about. In the cupboard, he found a couple cans of Van Camp's pork and beans. He opened one and ate the beans cold. They were surprisingly good. The bacon and fat were especially tasty. He ate half the can standing there.

When he set it down on the table, he heard a clicking sound. His hackles were raised instantly because it reminded him a little bit too much of the *ticka-tick-tick* noise of the caterpillars. Even now, the idea of them crawling on him made his skin crawl.

But this was different.

A constant clicking.

He traced it to the door leading down into the cellar. He stood there indecisively. He wanted to get a couple hours of rest. He needed them badly. But there was no way he'd sleep until he knew what that weird clicking was.

Sighing deep from his core, he went over to the door.

And went down there.

## 48

Frank was aware of the sounds of his boots thudding on the wooden stairs as he started down, the creaking of the steps themselves. The lantern threw bands of light about, making shadows seem to reach out at him. That was unnerving. But the thing that really troubled him was the fetid stink coming up from below. He'd been around death too much as a farmer not to know what it meant.

*Whatever it is,* he thought then, *it's not recent death. It's three or four days old.*

That hardly did anything to buoy his plummeting spirits or to soothe his rattled nerves. The clicking sound got louder and louder, and it reminded him of being a boy at his Uncle Bart's barbershop, paging through comic books as he waited his turn, the clippers going nonstop atop someone's head.

At the bottom, he stopped.

He breathed, his stomach tightening, his airway shrinking. Holding the lantern up high like a stock character in an old movie appraising a grim tomb, he moved slowly over the cracked stone basement floor, eyes wide, breath clutched in his throat. A voice in his head asked him why he was so damned interested in this. He had no good answer. Curiosity? Maybe. He told himself he'd never sleep with that odd clicking, but he knew it wasn't so. He would sleep. He could have slept in a cave with a hungry bear he was so tired.

There.

Wait.

A little ell led from the main room into a laundry room. There were still heaped, moldering clothes waiting to be washed. Bottles of Tide and Downy, a couple boxes of dryer sheets. And there, just on the other side of the dryer, was a corpse sprawled on the floor. He knew it was Bonnie Nordstrom; he did not need to study the remains in any detail to know that. The sweep of red hair told him all he needed to know. So it was not the identity of the body that held his gaze, but the things that were feeding upon it.

He guessed they were maybe a foot in length, muddy brown centipede-like insects with flexible segmented bodies and huge pincers. Their black beady eyes reflected back the light as they feasted on the ruined face of Bonnie Nordstrom. They were also at her throat, swarming—it seemed—beneath her shirt, feeding on the soft tissues of her breasts and belly. He didn't know what they were, but they looked more than a little like hellgrammites, the scary, predatory larva of the Dobson fly.

But no hellgrammite ever got this big. And hellgrammites were aquatic insects. They didn't live in people's basements. But day by day, The Food was rewriting nature's book. Where would any of it fucking end?

*Oh, Bonnie, oh dear God.*

He turned away when one of them crawled out of her mouth. He figured he should do something...but what? Should he have fought them for her body? Tried to pull them off her? Maybe, but judging by the size of their pincers, they wouldn't take kindly to it, and he rather doubted any bug spray in the world was going to slow them down.

He turned away, going back to the stairs.

And it was then that he heard the front door open above and the sound of many feet enter the house.

49

Frank waited there, lantern extinguished, wondering how he was going to handle this. Part of him wanted to charge up the steps and find out if whoever it was had seen Candy and the kids. But another part recommended caution. It wouldn't do any good to get shot by some weirdos.

Making as little noise as possible, he crept up the steps. He could hear them chatting, stomping about, making no attempt whatsoever at stealth. He saw that as a good thing. Then again, maybe they were just bold.

*You gonna cower in the darkness or you gonna man up and get this done?*

The gun in his hand, but held low at his side, he opened the door, expecting them to come leaping out at him. But that didn't happen. In fact, they didn't even know he was there until he stepped into the kitchen and surprised them as they went through the cupboards. There were four of them—a stout, smiling woman, her gray hair pulled back; a white-bearded gent at her side that might have been her husband; a young twenty-something woman with long black hair and eyes to match; and a middle-aged guy, balding, that looked pissy, ready to fight.

"Another one," he said. "Another one with a gun."

He had a fry pan in his hand, a heavy cast iron skillet. Cords were standing out in his throat, his eyes large and white, his mouth pulled into a severe line. He was going to throw it. Frank could see that. Whatever this guy had been through, it was bad enough that he was willing to take a chance on an armed man.

"It's okay," Frank said, keeping his body limp. "I was down in the basement. There's a body down there."

"Who it belong to?' said the old guy.

Frank sighed. "Bonnie Nordstrom, I think. This was her house. There's…things on her. Bugs."

The old man looked at the gray-haired woman and nodded. "Critters. I've seen 'em. Like centipedes with big pincers, eh? About so long?" He held his hands out to indicate about a foot in length, maybe more. When Frank nodded, he said, "Like hellgrammites, ain't they? But real big? Hate to get them pincers into my skin. Been seeing a lot of 'em these past few weeks. Have a liking for dead things, but not the living. That's the good thing. I used to fish brown trout on the Wolf River with hellgrammites. With a bent hook and a dead drift, they're real wooly buggers in the water! Trout eat 'em up! Took a twenty-four-inch brookie on one back in '77—"

"Enough, Mick," the gray-haired woman said. "I'm sure Mister...ah..."

"Bowman, Frank Bowman," he told her. "I got...*had* a farm up near Frenchman's Pond."

"Nice to meet you, Frank," she said. "I'm Maribel Carpenter and this is my supposed better half, Mick."

"Pleasure," Mick said.

She introduced the young woman as Ruby and the intense guy with the frying pan as David.

Frank sighed. "Nice to meet you all," he said, sliding the gun into his pocket and setting the lantern on the table.

50

Maribel said that Mick and she were from up north in Price County, as was David. Ruby was from Michigan. She was a schoolteacher. That's what they told him and Frank figured it was all he really needed to know.

He sat down at the table while they scavenged canned goods from the cupboards. *If my house was still standing,* he thought, *this is what it would be like. Strangers would be looting it for pork and fucking beans. I'm sorry, Bonnie, but they're hungry, and I don't have the heart to tell them no.* Which got him to thinking about The Food and nature gone crazy and wondering if there could possibly be any end to this or if the zone would just keep expanding.

David did not join the others in hunting down food. Still holding the fry pan, he eyed Frank suspiciously, intently. Had it been under any other circumstances, Frank would have told him to quit eyeballing him or he would have knocked his teeth out. At least, he told himself he would have. David held the fry pan like it was a dangerous weapon he was waiting for the opportunity to use. Feeling the .45 in his pocket, Frank thought, *Try it, you idiot. I'll drop you before you get it six inches.* And thinking that way made him feel worse as if he were one of those inbred redneck idiots that drove around with one of those bumper stickers that showed a target and said, THIS IS MY PEACE SIGN. He remembered his dad saying many years before, *a man with balls says it to your face, a man without any says it with bumper stickers.* That made him smile thinly. *The ball-less wonders do it on the internet these days, Dad.*

"Why don't you and Ruby go sit by the fire," Maribel told her husband. "I'll get us something to wrap our bellies around. Let's see…we got pork and beans, chicken noodle soup, canned spaghetti…where are those eggs?"

"Right here," Ruby said. She produced a paper bag that was coming apart from the rain. In it was an egg carton wrapped in a towel for some reason.

"Farm fresh," Mick said. "We liberated them from a farm down the way. Looked like it got hit by a bomb."

"Wasn't no bomb," David said. He looked around at the others in the yellow light of the kitchen. "You know it wasn't a bomb. It was one of those things out there. Same as got Carolyn." He looked at Frank. "We were in our SUV, me and Carolyn…she was my wife…something came out of the dark…it was big…it had lots of legs…it rammed right into the SUV, flipped it into the ditch. Then it tore the door off, pulled her…pulled Carolyn out…*it took her into the fucking night and I could hear it eating her! I could hear her scream! I could hear her bones crunching!*" When Mick opened his mouth to say something, he silenced him with a look. "That's what happened, Frank. That's exactly what happened. Some kind of monster…and if you tell me I'm crazy—" he looked down at the black cast-iron skillet in his hand and hefted it "—I'll smash your head in."

"Easy, David," Maribel said.

Frank shook his head. "That's all right. I know how it is, I understand—"

"You don't understand shit!" David cried.

Enough, enough, enough. Frank had sympathy for this guy, but there was a limit. He stood up to his full height, towering over David by a good six inches. "Now you listen to me. I watched that goddamn Food destroy my house. Destroy my farm, destroy everything my family worked for for five fucking generations. I've been on the run since. Today, I got into some shit, and when I got free of it, my kids were gone. Them and the woman who was watching him. I got a little boy and a little girl missing out there." By this point, Frank had stepped forward, feeling the antagonism building in him. He was bearing down on David without consciously meaning to do so. "So don't *you* tell me what I understand or don't understand, okay? And put that fucking fry pan down or it'll take 'em three hours to pull it out of your ass!"

David looked like was actually going to swing it, then he set it on the table and went out into the living room. Mick went with him. Ruby just watched Frank. Her dark eyes were curious.

"He's been through some…trauma," Maribel said.

"So have we all," Frank said.

He didn't waste any more time. He described Jerrod and Jasmine to them, giving them a good description of Candy as well.

"So many people we saw on the move today," Maribel said. "Everyone headed south. Trying to get away. Been going on for weeks, but today the roads were really crowded. I saw kids, lots of them…I just don't know, Frank, if I saw 'em or not."

"I don't think so," Ruby said. "I'd remember that woman, I think. Most of what we were seeing were big groups of people. Cars, trucks, you name it. A couple buses, too. They're heading down to Volk Field. It's supposed to be safe there."

*Volk Field, Volk Field,* Frank thought. *It's starting to sound like Shangri-la. Even if it is safe, how many people can it possibly hold? How many can it feed and shelter?*

"I'm sorry," Ruby said. "Wish there was something I could tell you."

Frank said nothing because there really was nothing to say. He thought of Janet, dead nearly two years now, and how disappointed she would have been in him, leaving the kids with a complete stranger. He kept telling himself that they were not dead, but it was getting so he no longer believed it.

Maribel lit the gas range with a stick match. "You're certainly welcome to eat with us, Frank. In fact, I insist."

"I'm not hungry," he told her, wondering if he would ever be hungry again.

## 51

"I heard something," David said about thirty minutes later as the others, save Frank, scraped their plates clean of eggs and beans.

All eyes were on him then. Heads were cocked, listening. Nobody spoke. Nobody did anything. They all waited there with forks in their hands, fearing for the worst. After a couple of minutes of guarded silence, there was nothing.

"Maybe the rain, the wind," Mick suggested.

There was a sort of communal sigh and everyone finished eating and sipped coffee.

"I tell you I heard it!" David said. "It was there! Something outside! It sounded like something brushed up against the house!"

"Easy, David, easy," Maribel said in that wonderfully calming voice that Frank thought would sound wonderful and enchanting reading bedtime stories to kids. "It could have been just about anything...just relax."

David apparently did not like being told what to do. He got to his feet, cussing under his breath, parted the curtain, and peered out the window. Apparently, he couldn't see anything in the blackness and rain because he shook his head and returned to the fire. He fed a few more logs in until it was burning high and bright, chasing the shadows from the room.

"I don't care what you people say: there's something out there," he said.

"All right, David," Mick said. "Enough. If there is something, I'm sure it'll make itself known. If it doesn't, then we won't worry about it. No need to be scaring people."

"I'm not trying to scare anybody! That's not my intention! I'm just trying to warn you! I *saw* one of those goddamned things firsthand! I *saw* it take my wife! And, goddamn you all, *I listened while it tore her apart!*" He was nearly hysterical, fueled by his own grief and guilt and rising anxiety. What was inside him could not be contained—it needed to be set free. "Do you people have any idea what that was like? Sitting there in that fucking SUV, upside down in the ditch, wondering when that fucking thing was coming for me?"

"It must have been...bad," Maribel said.

"Oh, it was! It was! You have no idea how bad!" His point had been made, some of the horror in him absorbed by the others and that, it seemed, was what he needed. When he went on, he sounded much calmer. "I guess...that is...I'm just trying to safeguard everyone. Even if you think I'm a nut, just try and understand I'm trying to protect you."

Frank understood that perfectly. He had never really doubted it. And unlike the others, he was sure he had heard something, too. He couldn't say what.

Ruby was watching everyone with her dark eyes. They were huge and shining, catching the firelight. "I saw one of them. It got my boyfriend," she admitted. "Two days ago. Something hit the roof. It shook the whole house. Tony went out there...I told him not to go out there...he was standing in the yard, just standing there. I came out of the door...I told him to get back inside, you know, with everything people were saying...then I smelled something, a burnt rubber sort of smell...and something grabbed him. I heard him cry out. Something came out of the sky, something big and dark like an owl...I couldn't see, not really...but it had a big claw like an owl and took it Tony up into the sky. He screamed." She stopped, licking her lips. "Have you ever heard a man scream? I did. It was up high, over the rooftops."

"You poor thing," Maribel said.

Mick reached over and patted her arm. Ruby tensed instantly. She did not want anyone touching her, that was for sure. Frank just watched her. He could feel the pain coming off of her. It was practically toxic. He didn't know anything about her and he didn't figure the others did either. She was a schoolteacher from up north in Michigan. That's all anyone knew. She was very attractive, darkly pretty, possibly Indian, Hispanic, or even Middle Eastern. As he watched her, he was more than a little intrigued by her—her smoldering dark eyes, her deep olive skin, her full-lipped sensual mouth. He was trying not to notice these things. Trying not see her long legs or the exotic beauty of her face. He had no business noticing any of that. He had two missing kids out there.

*How dare you think about anything else.*

Still, it lingered in his mind, how she would feel pressed up against him, his lips pressed to hers. It was a delightful fantasy, but one that made him feel ill with self-loathing for allowing it in the first place.

He felt someone should say something to her. He was no good with things like that, so he said the first stupid, inconsequential thing that popped into his head. "Where are you from in Michigan?"

He was certain she would ignore him because it was a blatantly ridiculous thing to say after what she had just told them. But she didn't. She looked at him, almost smiled even. Maybe she was glad for the distraction. "I work in Ironwood, but I'm from New Mexico—"

"*Listen,*" David said, holding out his hands to shush everyone.

Everyone listened. Frank was certain he had heard something again. But like before, he wasn't quite sure what. Maybe a scraping sound…but he couldn't be sure. David stood in the middle of their little circle, back to the fire, hands still held out. He wanted no talking and he didn't get any.

The sound came again and they all heard it. It was a scraping as Frank had thought. As insane as it seemed, he thought it sounded like someone out there peeling the old paint away with a hand scraper. Then it started to get louder. The window rattled momentarily in its frame. But whether that was from the wind blowing out there or something much more nefarious, no one could say. Maybe no one *wanted* to say. *Scrape, scrape, scrape.* It got even louder as if it was not something out there scraping really, but gnawing on the outside of the house, trying to chew its way in.

"Like teeth," David said before anyone else could. "Sounds like…like teeth."

"Like a dog gnawing on a bone," Mick chimed in.

But Frank wasn't even sure if that was adequate. It had gotten so loud that it was canceling out the wind. It sounded like someone was cutting a plank in half with a saw or running a large (very large) sawtoothed file over the siding out there.

David stepped carefully to the window. His stride was stealthy and catlike. His eyes looked like they might explode out of his head.

"Don't," Ruby whispered.

He held a finger to his lips as he approached the window. Swallowing, looking back at the others, he reached for it.

### 52

Frank could feel the tension in the air. It was strung like hot wires. He could feel it going right up his spine like static electricity. He could barely sit still. He wanted David to stop what he was doing, but his mouth was too dry to speak. The fire blazed up suddenly in the hearth and Ruby made a gasping sound. Shadows that were serpentine and thick-bodied slithered over the walls.

Mick and Maribel seemed to pull in a little closer to one another. Ruby looked over at Frank and her eyes were huge and unblinking. She was frightened. They were all frightened. David reached for the curtain to get a look at what was out there, if anything. His hand was shaking. It was as if he were reaching to open a casket lid, to find out what was scratching in the darkness of the box.

Thunder crashed out there and Frank tensed. *Listen to those boomers out there. Keep your head down, Jasmine. Keep it down safe, baby.*

David gripped the curtain, pulled it aside a few inches. Rain beat against the pane, darkness pressing in. It was hard to say whether there was anything out there or not it was so murky. Thunder rumbled in the distance. Lightning flashed off and on.

David sighed. "I don't see anything…it's so damn dark out there, though."

But Ruby who wasn't too far away started to rise from her chair. "I saw…I saw something shiny out there. I know I did."

"Maybe you better just close the curtain," Maribel suggested.

"I want to see," David said.

"Please," Maribel said.

But David ignored her supplication and that was the worst thing he could have done.

### 53

And it was at that moment that that grinding/rasping/gnawing sort of sound rose up with some volume, freezing David in place.

Ruby stepped back and away, standing over near Frank, just behind his chair. He felt her hand on his shoulder. He rather doubted she was even aware that she was gripping his shoulder blade so tightly it was nearly painful.

Then the lightning flashed, very much closer, and Ruby made that gasping sound again, and this time Frank did it with her because he caught a glimpse of something immense out there, something shiny and wet-looking that made his heart feel like it dropped three or four inches in his chest.

David stepped back now and Frank thought, *Close that curtain, you idiot, close that fucking curtain!* Thunder rumbled and that rasping, sawing noise increased, ratcheting up as if to mask the booming of the heavens. Then the lightning flashed, and it must have been right on top of them for it strobed brightly in the window and they all saw something. Just for an instant, they saw an eyeball about the size of a tractor tire staring in at them…it was bleary and yellow, stitched with bleeding red veins with a pupil that was an iridescent silver, like wet chrome.

David screamed.

Screamed the way Ruby's boyfriend Tony must have screamed when that winged nightmare took him off into the sky. Frank leaped to his feet. Maribel and Mick practically fell over each trying to get as far away from the window as they could.

"David!" Frank cried.

And as he did so, the window exploded inward as if it were hit with a battering ram, shards of glass flying like shrapnel. David got hit by a dozen flying fragments, crying out in pain. That's when the entire side of the house collapsed. It didn't collapse inward; it was pulled *outward* into the night. There was a deafening cracking sound followed by an immense crash…then the night was blowing in, wet and black and windy. David, bleeding and stunned, tried to climb to his feet and fell over the chair Ruby had been sitting in. *"Can't see…can't see…it's in my fucking eyes…it's in my fucking eyes…"*

Frank went to help him and Mick grabbed hold of him. "Don't!" he said.

Something came into the room which, at first glance, looked like an undulant power cable, long and sinuous and wet. But it was no power cable. It was part of something living. Not a tentacle, but a whip, bright red and glistening. It was thick around as a man's thigh where it came out of the night, tapering to a needle-like protrusion. It went wild, whip-sawing in every direction, slashing at the walls, slitting the wallpaper, knocking clocks and prints down, overturning furniture, upending the TV set.

And out there, out in the storm, whatever it was connected to roared with an eerie, shrieking noise that seemed to make the very air vibrate.

In the doorway, across the room, squatting down low with the others piled up behind him, Frank thought, *He's a dead man.*

David struggled to get out of the whip's way and it looked like he might make it. It came around in a blinding arc and he ducked under it. It hit the sofa and split it in two as easily as a cleaver splits a melon. He tried to crawl away towards Frank's shouting voice and the whip grazed his back. He screamed like he was being burned alive, flopping and gyrating on the floor.

He was literally out of his mind with pain

His shirt was gone, as was the skin over his spine. They had not been sliced away, but *burned.* The ragged edges of his shirt were on fire, and there was a burnt, sickening stench in the air like scorched meat. In the firelight, Frank saw the tendrils of smoke rising from David's back. He was laid open and raw right to his spinal vertebrae, the red flesh looking lightly seared.

There was a great impact that shook the house, knocking Frank out of the doorway right on top of Ruby. Whatever had butted into the house must have been of colossal proportions. He scrambled to his knees and made it to the doorway in time to see something he would never forget.

The rain was hammering down with such intensity that the living room floor was flooded, water blowing in a scathing mist from the wind funneling in with it. The fire was dying, being slowly extinguished. Thunder rumbled and reverberated, and it was hard to tell what was the storm and what was the leviathan out there hovering over the house.

Frank couldn't be sure where David was. The storm was so loud that he couldn't be sure of anything. Lightning flashed, and he caught sight of a great form outside the missing wall of the house. It was hard to say what it was in that momentary glimpse…only that it stood on four or perhaps six segmented legs and that its body was streamlined, plated, and the color of a boiled lobster.

That whip came into the room again, only this time it knew right where to go. It came sweeping in through the curtain of rain, making a snapping/cracking sound like a real bullwhip. Then the lightning flashed again, and Frank saw an immense, elongated head on a projecting neck like an elephant's trunk. When the lightning flashed again, bare seconds later, the head was where the wall had been. He caught sight of its immense aqueous eyes and its mouth yawning open like a train tunnel, exposing four teeth that looked to be the size of fence posts, but were sharp as swords.

Frank fell back out of the doorway.

The lightning flashed and he saw the whip curled around a smoldering, blackened hulk that must have been David. When it flashed again about six or seven seconds later, he caught sight of the creature retreating into the distance. It was like watching a tractor-trailer skitter away on many legs save that its body was serpentine and fluid, creeping away with a snakelike motion.

When the lightning came again, there was no sign of it.

It was gone.

Just…gone.

The only evidence was the battered farmhouse with a missing wall, the living room that looked as if it had been kicked by a giant, and four frightened people pressed together in the gray half-light of the storm.


## 54

"There's one possibility you should consider," Mick said some time later as they waited out the storm, the four of them huddled together under a blanket to keep warm, not daring to light a fire and draw something in again.

"What's that?" Frank asked him.

"The Army. They've been moving through here the past couple weeks evacuating people. They've been coming in helicopters and trucks and APCs. They gathered up a lot of folks."

Maribel nodded. "Been taking 'em over to Montpalk, I hear. Got some sort of camp set up there. A temporary camp. Gathering up the stranded and what not, bringing 'em to Montpalk before they fly 'em down to Volk Field."

"That could be where your kids are," Ruby said next to him. "I heard helicopters yesterday."

"Sure. They asked us if we wanted to come along three, four days ago," Mick said.

"Why didn't you take 'em up on it?" Frank asked.

Maribel made a snorting sound. "Because of certain hardheaded people."

That got a small, very small, chuckle out of Mick. "Yup, it's my fault, all my fault. See, I have a cousin in these parts. I thought I'd go down to his spread and we could wait this madness out."

Frank, intrigued, said, "Who's your cousin? I might know him."

"Ray Trawley," Mick said.

*Shit.*

Frank swallowed and then swallowed again. He wondered if Ruby sensed him tensing next to her. "Ray? Sure, I know him. Him and Madel. Good people. I think…I think they moved on weeks ago."

"See?" Maribel said. "What did I tell you?"

"Damn," Mick said.

The lie came easily, perhaps too easily. Frank didn't like lying on general principles, knowing full well that sooner or later lies trip you up every time. *Idiot,* he thought, *why didn't you just keep your mouth shut?* Even he wasn't sure. He supposed he felt sympathetic to the old guy. Mick was good, so was Maribel. Something in him just found it necessary to throw something out there, if for no other reason than to keep them away from the Trawley farmhouse.

*And what if they decide to go have a look?*

He'd cross that bridge when he came to it. Hopefully, they wouldn't.

There was silence for a time as each maybe thought about what it was they were going to do now. Ruby had lost her boyfriend. Mick and Maribel had no set destination. And Frank? He didn't know. He really didn't know. Montpalk sounded like a good idea.

The kids could be there or maybe at Volk by now. *Or they could be dead.* That was the blade that kept cutting him.

"Why didn't you leave?" Ruby asked him. "You knew it was getting bad, but you hung on. Why?"

He sighed. "There's lots of reasons, but none of them make any sense now. In retrospect, what I did was dangerous, foolish, and might have cost the lives of my kids." He had to hold it together after he said that; it brought him close to tears. He could barely contain the anguish in his soul. "I was worried about the farm, I guess. It had been in our family for generations. I grew up there. My dad grew up there. *His* dad grew up there. It's hard to understand, but I feel a strong connection to it, like I'm some kind of steward of it and I had to protect it." He shook his head. "It makes no sense. You don't endanger the lives of people you love for reasons like that. I built our house there. We, Janet and I, raised up our kids there. I just couldn't let it go. Like I said, it makes no sense now."

"You're wrong, son," Maribel said, reaching for his hand under the blanket and giving it a squeeze. "It makes all the sense in the world."

"It does," Mick said.

Ruby said nothing and was that because she thought he was a fool or because she really didn't care one way or another? Frank supposed it didn't matter. She was young. Twenty-four? Twenty-five? Something like that. He had fifteen years on her. There was no way she could understand him. It was easier for Mick and Maribel because their age gave them wisdom and a bird's eye view of things; Ruby didn't have that.

"You miss your wife, don't you?" she asked.

"Yes," he admitted. "Every day."

"That's...nice."

But he wanted to tell her, *No, it's not nice. She's been dead two years and I still can't move on. I wake up in the night reaching out for her, thinking she'll be there. But she's not and she never will be again. Sometimes, I'll open my eyes in the morning and I'll feel really happy for about ten seconds until I realize she's gone and it's not all some fucked-up dream.* He wouldn't admit to any of that. He was old school in many ways, very working class. Where he came from, men didn't piss on about their feelings. It just wasn't done.

"In the morning, I think we should get moving," Mick said. "Make our way over to Montpalk. That'll be a start anyway."

The others agreed, but Frank said nothing. He didn't have the heart to tell them he wouldn't be joining them. There was no way he could leave. Not until he had searched every square inch of the county for Jerrod and Jasmine. He hoped to God they were in Montpalk or down at Volk, but he had to be sure. Before he left, he would make damn sure he had looked everywhere. In every house and under every rock. And God help anybody or any*thing* that got in his way.

### 55

Janet died in her sleep. She went easy in the middle of the night. By God or fate or providence or silly haphazard coincidence, the kids weren't home. Jasmine was at a Brownie sleepover and Jerrod was with Danny Nordstrom and his family up at their summer camp on Two-Finger Creek. That was the only real blessing about any of it. Frank was tired after a long day in the fields and he went to bed just after supper. Janet decided to stay up and watch TV. He found her on the couch the next morning at six, cold as a brick. After that, things got confused and near-delirious, as if it was some fever dream he was wading through. The police and coroner and funeral wagon were gone before the kids got home. That was another blessing. When Jerrod walked in the door, he said, "Hey, Dad. Where's Mom?" *Where exactly?* a voice in Frank's pain-wracked mind had asked. "Come here, son. Sit down by me. We need to talk." That nightmare was played over again with Jasmine. And by that time, friends and relatives were filling the house and time became loopy and lopsided. He sat there while people poured out their sympathy to him. They held him and touched him and cried on his shoulder. He was cold as stone. He said very little and then finally nothing at all. He didn't think he'd ever speak again because there were no words worth saying, nothing that could touch the pain he felt deep into his marrow. Then one night, poor little Jasmine, eyes red from crying, her entire little world torn asunder, came and sat on his lap. She wrapped her delicate little arms around his neck and said, "I had a dream that Mama was with the angels and she was very safe, but she was worried about you. She told me to take care of you and I told her I would." She pressed herself tightly against him and he could smell the soap from her bath and the fresh shampoo smell of her hair. He felt her tears break warm against his cheek. That was when he first cried. He had cried the first time he held her as a baby and then not again until that night when she held him and made him feel so very loved. Now he feared that he would never hold her again.

And that was the most unbearable pain he could imagine.

Thinking back, Frank could not remember what was real. Janet's death was the worst thing he had ever gone through in his life. Not only had he lost the woman he loved and respected more than any other woman on the planet, but the kids had lost their mother. The grief and torment went on for many months and even these days, two years later, it would creep into their lives as if it had never really ended and, as far as he was concerned, it hadn't.

That night as he huddled with others, trying to close his eyes he thought about Janet and their children and how he had lost her and might have lost them, too. *Oh, baby, what can I do? I just don't know what to do.* And he could almost hear her voice in his thoughts, telling him to follow his heart and trust his instincts; neither would let him down. *Janet, Janet, Janet.* Gone now, so far gone. She slept in time and walked only in memory.

## 56

The rain, the constant rain.

It went on for many days. It ran and pooled and seeped and the world became green and fungal, bursting with spores and budding with flowers and clustered with noxious tangles of reedy undergrowth. The Food and the rain nurtured new forms of life, making things grow like they had never grown before, bringing forth chimeric life forms and even entirely new organisms from the mildewed bones of old ones. Every day, Frank would march out into it, searching, searching, searching. He found a truck and he used it to go from house to house, farm to farm, towns and little villages, looking for his children and asking anyone he saw if they'd seen them. Out there on the hunt, he did not like what he saw—the bones in the streets, the corpses in houses, the signs of gunfire, and the plant life which engulfed yards and grew up the walls of homes and buildings, vines and creepers and funguses of the sort he had never seen before. He found entire houses that were soft with some sort of infesting black rot. You could sink your fingers into the walls, into beams and struts as easily as you could the soft spots on a rotting pumpkin.

He encountered colonies of corpse-white mushrooms growing in cellars whose caps were big around as dinner plates. When you bumped into them, they mewled like kittens. He saw birds soaring high above like giant condors. He found bats hanging inside a church that were big as men. In rivers, he saw huge shadowy forms moving just beneath the surface, and once, out in the middle of an inland lake, something with many humps that looked like pictures of the Loch Ness monster he'd seen on TV.

At night, he would come back to the farmhouse and eat dinner with the others, trying to convince them to leave, but they wouldn't. Maribel treated him like he was her son and Mick acted like he was his father or a favorite uncle. Ruby was harder to gauge. She studied him closely as if she was looking for the first signs of impending mental collapse.

During the long watches of night, you could smell things growing out there, sweet and rich and green, far beyond anything Frank had ever known. There were strange noises of the sort he knew only from the soundtracks of jungle movies—squealing and whooping, shrieking cries and shrill droning noises, now and again an unearthly roaring from creatures that must have been massive and primordial. In the morning, sometimes alone and sometimes with Mick or Ruby (something he didn't like, but they couldn't be talked out of it) he would go off searching, searching, encountering myriad horrors that perched on roofs, swung in the trees, hopped and crawled across roads. The things that bothered him the worst were the prints he found pressed into yards and fields, the mud at riverbanks and sometimes even into the pavement of roads, prints left by monstrous things that had passed in the night.

He found more guns—pump shotguns, revolvers, 9mms—and he went out each day looking like a mercenary. He found few people. Most were crazy and some shot at him or tried to attack him, but he did not stop. He knew in the deadness of his heart that he could never stop. He would keep going until he was dead.

The rain hampered things, of course.

Roads were flooded out and some were even washed away. Others were cracked right open, blubbery white tangles of The Food oozing out, spreading over the ground like the webs of gargantuan spiders. It got hard to get places with the truck so he used a four-wheel ATV he found in a garage. With it, he could cut through woods and fields, follow trails and ford creeks, get places the truck just couldn't get him.

Ruby particularly liked to come with him and he found a second ATV for her. She was a very nice woman, very motherly and funny at times. And attractive. That wasn't lost on him. Her friendship was welcome, but her closeness disturbed him. Part of it was that she was so much younger than he, at least fifteen years. But the real problem was Janet. She still lived in his heart even though she'd been gone two years. Every time he felt himself being drawn towards Ruby, the guilt tugged at him, finally pulling him away or building a wall between them.

He was fighting against his emotions.

Not just feelings he was slowly developing for Ruby, but the horrendous guilt he felt over Jasmine and Jerrod. If he had indeed lost them, there was no point in living. Sometimes he laid awake at night listening to the sounds of nature gone absolutely berserk outside, thinking about Candy. Imagining that she had done something terrible to his kids and that he had caught up with her, killing her with his bare hands.

But he could never hate her for long. Some part of him still clung to the idea that she had taken the kids away to protect them. It was this and only this that tempered his anger and need for retribution.

They were out there.

They *had* to be out there.

## 57

There were no limitations to what The Food could do, the changes it wrought, or the multiform horrors it bred in the moist, hot darkness of its womb. In the week after the events at Ray Trawley's house (and the loss of his kids), it was like Frank was living in some kind of nightmare. It was as if every 1950s B-monster-movie he'd seen as a kid was finally coming into its own. But even that didn't really cover it. At night, the constant shrieking and roaring kept him awake, always fearing that the monstrosity that had lunched on David would come back for seconds. It sounded like the Mesozoic world out there, or at least, the way he had imagined it as a boy as he built plastic Aurora dinosaur mode kits.

He was cutting through an overgrown pasture one day when something immense like a Jurassic flying reptile swooped over him. It was fast. He saw its vague shape but little more as it flew by, but he wondered if it could have carried him off. Things like that were disturbing, but there were other smaller things that frightened him worse. He came across a peach orchard one morning that appeared unnaturally verdant, the trees thick-boled and oddly leafy. The peaches themselves were huge, swollen and ripe. Almost repellently so. He plucked one free and the broken twig gushed a sticky, clear sort of sap over the back of his hand. It felt almost hot. But the fruit itself...that's where the real, true horror lay for it pulsated in his palm like a living heart. He tossed it with a cry.

The important thing was to be careful.

Careful of where you went, where you stepped, and to be aware of what might be watching you.

## 58

"This whole damn county's going to be a lake if this keeps up," he said one afternoon to Ruby after they crossed a flooded county road.

They had pulled their four-wheelers beneath the limbs of a massive oak tree to get out of the downpour. Frank just hoped nothing weird would drop down on them.

Ruby unbuttoned her yellow rain slicker a few inches and pulled the hood off her head. It was hard to tell which was darker—her eyes or her hair. To Frank, they both glistened like onyx. Brushing rain from her face, she said, "Frank, I'm just going to come out and say this. I don't want to hurt your feelings or anything—"

"Don't worry about that; I can take it. You should have heard the way Janet used to lay into me sometimes when I aggravated her."

Ruby smiled. "I would have liked to have known her."

"You guys would have got on great. You're so much alike. Both so patient, so understanding." He shrugged. "I know what you're going to say."

"Do you?"

"Yes. You want to know how long I'm going to carry on like this before I give in and go down to Montpalk."

"Something like that."

He nodded. "I just wish you guys would go without me. You don't need to wait for me."

Ruby gave him a withering look. "We're not about to do that and you know it. We understand what's keeping you here. It would keep us here, too. Don't ever think it wouldn't…"

"But…?"

She reached out and gripped his arm. "It's time to go, Frank. You've looked just about everywhere. If they were here, you would have found them or run into somebody who had."

There was no denying the logic of what she was saying. Of course, it made perfect sense. His brain understood what she was saying very well. His heart, on the other hand, had no use for common sense. It had only feelings. It was governed by them.

"You're right."

"And?"

"And I wish the three of you would push on already."

"Frank…"

He sighed. "All right. I guess it's time. But if I get there and no one's seen them or heard about them, I'm coming right back. You better understand that. I won't abandon my kids."

"I wouldn't want you to."

"All right. Give me two days and we leave. There's a few last places I want to check."

She was satisfied with that even if he wasn't. The idea that he might be abandoning Jasmine and Jerrod was the greatest pain he could imagine next to Janet's death.

*What if they're out there and they need me and I'm turning my back on them?*

He wasn't comfortable sharing his feelings, so he didn't tell Ruby about any of that. He had a feeling she knew anyway. Regardless, his guilt was becoming unmanageable. It was a raging monster that lived inside him, and try as he might, he could not get it under control.

## 59

The next day he went out alone. He liked it better that way. He could cover territory faster when he didn't have to worry about Ruby or Mick. One of the places he wanted to check was Franny Beckman's spread off Highway J, a huge working farm that was operated by Franny, his brother, his three sons, and two hired hands. It was a dairy farm and that's how it made its money, but it also had chicken and pigs and goats.

As he pulled the four-wheeler down the drive leading in, noticing with some unease the abundant insect life, Frank felt a lump rising in his throat because Franny had been a good friend. Without even entering any of the barns or the farmhouse itself, he could sense the desolation. It was thick with portent.

He parked the four-wheeler, facing it back towards the road in case he had to make a speedy getaway. It wouldn't be the first time he'd had to flee for his life from the local wildlife. He stood there on the drive, the blue-steel .45 on one hip, a Beretta 9mm on the other, a twelve-gauge Remington in his hands. He was trying to get a feel for things.

He checked out the house first.

If anyone was alive, that's where they'd be.

Swallowing, he stepped up on the wide porch that wrapped around the front of the house. In his mind, he could remember late summer afternoons when all the boys were lounging here, sipping lemonade that Franny's wife, Sherry, made from scratch. It was so good and so well-known that she sold gallons and gallons of it at the county fair in August.

He sighed.

There was no point grieving a way of life that was long gone now. Things were what they were.

He knocked on the door, first lightly and then with enough force that it made his knuckles hurt. "Franny? Sherry?" he called out, repeating the summons about three times before giving up.

He opened the screen door, then the inside door, entering a house that was silent and empty. Dust motes spun in a shaft of sunlight. He looked around the entry, the living room, the kitchen, and finally the dining room and Franny's little office. Everything was neat as the proverbial pin. Other than the settled dust, there was nothing to suggest anything terrible had happened there. The Beckmans might have been gone to church or out to a movie.

Nothing and nothing.

But in Frank's mind, there was definitely *something.* The atmosphere of the farmhouse felt yellow with age and time. That wasn't what he was feeling, though. Not necessarily. It was something else. Something more threatening.

He poked around upstairs, but there was nothing to see in the bedrooms or bathroom. He even looked in a linen closet and the attic above. Nothing. The feeling grew in him stronger and stronger that the menace was outside not inside.

He stepped through Franny and Sherry's bedroom and out onto the balcony. The air should have smelled fresh after the closed-in smell of the house, but it didn't. In fact, it smelled plain bad. And it wasn't the usual agricultural stink of manure...no, this was a pungent, fusty odor of death and maybe life, too, life growing and greening and ripening obscenely.

From his vantage point, he could see most of Franny's spread— the silo and corn cribs, the pole buildings, the two main barns which were immense and nearly a city block in length, fitted to handle several hundred milk cows. He could see the pig wallows and hog barn beyond—his mother used to call such set-ups "piggeries"—and, in the distance, fields of corn, barley, and alfalfa.

But no animals.

Even from this distance, Frank figured he would see something. A few strays, at any rate. It was possible they were all dead or had wandered off, but it seemed unlikely that there wouldn't be something.

He began to get a real bad feeling in his stomach. He suddenly knew many things and at the same time, knew nothing at all.

*Well, you better go see about it before you leave.*

Outside, the feeling of dread increased until it owned him. The shotgun felt oddly light in his hands. He could feel the beat of his heart in his throat. He was going into something absolutely terrible and he knew it.

### 60

The first things he investigated were the chicken coops. He found a lot of feathers and a tell-tale poultry stink, but no chickens. It was possible predators had gotten to them and not necessarily exotic ones. Coyotes, bobcats, and foxes were the usual suspects, along with wild dogs and even wolf packs coming down out of the big woods. Yet, he saw no signs of that. No partial carcasses or wings.

He moved on, peering into outbuildings and maintenance sheds, finding only tractors, feeders, and assorted heavy equipment.

Then he came around the twin silos and found the source of the death smell—seven or eight Holsteins rotting in the fields. They had been dead for some time by the looks of them. Crows and buzzards were picking away at them. The stench was hot and foul.

Okay, that was to be expected.

Ahead was the low, brick enclosure of the pig barn. The muddy wallows beyond were flooded out by the rain. As it was, Frank was ankle-deep in muck.

He stopped, listening.

*What was that?*

There was a sound coming from inside the barn. Not the usual grunting and squealing, but fleshy pulsating sounds, cooing and screeching and slithering. Whatever it was, it was coming from several different locations and it set his skin to crawling.

He stood outside the doorway, bile inching up the back of his throat. The shotgun trembled in his hands. He was not a man who gave into fear easily, but with the things he had seen by then and those others he dimly suspected, he knew very well to listen to what his instincts were saying.

And what they were saying was that there was danger here, terrible danger beyond anything he could imagine. In fact, his instincts weren't saying this, they were screaming it in his head.

But Frank was nothing if not pig-headed and stubborn.

He stepped closer to the doorway. A hot, almost yeasty odor blew back out at him. It was sickening. He edged in closer. He smelled straw rotting with pig urine and excrement and something far worse that he acquainted with blood and fungal rot. The rusted Orange Crush thermometer above the doorway held at an easy seventy degrees.

*Please just get out of here. This does not concern you.*

But he shook his head at that. It *did* concern him. If he was truly a living being and truly a steward of the land as he liked to think, then this most definitely concerned him.

Sucking in a draft of summer air, he stepped into the shadows and stench and heat of the pig barn. Light filtered in through skylights above, but its beams were clotted with dust motes and chaff. The stalls to either side were empty. Somehow, he expected that. He followed them for about forty feet, his breath coming in thin, short gasps.

It was at this point that the walkway cut off to the left. The barn was L-shaped, and now he knew he was about to see what was making that noise.

## 61

The heat in there was gradually rising the closer he got to its source, as if he was approaching some monstrous furnace. And the stink...dear God, not just nauseating, now it was completely repulsive. It was like a hand reaching down into his guts, trying to yank everything right up into the back of his mouth.

Once again, that mousy, frightened voice tried to warn him away.

He ignored it.

He stood there, steeling himself, trying in some small way to make himself immune to that rancid stench of delirious growth and vile, juicy propagation. The smell was sharp, sweet, and sickening—like fecal rot, potatoes decaying in the black heat of an August cupboard, and maybe even a wicked, fruity odor of putrefying, sugary pulp.

And it was about that time that he became feverishly aware of something else: a throbbing. An irregular pulsating that he could feel in the plank floor beneath his feet.

Gripping the shotgun and holding it high, Frank moved around the corner and looked upon what he had come to see.

It was unbelievable.

He saw the bodies of a dozen pink, plump porkers all jumbled in a central heap. Their fly-specked flanks appeared to be glistening, as if they had been rubbed down with oil or were sweating some sebaceous grease. They were not dead. Far from it—they were full and fat, thick veins standing out beneath their shiny skin.

They were pulsing.

They were the source of the awful throbbing.

They were pulsating like hearts, blood-swollen and so unbearably bloated it would have been near-on impossible for them to right themselves and stand. Frank saw that there were something like roots growing out of them, clustered roots that were fleshy and vibrating. They led from the hogs to some impossible, grotesque bulk that was growing up the wall and possibly right into it. It looked like a gigantic operculate seedpod with a brown, furrowed, fibrous calyx or outer shell. It had sprouted dozens of pale green tendrils that hung in wiry bunches, poised as if they were seeking prey. Whatever in the Christ it was, it seemed to be budding as he watched, pollen tubes branching from the central ovule, ovaries bursting with seed and putting out great vibrantly purple flowers like those of hothouse orchids and canoe-shaped fan leaves that were pink as the hogs, fuzzy and veined.

And it was moving.

The entire fucking thing was throbbing and undulant, tendrils coiling and petals wavering. The pod itself seemed to be expanding and deflating like a bladder. At its apex, there was a sort of terminal bud that was spherically lobed like a false morel, giving it the hideous look of an exposed, exaggerated brain. And sprouting from the top of this were globular berries on narrow stalks that looked unpleasantly like human eyes.

And Frank was nearly certain they were staring right at him.

This was no plant any more than it was an animal; it was some terrible hybrid of the two. It was still growing, still evolving, still...*becoming.*

Frank slowly began to back away from it and the eyes seemed to follow him. There was no doubt that they were aware of him.

It offended him right to his core, and he wanted to start blazing away at it with the shotgun; but that was pointless. The thing was huge, easily the size of a pickup truck standing on its bumper. The buckshot in the Remington would be little more than an annoyance to it.

*Look at it,* he thought then. *I mean, just fucking well look at it! Do you want to piss it off? Do you want to give it a reason to come after you?*

But that was silly. Plants couldn't move, they couldn't walk...they were just plants.

*But what about this? Think about it. That's it, think about it.*

But he found he was unable to think about it. The air was suddenly redolent with a sugary sweetness that made him want to swoon. It reminded him of...of cherries. Not real cherries, but chocolate-covered cherries, those red juicy balls drenched in syrup. It was like that. It was insane, but he could not only smell it, but taste it on his tongue. It filled his head. It sank him in a weird, dreamy fugue in which he could see those many heaped pigs seemingly coming to life.

They were standing up uneasily, quivering, porcine, swollen like barrels. Their jaws opened and closed with a sort of mechanical slowness, black slime dripping from them. They were moving towards him with stiff, zombie-like strides. They didn't seem to have eyes, just puckered holes where the eyes should have been.

And what was infinitely worse was that plant thing had crawled down the wall and it was moving, too, in some impossible rustling mutiny of stalks and slithery tendrils and blossoms that wiggled like fingers. The brain-like lobes of the terminal bud at the top were fluttering.

As Frank stood there, it reached a long suckered sarcous filament in his direction.

And that was when he snapped.

The thing was running with a jellied greenish sap that was sweet and narcotic, making him drunk on its odor.

He squeezed the trigger of the Remington either on purpose or purely by accident—even he wasn't sure—and one of the pigs' heads vaporized. But it did not fall. No, it kept coming with the same relentless, robotic tread of the others. That it no longer had a head didn't seem to make any difference. Strings of bloody mucilage draped from the stump of its neck, swinging from side to side as it came on.

The plant-thing was indeed animated.

As it came ever forward, still rooted to the hogs, it looked as if it was walking them.

Frank cried out and ran.

Behind him, cooing and squeaking and guttural cries rose to manic levels. He ran from the hog barn and behind him the double-doors on the side burst open and that viscid, pulsing monstrosity pulled itself out into the light. It shambled. It squirmed. It crept. It threw out an insane array of appendages that dug into the earth and pulled the mass of the thing ever forward.

By the time he reached the four-wheeler, jumped on it, and turned it over, he relaxed a bit.

There was no way it could catch him.

But that no longer seemed to be its primary motivation. No, now it burst through the fence to one of the pastures and just waited there, pulling the pigs back towards it on their cords.

What the hell was it doing?

Then he saw and knew. And in knowing understood even less than he had before. It was putting out a forest of writhing white rootlets that sought the ground and anchored the creature to it.

It was rooting itself.

He stood there for maybe another five minutes or so, curious as he was horrified. As he watched, the monster plant unfolded its leaves and shook free its tendrils. Stalks rose from it, buds opening to take in the sunlight, it seemed, those vibrantly purple flowers fanning out. The pigs laid down at its feet...if it had any.

There was nothing more to see.

Frank didn't know what was going on, but he was certain of one thing: whatever weird anomaly allowed a plant to take on the characteristics of an animal, one thing was for sure—the creature was changing, it was in the process of becoming something, maybe an entirely different life form.

And that was one thing he did not want to see.

## 62

They set out in the truck the next day. It was slow going because as Frank had learned the hard way, via Claw-Face, it was important to scope out the path ahead long before you got there. So he didn't push it. He took it slow and easy, always keeping Jerrod and Jasmine in his sight. If they were in Montpalk, then he needed to get there. It would not serve the cause of that by driving fast and winding up in a ditch being chewed on by something.

Mick drove up front with him, Maribel and Ruby in the back of the extended cab. Frank found that funny. When he was a teenager, double dates often started like that, girls in the back, boys in the front. Then, somewhere during the evening, couples were paired up.

His smile didn't last long.

He had too much on his mind. And if he was entertaining some half-baked fantasy about romancing Ruby, well, then that's all it was, a fantasy. There was no time for such things in his life right now, and why would she go for a guy fifteen years her senior?

*You've been alone too long,* he cautioned himself. *You're not thinking straight. You need to get your shit together and quit with the puerile romantic bullshit. Jesus Christ, act your age.*

"I'm thinking we're making the right choice here," Mick said, studying the countryside. It had not rained in over twenty-four hours now, and he had a pretty good field of vision showing him meadows and pastureland, encroaching dark thickets that looked to be decorated in a lace of mist that the sun hadn't burned away yet. "Sooner or later, they're going to come in and bomb this county and you know it. They're going to hit it with napalm and burn it flat."

"Maybe."

"No maybes about it, Frank. You can't think for a moment that they're not watching what's going on here real closely with their satellites and drones, targeting where The Food is boiling up out of the ground and where the wild things are growing."

According to Mick's scenario (which made perfect sense), they were going to burn the county, then the boys in their white space suits were going to show up, start poisoning out the rivers and lakes and ponds.

"Then I figure the real Army'll roll through with mechanized infantry, troops, and helicopters, close air support and mop-up anything that moves."

"It would be quite an operation," was all Frank would say. He knew it was probably true...but the very idea left him cold. If they wiped out the county that meant everything he'd known his entire life would be erased.

*It would be for the best, wouldn't it?* he thought then. *This can't be allowed to go on. It has to be contained. It has to be stopped. It has to be cut out like a malignant growth.*

"You don't pay him no mind," Maribel said, in that not-so-subtle way women have of scolding their husbands. "He thinks he's still fighting in Vietnam."

"Damn, woman, I'm just saying. And don't be knocking my service record. We gave 'em hell at Dak To in '67."

She sighed. "Oh boy, here we go."

"God," Ruby said, "you two fight like an old married couple."

They all got a laugh over that and it felt good. They made light small talk. Not once did Frank mention his kids and nobody asked him about them. But like him, he knew they were thinking about them and doing everything they could to distract him from the subject. They were good people, all three of them, and he was lucky to hook up with them.

About ten miles from the farm, Frank started driving even slower because he began to see cracks in the pavement and not the usual sort from weathering and sun-bake. These were pronounced. He was seeing just too damn many of them to believe they weren't caused by something pushing up from below.

63

There was standing water everywhere.

All the rain had flooded the countryside, turning low-lying fields into lakes and meadow into ponds. They saw the tops of fences rising from murky waters. Tractors in the fields were sunk up to their cabs. It would take many, many weeks of sunshine to dry it all up and some of it would just become swamps or boggy hollows. What was of most concern were dips in the road and the bottoms between hills. The road was completely flooded out and they had to drive through them. Even in four-wheel drive, it was dangerous. If the truck got inundated and conked out, they were going to have to swim for it.

Luckily, that didn't happen.

What did happen was that the ground began to shake and heave. Frank brought the truck to a stop. The rumbling came and went.

"Heck was that?" Maribel asked.

"I don't know," Frank said. "But the sooner we get off this damn road, the better."

"Yeah, she's coming apart," Mick said.

And it was. Frank was seeing even more cracks and hairline crevices that widened considerably just off the road. One of them split into a gorge that took hills and part of a forest with it. It was not a good portent. Now and again, they felt the rumbling. Once, it shook the truck so badly that Frank could not keep it on the road.

"This isn't looking good," he said.

"Just keep driving," Ruby told him and there was clear desperation in her voice. "Please."

He drove on and things were okay for maybe fifteen minutes other than the occasional crack in the road. Then, the rumbling really hit. It struck the truck like a shockwave and Frank skidded it to a halt right there on the centerline. The rumbling continued, the truck shaking on its springs. It was hard to say where the epicenter was; it seemed to be coming from every direction at once.

And then, about forty feet in front of them, the pavement not only cracked but opened up like a yawning mouth and the road fell into a sort of crevasse. By the time that registered with everyone, the rumbling shook them again...then The Food came bubbling out of the chasm. In fact, it came surging out, exploding in ribbons and clots and great blubbery masses of whiteness like the dough from a can of biscuits when you press a fork down on the dotted line of the tube. Like that, it came up with enormous pressure, sending out spiraling arms and pillars that crashed back to earth.

"Get us the hell out of here!" Mick cried out.

Frank threw the truck in reverse, burning rubber and swinging around. He drove about a mile down the road and pulled to a stop.

"We're pretty much out of options," he said. "If we want to get to Montpalk, we're going to have to walk."

"There's no side roads?" Maribel asked.

Frank shook his head. "I know this county good. I've been keeping an eye on them and every one I've seen is flooded right out. We leg it or we go back."

"I guess we don't have a choice," Ruby said.

## 64

They followed Frank because he was the only one who knew the lay of the land. After they packed as much of the gear as they could reasonable carry on foot, stuffing it in old olive-drab Army rucksacks that Frank had found on one of his scavenging expeditions, they moved off into the forest. They walked for several hours, Mick bitching that he hadn't had to "hump a ruck" (as he put it) since the war.

It was one thing for Ruby and Frank to walk hour after hour—she was young and athletic; he was wiry from a lifetime working in the fields—but it was a different story for Maribel and Mick. It was especially hard on her because her knees weren't so good. But it was no picnic for Mick, being that he'd passed his sixty-fifth year and had the bad back to prove it.

Frank let them rest finally.

Mick and Maribel sat down on a log. Both were red-faced and sweaty from exertion.

Ruby took Frank aside. "You're pushing them too hard," she said.

"I guess I am."

"You have to keep their age in mind. Last thing we need is for one of them—or one of us—to collapse out here."

"What do you suggest?"

"A break every hour on the hour. Don't push too hard."

"Okay."

She stood there staring at him. Was she sensing his impatience with this whole situation? He figured she was. He couldn't help himself. It had been their idea to go, and now because of them, he was not covering ground the way he wanted to. He had been hesitant to leave the general area where Jerrod and Jasmine had disappeared. But now that he had, he wanted to make tracks.

"I know you're worried to death about your kids, Frank. We all know that. We all feel for you," she said, her voice very soft; he wondered if this was the tone she used with rambunctious students in her classroom. "But you need to keep other people in mind. We've done everything we can to help you. Just go easy, okay?"

He nodded, feeling some tension unwinding inside him. "All right. But I was hoping to get out of these woods by dark and I don't think we're going to be. It's hard to say what might hunt out here by night."

"We'll have to take that chance."

He shrugged. "Okay. If it was just me, I wouldn't care what I faced. But I worry about the rest of you."

She chuckled. "You don't have to be a hero."

"I'm not a hero, lady. It's a matter of survival now."

## 65

Just before sundown, after a hard day of trudging, Frank spotted a lone cabin atop a ridge. He didn't see anyone around, but that didn't mean anything. He toyed with the idea of sneaking up there on his own and scoping things out, but he didn't like that idea. The last time he did that, those he was with disappeared.

"What do you think?" he said to Mick.

"I think we need to get some cover over our heads before nightfall."

"I'm all for that," Maribel agreed.

Ruby looked unconvinced. "Shouldn't one of us check it out first?"

Frank smiled. "Good thinking…but I don't like the idea of us separating. If there's something bad there, then we're all armed and we can face it together."

"Makes sense," Mick said.

There was no more discussion.

Whoever lived up there must have needed a tremendous amount of privacy because there was absolutely nothing in any direction. As they climbed, Frank could not even see so much as another shack in any direction. The woods were thick and dark, so it was hard to be sure, of course.

They took two breaks climbing up the ridge because it was a near-vertical ascent. They had to use saplings and tree trunks to pull themselves up. But finally, they made it.

Although he didn't like the idea of them splitting up, Frank said to Mick and Maribel, "Why don't you two rest for a couple minutes? Ruby and I can check it out."

"It would be welcome," Maribel said, massaging one of her knees.

Ruby nodded and smiled; she liked the idea. Frank did, too. He liked it a lot. Whether it was the fresh air and exercise or not, he didn't know, but he was suddenly very aroused. Just the sight of Ruby was exciting him in a way he had not been excited since Janet had been in his arms. Although under the circumstances it seemed crazy, he badly wanted to get Ruby into that cabin. He wanted to get her in there and tear the clothes off her. The very idea was making his heart pound and his breath come fast. As they hiked up the last twenty feet to the cabin, she kept looking back at him and he could see the heat in her eyes. She was thinking the same thing. As she climbed, he studied the round globes of her ass in her khaki shorts, her long tapering legs, the give and take of her muscular thighs. Her skin was such a perfect olive hue it made his mouth water.

"Hurry," she called down to him.

*Are we really on the same page?* he wondered with excitement. *Are we really going to do this? Slip off into the cabin like a couple horny teenagers for a quickie?*

By God, he was certain they were.

When they reached the top of the rise, he peered around and saw no signs of life. Ruby came to him and he took her in his arms roughly. He arched his head so his lips would meet hers and then he stopped.

"What?" she said.

"Listen."

The cabin was just through a fringe of hemlock and red maple, and from that direction, there was a very audible hissing sort of sound, a low susurration of the sort you might hear on a windy night—tree branches brushing against a house. It was busy and consistent.

Ruby went noticeably limp in his arms.

She pushed away.

"What now?" she asked, as if this was a minor annoyance like a phone call or a knock at the front door.

"We better find out."

He pulled out his .45, and by then, she already had the Beretta 9mm in her hand. Her eyes were dark and bright, her mouth set. Her long neck was corded with tendons. She was ready to fight and he knew it.

## 66

He led the way through the trees and neither of them spoke. They could see the cabin just ahead. A winding dirt road led off behind it through the woods. It was a fairly large structure, he saw, more of a lodge than a cabin. As they approached it, something looked very wrong about it. It was like one of those houses that Frank had run across that were soft with black rot.

"Did it...did it just wiggle?" Ruby asked.

He couldn't say that it did, yet he wouldn't have been surprised. A rank, near-suffocating sort of heat blew off of it that reminded him of attics at high summer: stifling and unnatural. A light rain began to fall from the sky. It ran down Ruby's face like teardrops.

Whether it was the rain or not, a poisoned sort of stink came from the cabin, one like mildew and backed-up sewers and standing pools of gray water.

Ruby recoiled and so did he.

Although Frank didn't say so, he was certain that as they got closer that it stunk like an infected wound. He could imagine terrible life forms being born in its haunted, oozing spaces.

The real question here was, did they get closer and dare to look inside or did they call it a day?

It was obvious from the dark, evil stench of the place that it was not somewhere they would want to spend the night. Even huddled under a tree against the falling rain would have been better than the septic, rotting depths of the cabin.

Yet, as much sense as turning away made, he did not turn away. And surprisingly, neither did Ruby. In fact, it seemed that they were both independently drawn to it. There was something about it they had to know, as awful as it might be. It was like wanting to yank the sheet off a ghost at midnight to see if there was indeed anything corporeal beneath it.

Frank was the first to reach the door. He felt dizzy from the fumes, his stomach all woozy, clenching like a fist. The cabin rising above him seemed to be moving, *wiggling,* as Ruby had said.

Was he seeing that?

Was he really fucking seeing that?

Yes, now the cabin was jiggling like a Jell-O mold. The entire thing seemed to be in motion. The heat, the stink, they were debilitating. His thoughts were mixed up, and he wasn't sure what he was doing...other than the fact that he was reaching for the doorknob (and knowing it was a terrible mistake).

"Open it," Ruby said and her voice was deep and husky. In some distant room in his mind, he was certain she was sexually aroused. And the perfectly insane thing was, that he was, too. This is what they had both been thinking of, and now they were going to do it in the hot fungal depths of the cabin. *"Open it, goddammit,"* Ruby ordered him breathlessly. Her hand was on his back. She was rubbing it up and down his spine. She was pressed up close to him, so close that his arm was wedged in the valley between her breasts. He could feel the heat of them through her thin T-shirt, but it was nothing in comparison with the heat emanating from her groin as it was pressed against his leg.

A voice in his head that sounded drunk and hungry said, *Get her in there. Get her in there and fuck her. Fuck her the way she wants to be fucked. She's begging for it.*

Then the door was open and he wasn't even sure that he had opened it, only that they were now inside. The interior was lit by a pale greenish light that guttered like a candle. The rafters above were invisible amongst yellow glistening strands and ribbons of some fleshy material that was shivering. It looked like the seedy, webby guts of a pumpkin. It grew in an amazing profusion, thick and knotted and tangled and draping down like confetti at a birthday party. And the walls...they were bowed and uneven with some lumpy growth that was orange and fuzzy. They seemed to be breathing. A watery fluid dripped from them, some sort of sap that smelled sweet and absolutely luscious.

As he pulled Ruby into his arms, he looked around with dizzying hallucinogenic delight. He noticed that there were bulging toadstool-like masses growing from the walls and that they were oddly human-shaped. Dozens and dozens of yellow threads were connected to them from the network high above. They looked like they were wired like old-time switchboards.

*Am I seeing this? Am I really seeing this?*

He blinked and they only grew clearer—bulging, throbbing, tumescent forms that were breathing as the walls breathed. He saw the vague shapes of arms and, yes, faces. One of them—he thought it might be female—opened its eyes with a dusty, tearing sound and looked at him. The eyes were not aqueous, but made of fine scarlet fibers. There was no malice in the look. They just seemed to be saying, *Hey, man, what took you so long?*

And something in Frank's head was wondering the same damn thing. Feeling dreamy, detached, almost like he was watching a movie (but one with mind-bending clarity), he took Ruby in his arms yet again...only this time maybe it wasn't him taking her, but meeting her, crashing into her because she seemed to throw herself at him. They were like two molten objects colliding, welding into a common whole.

He kissed her hungrily, her tongue like hot neon in his mouth, his hands up under her shirt, squeezing the cones of her breasts as she ground her hips violently against him. It was like melting. He was in his body and beyond it, tripping out in some cosmic, kaleidoscopic hyper-reality, his brain rioting with colors and visions and a warped reality that was not only consuming him, but bending all around him and folding over him. The touch of Ruby's skin was burning hot beneath his hands. It was made of mercury and hot butter and smoke, psychotomimetic secretions boiling out of her and drawing him in deeper and deeper into a euphoric, mind-bending crystalline anti-reality. His fingers seemed to slide into her furnace depths. They tingled with tactile eruptions of sensory delight as he explored her body which was an electric flesh mosaic that his hands needed to describe—

*No, no, no,* a voice cried in his head. *NO! NO! NO!*

And he felt as if he had momentarily awoken on a sterile plain of suffering where the joy and beauty and organic bliss evaporated, leaving the harsh, biological reality of the cabin. No longer were stars exploding in his eyes and nebulas sucked into the hallucinatory angles of his mind…no, now there was just the cabin which really wasn't a cabin at all but a mantrap, a great No-Pest Strip, a Venus Fly-trap drawing in the unwary with promises of sweets and manic eroticism.

He had been doped.

They had both been doped.

He stood there on rubbery legs, trying to pry Ruby from him with limp fingers. And it was at that moment, as he rejected the reality the cabin offered him, that the hot, mucid stench of the place overwhelmed him and pushed him to his knees, tangled with Ruby, the entire cabin like a pulsating bladder around them. They were webbed in the yellow threads which were glued to their skin and tangled in their hair. The threads roped their bodies and moved over their skin like snakes, sliding and looping and seeking.

Ruby was completely out of it.

Frank, gathering up what self-control and strength he had left, slapped her across the face again and again until she snapped out of it. And when she did, she sprang at him like a feline, clawing and hitting, and he fought to get her under control which was no easy bit.

In that fluctuating green light, he saw reality take control. He saw her eyes widen and her pupils focus. That's when she screamed. She rose to her feet, tearing through plaits of the fibers that held her in place. She ripped and tore them. Then she sank to her knees next to Frank and vomited her guts out.

Then they were both fully awake and fighting in the hot, pulsing belly of that which was attempting to ingest them. The walls were pressing in and the ceiling pushing down. They clawed out chunks and scraps of the soft, fuzzy walls, digging trenches in them as their air supply was sucked away and the living fungous threads wrapped around them, unwilling to let them go.

They were being buried alive, and worse than that, their hands and faces were stinging from digestive juices and they could not see as the rank, moist darkness of the creature closed down on them.

But still they fought, tearing out gooey, spluttering hunks of tissue—

And then whatever held them, regurgitated them out in a wash of slime and tissue. Hands took hold of them and pulled them entirely free, and they both saw the hands belonged to Maribel and Mick.

## 67

After they had cleaned up, they hiked well away from the ridge until they found another hilltop. Here they built a fire beneath a huge elm and waited out the night.

"Like some sort of fungus," Mick said. "That's what it was. It showed us what we wanted to see, gave us what we were looking for."

Frank nodded, still having trouble wrapping his brain around it all. "The crazy thing was that we both saw it move. We both knew better than to go in there, but we did anyway. It had us. That easily, it had us. I remember the sweetness. It smelled so sweet."

"By that point, it was probably too late."

Ruby was on the other side of the fire with Maribel, just staring at the blaze. She had said very little since it happened. Frank was having trouble gauging her. Was she still, understandably, disturbed by it? Did she feel guilty somehow? Or did she feel ashamed by it all because, doped as he was, she had lost control? He couldn't be sure.

When Mick and Maribel had pulled them free, at great risk to their own lives, Frank had seen a great fungous mass of yellow and orange and green that seemed to melt back into the ground. And so quickly that he was not even sure any of it had happened.

It all seemed like a dream now.

Like Ruby, he just stared into the flames.

*It imitated a cabin. A cabin for God sake.*

That was the tough part to accept. Sure, The Food was mutating everything. He understood the weird bugs and oversized wildlife and chimeric forms...but a fungi that could pretend to be a house to draw you in so it could drug you up, trip you out, then consume you...that was so fantastic, it squeezed out the brain trying to make sense of something like that. He wondered if those human forms growing from the walls had been real or not. If they were indeed real, then they must have been people that were drawn in like Ruby and him.

Sighing, he finished his coffee and went over to Ruby. She did not look at him. "Listen," he said, trying to be as compassionate as possible. "We survived it and that's all that matters. I can't pretend to know really what that thing was, but now we know about it. We'll be on guard. We survived it."

She barely nodded.

"Are you all right?" he finally asked.

She kept staring into the fire. "No, I'm not all right at all."

## 68

It was another hard hike the next day that was made worse by the falling rain. No matter where you went or what you did, you could not escape the wetness. The good thing is that they had packed rain slickers. Without them, what was a misery would have become sheer torture.

They walked up hills and down hills, fording streams that might have been less than a foot deep months before but now came up nearly to their hips. The forest was sodden, the fields muddy, the trees dripping. The rain came down in curtains and sometimes a fine mist, but it never, ever stopped. Now and again, they took shelter beneath a tree when it got really bad. That was better, but it was hardly dry. Sometimes Frank thought it was better out in the downpour than beneath some lone spreading maple. Out there, at least you were moving, gaining ground, going somewhere and doing something. Beneath the trees, the branches dripped with a maddening slowness on top of your head ceaselessly—*drip, drop, drip*—and it was enough to drive you mad.

The vegetation was unbearably thick and congested, a tangle of bushes and low-hanging limbs, wildflowers and weeds and draping vines. It was like cutting through rainforest, which, Frank figured, it was going to be if the rain did not stop falling. There were stands of huge, bloated corpse-white toadstools and mushrooms of the sort Frank had never seen before. They looked much like inky caps, but their bells were the size of milking pails. He saw stands of juniper that were oddly pale as if the color had been washed out of them. Weird outbreaks of root rot and shelf fungus, whose individual brackets were the size of dinner plates.

It was all very disconcerting.

And still the rain fell, and you could almost hear things growing, blossoming and budding. The air was heavy and humid, absolutely rank and rotten with the stink of germination. Immense puffballs grew from the soil along with unidentified spongy masses, gelatinous secretions, and wiry strands of mycelium that seemed to be consuming tree trunks.

What was happening to the world was not only disturbing, it was downright scary.

## 69

Around noon, they took a break beneath a huge mulberry tree and ate some canned food and brewed some coffee to take the chill out. Nobody was in the best of spirits. They were dog-tired and irritable, but making a concerted effort not to pick at one another.

Frank stared out in the rain, thinking of his kids, as he always thought of his kids, and missing his dead wife. He tried twice to engage Ruby in conversation, but it was like chatting with a stump. He gave up finally. Maribel gave him a questioning look, implying that she had no idea what was going on with Ruby either.

Mick, who was usually chatty, was tight-lipped. Now and again, he would look at Frank in a most ornery way.

Finally, Frank said, "Say what's on your mind. Get it out."

"Well, now that you mention it, I'm kind of wondering if you have any idea where we're going," he said. "I'm starting to get the feeling we're lost and getting loster, if that's a word."

"It's not," Ruby said and said no more.

Frank understood. "We're not lost. Trust me. Cutting through the woods is the shortest route to the highway on foot. I told you all this wouldn't be easy."

"Well, it's just that we don't seem to be getting anywhere."

Frank had to bite his tongue. What he wanted to say was, *I invited none of you. I could have done this all by myself in half the fucking time. You think I like playing boy scout leader to you people, you're wrong.* But he didn't say that. He decided diplomacy was the best way. "I told you it would be tough. If you can't take it, we can cut back to the road. I'll put it up to the vote. Whatever you guys want."

"We'll continue on this way," Maribel said. "And I won't hear any more about it. And you quit being a bitter little cocksprite, Mick."

"Shit," he said.

*Cocksprite?* Frank didn't know what that was, but he liked it. It was right up there with "weasel-dick" and "monkey-skull."

"Ruby?" Frank said. "You get a voice in this."

He didn't think she was going to respond, but finally, she licked her lips and said, "I'm tired. I'm beaten, that's all. I just want to go home. I want to sleep in a warm bed. I feel so…dirty."

"When we reach Montpalk, there'll be beds," Maribel assured her.

Frank agreed silently.

He didn't know about beds, but he had the most awful feeling that there was going to be *something* in Montpalk. Something bad.

Mick was poking around in the dirt with a stick. Intrigued, he grabbed a tuft of grass and pulled it up. Where its roots should have been, there were fine white fibers that were shiny and waxy like corn silk. "See? Now that's what we're dealing with here, people. The Food and all this damn rain, this humidity…it's making these funguses grow. They're going to get into everything. Even us."

## 70

Frank made them push on whether they liked the idea or not. They still had many, many miles of hard country to cross before they could get within sight of the highway. He tried telling them that, but either they didn't understand or didn't want to. The forest they were cutting through was very deep and dense. He feared what might live in it.

Still, the rain fell.

It ran down their faces and got inside their raincoats, soaking anything that wasn't already soaked. It got in their ears and mouths. It turned what they carried into cumbersome bags of wet cement. Whenever they paused, it rolled off them like rushing waterfalls.

They plodded on through puddles and pools, crossing creeks and streams and steaming black mires that tried to suck the boots off their feet. The vegetation all around them was unwholesomely abundant, thick and tangled and vibrantly green.

As the canopy overhead opened, the rain rushed down all that much harder, inundating them, forcing them to seek the trees whose boles were green with networks of fungi and thick mats of green moss.

"Look," Mick called out, trying rub the water from his eyes. "A shack."

Frank saw it. A little tarpaper shack with the rusting spout of a chimney rising from it. It leaned badly to one side. But if it was dry inside…

He told Mick they better approach it carefully after the cabin, but the constant falling rain had washed away his common sense and he rushed forward eagerly. Maribel joined him. Ruby hung back with Frank.

"I don't smell that sweetness, do you?" he asked her.

She shook her head.

He tried to take her by the hand and lead her over there, but she nearly cringed at his touch. The episode at the cabin had seriously undermined something in her. It had broken something vital and necessary. She was not the woman she had been. He wondered if she ever would be again.

He left her standing there and joined the others at the shack.

"Well?" Mick said.

He was planning on going in there, but he didn't like the idea of doing it by himself. Frank joined him. Maribel hung back with Ruby. Mick opened the door and they stepped inside.

"Shit," Mick said. "Dirty motherfucking shit."

It was wet inside. The warped floor was a lake, water running through numerous holes in the roof. They went in anyway because it was still a little drier than standing out in the deluge. There was a sort of pale yellow moss all over the walls crowding for space with colonies of toadstools whose caps were the size of teacups.

Nobody said anything because there really wasn't anything *to* say. They stood there, shivering in the dampness. What furniture there was was infested by black rot that seemed to be devouring the upholstery.

"What now?" Maribel finally said.

"We get out of the rain for a bit, then we start again," Frank told her.

Ruby was studying the toadstools on the walls.

"Just leave those things alone," Maribel told her as if she were a child.

Maybe she was, because she completely ignored Maribel's advice. She began poking the toadstools with the tip of her finger. Finally, she plucked one off and held it in the palm of her hand.

"Feels like cheese," she said. "Just like cheese."

Frank was paying little attention to that. He saw several gray objects floating in the water on the floor. He crouched down to examine them. They were dead; there was no doubt of that. He took out his knife and flipped one over. It was about the size of a fifty-cent piece, but had legs like a spider.

"Goddamn tick," Mick said. "That's what. And look at it! Get a dozen of them on you, they'd suck you dry."

Ruby dropped her toadstool and stepped back out in the rain.

"Let's go," Frank said.

Out they went again, moving through a misty vale where creeks and streams converged into a frothing maelstrom that came up above their knees. They pushed on through and crawled up a green hillside into the forest again, They marched another ten minutes, Frank leading, when they stopped.

"What is that?" Maribel asked.

Thing was, Frank wasn't really sure. About fifteen feet above the ground, there was a net above them. He at first thought maybe it was some sort of colossal web for a giant B-movie spider, but that wasn't it. It didn't look to be made of silk, but something pink like strands of tissue and hanging from it were creatures that looked roughly like bats. They were the size of small dogs, completely hairless, pink as the web that held them. They had wings folded underneath them and huge, lidless eyes and the snarling snouts of weasels. Whatever they were supposed to be, they hadn't finished yet—they looked fetal, like some weird freak birth you would see in a laboratory jar.

Frank, unable to help himself, prodded one of them with a stick. It trembled. Its jaws opened, trembling as if they were weak, showing tiny yellow nubby teeth. It let out a high-pitched squeak.

"No, no, no," Ruby said, backing away. "This is enough! Do you hear me? I've fucking well had enough of this! I won't see any more of this because it can't goddamn well be real and you all know it! *THIS IS INSANE! IT'S ALL CRAZY AND YOU CAN'T—*"

At that point, Maribel slapped her across the face.

Suddenly, the fetal bats were of little interest.

"You…you slapped me," Ruby said, anger boiling up inside her.

"Yes, dear, I did. And if you get hysterical again, I will slap you a second time."

Ruby looked very much like she was about to give the older woman not only a piece of her mind, but a good thrashing. Frank made ready to intervene. Ruby calmed and turned away. She walked off into the rain and the others followed.

## 71

As it turned out, the bat-things were only one of many revelations that day. And not a one of them turned out to be good. Frank managed to steer Ruby in the right direction before she led them astray, but she didn't seem to care one way or another. He was beginning to believe that the cabin fungi (or whatever it was), had snapped something in her. If this was an ordinary situation, he knew, she would probably need therapy.

He pushed on through the rain, constantly stopping and looking behind him to make sure the others were following. He did not trust them not to wander off or sit down on a log and give up.

He moved ever forward, seemingly indefatigable. He knew the Cane River would be somewhere ahead, but whether they would sight it in an hour or four, he really didn't know. Goddamn woods were murky even in the afternoon. The sheets of rain were making the vegetation steam, coaxing a hazy ground mist from the soil.

"Listen," Mick said. "We need to take five."

Frank nodded. The three of them pressed themselves under a tree. They were pathetic and drenched. He wished—not only for his sake, but theirs—that they would have just went their own way after the first night in the farmhouse. He was beginning to feel like he was their keeper, that they were children he needed to mother over.

"I'll scout ahead a bit," he told them.

"Jesus Christ, Frank," Mick said, "don't you ever get tired?"

The rain running down his face, a chill up his back, Frank felt anger seep into him. By nature he was a pretty calm, cool guy, but even he had his limits. When he opened his mouth, he knew damn well he was going to say the wrong thing. "Tired? Yeah, Mick, I'm fucking tired. I'm real tired. But you know what? I'll have the rest of my life to sleep. Right now, I've got two kids out there who need me. I'm going to Montpalk to find them. Remember *Montpalk?* Remember how the three of you wouldn't get off my ass until I agreed to go?"

He realized he was inching in closer to Mick, suppressing a very real need to belt him in the mouth.

"Well, that's where I'm going, Mick. And if my kids aren't there, I'll look somewhere else and then somewhere else after that. But the one thing I won't do is sit around polishing a log with my ass when there's things that need doing."

He didn't wait for a rebuttal.

He'd had enough of them for one day.

Having them with was like dragging a fucking anchor behind him. But as he wandered off in the forest away from them, the tension ran out of him. He stood there, soaked and miserable. It wasn't their fault. Not really. Something was eating away at him and he was not going to slow down until he found those kids. That's just the way it was. Until then, he was not going to be good company.

True to his word, he scouted ahead a bit, slogging up one hill and down another, bored by the sheer repetition of the forest. He paused atop a wooded slope, staring down through the veil of rain at a confused run of boggy hollows, black pools of water, and thick, dripping undergrowth. He could barely see anything in the haze.

*What if I am lost?* he thought then. *What if I'm leading these poor people in a circle, running them hard until they drop down dead?*

No, he trusted his instincts. Unless The Food had subverted the laws of physics, too, and not just biology, they were moving in roughly the right direction. Once he caught sight of the Cane River, he would feel better, though.

Sighing, he made to turn back to join the others when he heard a buzzing sound. It came and went. It sounded like hornets—a lot of fucking hornets. But out in the rain? He knew enough about wasps and hornets to know that like most flying things they were real pussies in the rain.

The buzzing continued.

*Leave it. It doesn't concern you.*

But this is the way he had to bring the others, and if there was something dangerous here...no, he had to see what this was about. He moved away to the left, fighting through unnaturally lush stands of juneberry and sumac. It would have been easy to lose himself in them completely. In the back of his mind, there was an image of his white bones tangled in creepers and stalks.

The buzzing was louder.

He emerged from the sumac, scratched and sodden, and right away he smelled a horrendous, gut-churning odor of putrescence. The only reason he hadn't before is because the breeze was carrying it away from him. He stalked through some high grasses, tightly packed scrub and dwarf pine...and there it was, a carcass jumbled in a flooded cut in the earth that was practically a grave.

It was hard to see at first because of the flies. They were immense things, black and shiny and buzzing stridently, their bodies the size of jelly beans. Then they lifted like a shroud and he saw maggots, what looked to be hundreds of them, feasting on what lay beneath.

But what exactly was it?

He couldn't be sure. It looked like it had been a large animal, like a bear maybe. He saw tufts of fur and exposed rungs of bone, a set of fanged jaws opened wide. Other than that, the creature was just a festering, fly-specked mass of carrion, half-submerged. The only thing he could be sure of was a furry limb with saber-like claws.

Whatever in the fuck it was, he wouldn't have wanted to meet a living version of it.

The stench of rot pushed him away, and he made his way back to the trail as fast as he could. He didn't like the idea of leaving the others alone a second longer than he had to.

## 72

Just after three that afternoon, Frank spotted two things of interest.

One was the Cane River, which had burst its banks and then burst them again. The little valley it ran through was pretty much flooded. There had been a town down there, a little village called Ebbeton, but it looked to be entirely gone, drowned. He could see the tops of trees poking from the murky surface and what might have been the tip of a church steeple. The Cane had swollen to nearly five times its size, the surrounding countryside inundated by a series of misty bogs.

"How in the hell are we supposed to get through that?" Mick asked as they stood there on the high ground, rain beading his face. "Even the bridges are underwater."

"We'll find a way," Frank told him, studying it all through his binoculars.

The second thing of interest was a small cabin, which must have been well away from the river and its attendant swampland at one time, but was now perched on the edge of some very dark pools.

"Another cabin," Maribel said when he handed her the binoculars.

Frank took the binoculars back and studied it for some time. He saw no reason to think it was like the other. But there was only one way to find out.

"I'm going down there," he announced. "Alone. If it's okay, I'll signal you. If you don't hear from me within, say, thirty minutes, get the hell out of here. Make west for the highway. Got it?"

"Sure," Mick said.

"You shouldn't go alone," Ruby said.

"It works better when I'm alone."

## 73

The farther he was away from Ruby and the others, the better he felt. Something about their presence was making him feel claustrophobic. He should have taken great comfort from their companionship, but he didn't. Mick was turning sour. Ruby had been very strange ever since the cabin incident and, as bad as that was, he was just sick to fucking death of her brooding. Maribel was okay. But more than once, as he and Mick disagreed with each other, he could feel her loyalty shifting to her husband. That was understandable.

Bottom line was, Frank did not have time for politics and petty bullshit. He had to find his kids, if they were even alive, and the others were slowing him down and wasting his energy.

He moved down the hillside, thinking how lucky they had been of late. Sure, the cabin incident was bad, but other than that and a few other bad scrapes he'd had out on his own searching (the Beckman farm came to mind), they hadn't had any real trouble with the wildlife.

He was counting his lucky stars over that.

He reached the cabin without incident, though he did hear something moving about in a thicket flanking a two-rut road. Maybe it was something and maybe it was nothing at all. A few oversized bugs were about, but nothing he considered dangerous.

About thirty feet from the cabin, he went down on one knee with the shotgun in his hand. He waited. He listened. He tried to get a feel for the place. It was small, probably one or two rooms at most. It had a flagstone fireplace and stacked logs for walls, mudded seams. A very Daniel Boone sort of hovel. But it would get them out of the rain, and that was the most important thing for their well-being at the moment.

He saw nothing about it or the two sheds and outhouse behind it that gave him pause.

It looked perfectly ordinary.

He smelled nothing sweet in the air, saw no weird growths. Still, he waited. Rain pattered against his slicker and beat on his head and ran down his neck. He needed to get out of this ASAP.

As he got closer, he noticed with some unease that there appeared to be gun slits cut into the walls."Anybody home?" he called out. "Name's Frank Bowman. Had a farm north of here, far side of Frenchman's Pond. Mind if I come in?"

He waited and there was no response.

*Well, either nobody's home or you're being baited in,* he thought.

He did the reasonable thing: he walked tall and easy up to the front door. If he came forward in a crouch, he'd look like he was thieving or something.

No guns were fired.

He rapped on the door and there was still no response.

He let himself in.

### 74

It was beautifully dry inside.

No leaks.

No fungi on the walls.

There were two rooms. One was sort of a kitchen/pantry. The other had simple bunk beds. A fireplace. A table and chairs. All very rough-hewn as if whoever owned the place had made them all from what he found in the woods. There was a stuffed Brook Trout over the mantle, a real monster, and a couple deer heads that looked very old. What interested him the most was that there was no dust or dirt, very few cobwebs. It was all well-cared for, clean and tidy. There was even a large wicker basket filled with blankets, pillows, and sheets for the beds. A crate of tools. Plenty of wood for the fire. Ample dishes and silverware, pots and pans, dry goods, and even a five-gallon jug of water and a blue-flake enamelware coffee pot that looked well-used.

*Whoever left it like this is going to be coming back and you know it.*

He saw an iron trapdoor ring on the floor.

He pulled it up and found more interesting things below.

## 75

Beneath the floor was a storage room of sorts of comparable size to the one above. It had a cement floor, concrete block walls. There were crates of military MREs, sealed jugs of spring water, dry goods, canned vegetables and fruits, toilet paper and paper towels, a rack of Army surplus fatigues and raincoats, boots and shoes. There were batteries, a variety of ammunition, lanterns and flashlights, waterproof tarps, cook stoves, and extensive first aid kits.

*Had to be some kind of survivalist or something,* Frank thought. *This much stuff.*

He climbed back up the ladder and closed the trapdoor. This was the perfect place to dry off for awhile. The only thing that bothered him was that the person who outfitted this place would be coming back. And if he or she or *they* had gone to this much trouble, they were certain to be willing to fight for what was theirs.

Strangers would not be welcome.

But it was a chance they'd have to take.

He went outside to wave the others down and that's when he heard the first gunshots.

## 76

Frank couldn't be sure, but he was almost positive they were coming from several different locations.

*Shit.*

He heard some shouting and then a loud scream that he knew without a doubt was Ruby. He started running in the direction of the others, climbing up the hillside as fast as he could possibly go while still hanging onto the shotgun. He heard a few more shots, then nothing save for another scream that sounded like it was coming from farther away in the forest.

He made it up the hillside and scrambled through the lush stands of chokecherry and bracken. What he saw took the stomach right out of him and nearly put him to his knees.

Mick was laying there.

There was no doubt that he was dead. He was sprawled in the mud, the side of his head blown away by what must have been a heavy-caliber weapon.

Frank went to him, knowing it was hopeless. The puddles around him had turned red. Clots of gray matter floated in the one near his head.

He heard Ruby cry out again and he went after the sound, plowing through congested stands of wild cucumber and bog rosemary, slipping in the mud, and splashing through pools of stagnant water that came up to his knees. And this was how he found Maribel—he tripped right over her corpse. He pulled himself up, turning away. She had taken at least seven or eight rounds at close range.

*Jesus Christ...*

As he moved into the forest, blind with rage and the need for payback, a scenario played out in his mind where Mick was shot and killed first and Maribel, out of her mind, turned to attack his shooter and was gunned down.

Then they took Ruby.

He didn't have to guess what they wanted her for.

He heard another cry and went after it. There was some shouting and swearing. Okay. Frank moved faster, leaping through the forest. The only advantage he had over them was that they were trying to drag Ruby with them and she must have been giving them trouble, lots of trouble.

*Good girl.*

He cut through a stand of birch, paused, sighted their trail easily enough. There were four paths cuts through the grass. He went after them, moving more carefully and as quietly as possible. The good thing was that he didn't think they knew about him. That gave him a slim advantage. He would have to play it.

## 77

After fifteen minutes of slow, careful stalking, he caught sight of them as they dragged Ruby up a deer trail cut through the ferns. They were heading into some hilly, heavily wooded country. Charging them from behind was pointless; he would need to flank them or get in front of them.

He cut to the left, picking his way through heavy undergrowth. He was dead even with them now. He kept moving, gaining some speed which wasn't easy as he went up one hill and down the other. They were below him now. He cut over to intercept them. There was craggy little hollow below full of green stumps and fallen trees, tangled deadfalls. He saw four men. They were wearing camouflage fatigues. Two of them had Ruby. She was fighting. They were dragging her, stopping to slap and kick her from time to time. Another guy was behind them. Another, a sort of scout was moving ahead of them.

The big problem was that all Frank had was a shotgun and the .45. Neither was any good for long-range shooting. He'd have to get very close to use either with any sort of accuracy. The men had rifles—the scout carried a .30-06. The two that were dragging Ruby had carbines of some sort. The guy in the back had what looked to be .30-30.

This was going to be sketchy.

While the other three fought through the mucky bottoms of the hollow, navigating logs and stumps, and swearing as they went up to their knees in mud holes, the scout was farther ahead.

Frank waited.

Then, carefully, he crawled through the wet loam and pine needles, silently as possible, cutting his hands on loose stones and snagging his rain slicker on outgrowths of bracken. He wedged himself between a slab of sandstone and a bushy sugar maple, peering down at the rolling hills below. The three men with Ruby were still trying to navigate the hollow, fighting through bushes and swampy runs, swearing and shouting. The scout was waiting on a narrow fern-covered ridgeline for them, wiping rain from his face and swatting at mosquitoes.

Finally, he shook his head and started up.

Frank waited for him.

He knew if he shot him, the others would start pouring rounds at him. And against those damn carbines, military-grade by the look of them, he wouldn't stand a chance. He had to take this guy out quietly as possible and get his rifle. With the .30-06, he thought he could probably pick off the others. It had a scope. He needed that badly. Using his knife on the scout was out of the question. Frank was big, but he knew nothing about knife-fighting. He was no goddamn Army Ranger or what not. He was a farmer for chrissake. He'd never been in the service.

But there was another way.

The scout, if you could call him that, was coming now. He was obviously frustrated and pissed off with the others. He was drenched and miserable and impatient. Frank had a pretty good idea by the scowl on his face, that taking Ruby was not his idea.

Closer.

Closer.

The rain fell down harder. It worked to Frank's advantage. It poured down, lashing at the trees above and sending leaves and loose branches spiraling down. It chewed at the earth, creating rivers of black soil. The scout was mumbling under his breath. He carried the .30-06 low at his side. He did not expect trouble. He neared the sugar maple. His boots skidded on slimy exposed roots. He swore.

Then he looked up just in time to see the butt of Frank's shotgun coming at his face. He made a yelping sound as it struck him with considerable power. There was an audible *crack!* as his nose was broken. He fell back, slipping and landing on his ass. He let out a cry of pain, then Frank kicked him in the face, tearing open his mouth and freeing him of several teeth. When he tried to get up, Frank hammered the butt of the shotgun into the back of his head. He trembled for a few moments and went still. The blood washed the blood from his face and head.

Frank picked up the rifle, took the man's web belt that contained a knife and .357 magnum handgun.

Now it was time to get the others.

## 78

He caught sight of them easily enough despite the rain and haze. They had made it out of one hollow and were traversing yet another, shoving Ruby in front of them through the mud, tripping over logs and branches, black with muck right up to their thighs. As he watched them through the scope, he could see that they were an irritable bunch, swearing at each other, swatting at mosquitoes, shouting at Ruby.

It was a real clusterfuck.

The guy in the back with the .30-30 put a hand to the side of his mouth and shouted what sounded like, "HAL! HAL! WHERE THE HELL ARE YOU?" And Frank wanted to shout back that Hal was in the same place he was going.

He decided he'd pick off the two guys with Ruby first. That was the best way to do it. That would give her time to go to ground as he wasted the guy in the back. It was going to take some fancy shooting even with a scope, but Frank didn't see a choice. He bagged his buck every November, and as a farmer, he had a permit to tag a couple does for meat. Once he got his target in his sights, he rarely missed.

One of the shitkickers was yelling at Ruby. When she didn't move fast enough, he shoved her down into the muck and kicked her. *Sonofabitch!* Frank sighted in on him, keeping steady and keeping calm. The guy had shouldered his carbine now. He had his hands on his hips and he was giving Ruby a piece of his mind (something he probably couldn't spare to begin with). The silhouette he offered was perfect.

Frank put the crosshairs on his chest and fired.

No hesitation.

The round caught him dead on and chunks of his spinal vertebrae exploded out of his back along with a lot of blood and meat, some of which, Frank knew, was his heart. He flopped over face-first into a pool of stagnant water with a splash.

The other two started shouting.

Frank worked the bolt and sighted the other guy. He fired and missed, splitting a log about six inches from his head. He had gone down low now in the muck with the other shitkicker. They were firing their weapons indiscriminately.

Frank shifted his position.

Still no good. They were obscured by ferns.

He moved again, getting closer than he wanted to and crept on his belly through the bracken until he got onto the lip of a slope which gave him a perfect bird's eye view of the string of hollows down there.

The shitkicker with the carbine launched himself forward, firing on full auto in every which direction. He seized Ruby and put a handgun up to her head. She was wailing and screaming.

"YOU UP THERE!" the guy shouted and his voice echoed through the woods. "THROW YOUR WEAPON DOWN OR I'LL KILL THIS CUNT! YOU GOT FIVE FUCKING SECONDS!"

Frank sighted in on him. This was his only chance. If he could clip this guy, the other one would probably try and make a run for it and he'd be easy prey.

But this had to work.

Frank knew that if he couldn't pull this off that Ruby was toast.

## 79

He sighted in on him, then through peripheral vision he saw something immense step out of the curtain of rain. Something impossible. And something the other two guys had not seen yet because it was behind them.

*"Shit,"* Frank said under his breath.

In those few seconds, he saw it standing there between two huge cedars, he doubted what the scope was showing him. The rain, the mist, the haze had distorted it and he was hallucinating the rest.

He had to be.

It couldn't be fucking real.

But it was. A bear like no bear Frank had ever seen. It was a huge, shaggy, massive animal that stood easily nine or ten feet in height. He doubted that two men could have circled their arms around it. Its body was lumped and mounded and hunchbacked, some of it covered by mats of red and silver hair, and spiky tufts that looked like the quills of a porcupine. Where it wasn't, an exaggerated, alien-looking skeleton was trying to push through bare patches of its pink membranous flesh that was striated with a network of blue and purple veins. Its head seemed to grow horizontal to its shoulders, protruding like a gargoyle from a cathedral. It was gigantic and grotesque, like the skull of a cave bear covered in the thinnest veneer of flesh, the snout hairless, interlocking teeth like those of a crocodile jutting from its jaws.

That's exactly what Frank saw through the scope in those two seconds before it leapt.

That's also when the two shitkickers saw it and realized that whoever was shooting at them was the least of their worries. Ruby screamed and scrambled through the swampy water. The bear bounded forward on all fours, letting out an unearthly squealing like that of a human infant, but guttural and deafening.

The two shitkickers were crying out, opening up with their weapons as the bear launched itself at them in a titanic blur, knocking aside dead trees and smashing through branches, the impact of its weight—which had to be well over a ton—sending water spraying up into the air. The guy with the carbine was screaming like a teenage girl. He stumbled over a stump, rose up, fell again, rose up one more time, and emptied his entire clip into the beast.

He hit it.

There was no doubt of that. The bear threw its head back, revealing a stringy pelt of yellow-white hair that ran from its chin down to its belly, letting loose with a primordial roar of rage. Then it moved with incredible speed, lashing out at its prey with an immense hairless paw. The flanges were webbed like those of a frog, tipped with deadly black talons.

The shitkicker barely had time to scream.

The claws laid him open from scalp to throat. The shredded remains of his face along with a great quantity of blood and meat went spraying into the foliage. The impact knocked him six feet.

The other guy tried to run, but the bear came after him, squealing and braying. He turned and got three rounds off with his .30-30 before the beast knocked him flat. It raised its upper body, then brought it down, paws first, with all its weight and force. The man's ribcage was smashed with a horrible wet crackling. The beast stomped down on him four or five times, then it sank its teeth into his throat and ripped about 90% of it out. Its face slicked with blood, its jaws closed on his head, shaking him from side to side, smashing him into stumps and logs, tearing him open and splintering his bones.

Then to began to eat him.

It opened up his body cavity, yanking out his entrails and gobbling them up with gluttonous fervor before scooping out his organs and scattering his ribs to get at what lay beneath.

While this was going on, Ruby was scampering away. The beast did not notice; it was gorging itself, slurping and crunching and licking. By then, Ruby was crawling up the hillside out of the hollow. What she was doing took an incredible amount of guts. The bear could have taken her at any moment.

Frank wanted to go to her, but it would have done her no good.

She was climbing in his direction and he didn't dare take his eyes off the scope. If the beast decided to charge her, he would have about enough time to put a couple rounds in it.

He had to stay put.

When she was free of the hollow, using roots and saplings to pull herself through the forest, he called out to her, "RUBY! RUBY! UP HERE! KEEP CLIMBING!"

The beast was so busy rendering its prey, it didn't even notice him shouting. At least he thought so, but then suddenly, it reared up on its hind legs and he knew it had spotted Ruby.

"RUN!" Frank cried out. "RUN FOR GODSAKE!"

Crying and screaming, she did just that. The beast growled, then let out one of its resounding roars that seemed to shake the forest. It stood there in the rain, the yellow-white ruff at its chin and chest red and pink with blood. It looked like some mutant polar bear standing there, filthy with mud and dirt, drenched in gore. Its mounded flesh bulged from bare spots like great pink tumors, pulsing and gleaming with secretions. Its great skull-like head was bifurcated at the crown like a brain, cocked to the side, its eyes huge and liquid green. In the scope, Frank could have sworn they were slit like those of a reptile. It raised its huge webbed paws up, claws extending.

It arched over.

It was preparing to charge Ruby.

Frank fired, struck it, and fired again. The beast stumbled back, but did not go down. It howled with pure wrath at the falling rain, swatting at invisible enemies.

And it was at that moment that they got a piece of luck. The shitkicker who had been swatted in the face was trying to crawl away. Regardless that he was flayed from scalp to chest, he was inching away like a slug. The beast could not allow that. It leaped on him, smashing him flat and the cracking of his bones was sickeningly audible. It grabbed him in its paws, lifted him skyward, easily fifteen feet in the air, and brought him down with fatal velocity against a jagged cedar stump.

He was nearly split in half.

The bear wasted no time in tearing him apart and stuffing itself with his viscera, smashing open his head and licking his skull clean like a particularly gruesome Winnie the Pooh with a honey pot. The sound of its teeth scraping against his skull was almost too much.

As it did so, Frank saw it in profile through the scope. Its spinal vertebrae were exposed, jutting out of its back in white serrated plates that gave it the look of a prehistoric monster.

He went down and reached for Ruby.

He gripped her hand and hoisted up from the dank, wet undergrowth. This was it. This was their chance. They either made good on this or they were going to be lunch.

## 80

He pulled Ruby into his arms and she clung to him like a wet kitten, trembling and sobbing. She was dirty with mud, face scratched and bruised, her T-shirt torn open from branches. But when she looked at him with red-rimmed eyes, he could see that if nothing else, the shock, the trauma of the fungus in the cabin was gone.

Survival instinct had canceled all that out.

What happened before didn't matter.

There was only now and that was enough.

"I didn't think I'd see you again," she said.

"I heard the shots. I was tracking you." He kissed her on the lips and she kissed him back. Hard. "Did they…did they abuse you?"

"They knocked me around, but I'll heal."

"Let's go. We have to get to the cabin."

No argument on that.

Then they heard a crashing from the forest like a bulldozer knocking trees aside.

"It's coming," she said.
And it was.

## 81

As they ran, they could hear it behind them, smashing through the forest like a bull, knocking down trees and tearing apart undergrowth as it came veering at them like a rocket. It could be stealthy when it wanted to, but there was no stealth in this.

They were prey.

It was coming to kill them.

It was howling and screeching, making a variety of terrible noises that sounded very un-bear like. The only thing that slowed it and bought them some time is that it came across the body of the scout and decided it could not just ignore it. It seized the man in its jaws and he screamed. They could hear the sound of him dying as the beast literally tore him to pieces.

But by then, Frank and Ruby sighted the cabin in the distance and it looked like they might make it. They passed quite near to the bodies of Mick and Maribel but they did not dare pause. They half-ran, half-stumbled down the hillside, tripping and falling, rolling and righting themselves. Then they were racing for the cabin.

Frank directed Ruby to get inside and he went down on one knee as the beast showed itself on the hilltop. It moved with a crazy lumbering sort of motion, a shaggy relentless bulk. Its head moved side-to-side like that of a swimming snake.

It paused.

It sniffed the air.

Ropes of gore and saliva hung from its colossal jaws. It rose up on two legs and roared, bristling with deadly intent, pawing at the air.

Frank didn't waste that opportunity—he sighted the beast with his scope and put a round right through its throat. Blood exploded, foaming out of its bushy ruff. It made a gurgling/squealing sort of sound and he thought, *I got it, I've got that sonofabitch.* Then it came down the hillside. Not as fast, its gait awkward, but it was definitely coming.

He got off another round, but he didn't know if he hit it or not.

Then he was inside and the door was bolted and barred. He had a pretty good idea what had happened to the original owner. Somewhere out there, there was a cave filled with bones, the lair of this mutant horror.

But it would end now because it had to end now.

Frank watched the beast through one of the gun slits. It had paused again at the bottom of the hillside. It stood up on its hind legs, then went back to all fours. It moved in a circle. It bashed saplings out of its way.

He tried to draw a bead on it, but there was too much brush in the way. He was not going to waste another round.

Now it had their scent again.

It sniffed the ground, it sniffed the air. It rose up, extending its massive paws against the sky, growling and making a shrill braying sort of noise. It was bleeding, punched with bullets, but on it came, plowing forward on all fours.

It charged the cabin with an insane wrath, powered by hatred and hunger and a primeval knowledge that man was its greatest enemy.

Ruby stood there by the fireplace, trembling. She looked as if she was caught between instinctual imperatives: run or find a nice deep hole and hide.

"Get that trapdoor open," Frank told her. "I'm going to put a few more rounds in that sonofabitch, then we're going below."

She nodded nervously.

Through the gun slit, Frank watched it getting closer, galloping full on, its huge body a mass of muscle and sinew, a living battering ram. He sighted in on it, fired. Sighted again, and fired. The second shot took out a hunk of skull. The beast skidded to a stop, went down, got up, went down again.

*He's done,* Frank thought. *He's got to be done this time.*

Then, growling low in its throat, its bulging green eyes blazing brightly, it rose up yet again. It made a gobbling, slurping sort of noise as gouts of blood and saliva rained from its mouth. As it breathed, bubbles of blood popped at its throat.

*This has got to be it, it's got to be—*

"Shit!"

It charged again. He fired, but his aim was way off. The beast hit the cabin full force and it shook, one of the old moth-eaten deer heads falling from the wall. The beast threw itself against the cabin again and again. Such was its fury that several of the logs were shifted, daylight spilling in.

"Get below!" Frank told Ruby.

She scrambled down the ladder and he joined her. As he shut the trapdoor, he saw the front door explode off its hinges as the slavering, wounded, blood-maddened beast hit it again and again. With its feral green eyes and near-exposed mutant skull, it looked very much like the demon from hell it was.

Then the trapdoor was closed.

Ruby and Frank clung to each other. They huddled in the darkness, pressed into the corner near a stack of green metal Army footlockers. Upstairs, the beast was going absolutely wild looking for them. It was in an absolute cacophony of bestial rage as it tore the cabin apart, flinging about furniture, hammering against the walls, casting pots and pans and tools about, smashing and breaking and throwing its girth about making the entire structure shake. The ceiling creaked and groaned from its immense weight.

Then silence.

*It's casting for us. It knows we're near.*

Yes, they could hear it sniffing around the trapdoor. The beast, of course, had no idea how to work a conveyance like a trapdoor; it only knew that it was the only thing that separated it from its quarry.

It let out a wild, almost deranged cry of seething rage that cycled up and up until it almost sounded like the shrieking of a woman who had completely lost her mind. Snarling, it began to stomp on the trapdoor, hitting it again and again with all its weight and strength. It wouldn't hold, Frank knew. It couldn't hold. It wasn't designed for that sort of punishment.

He got Ruby behind him.

He could feel her shaking and he wasn't doing much better himself. *Smash.* The beast slammed down on the trapdoor. The cellar space shook. *Smash, smash, smash!* Frank heard a distinct splintering noise. Then a cracking sound and the trapdoor collapsed inward, the beast coming with it like some sinister Jack-in-the-Box. At least, its upper body did and that seemed to be about as large as a small pick-up truck. It hung down through the trapdoor, not willing to drop down all the way. Its bloody maw was snapping and growling, dripping gore, one of its paws lashing out, knocking over racks of supplies, slitting open raincoats, anxious to find some flesh it could stuff itself with.

With what little light its gigantic body did not block out, Frank sighted on its mammoth head and jerked the trigger. The round went through one of its eyes, taking out a massive wedge of skull and gray matter. He fired again, putting this one right through its bleeding, exposed brain. Immediately, it yanked its bulk from the trapdoor, screeching and bellowing, rising up and then coming down with a final, wet-sounding impact that shook dust and splinters from the rafters over their heads.

It shook once or twice, then moved no more.

"It's dead," Frank gasped. "It's dead."

Still, neither Ruby nor he dared to move. They waited another twenty minutes as blood and slime and clots of tissue dropped from the beast into the cellar with a splatting noise, one of its great paws dangling through the opening, swinging back and forth.

## 82

They were lucky, Frank figured, in that the beast had not blocked the trapdoor in its death throes. If that had been the case, they would have had to saw their way through it. Still, climbing out was a frightening experience that he figured he'd relive in dreams for years to come.

He went up first.

The ladder was still intact. He climbed up it, his shoulder brushing against the beast's paw. He was close enough to see its claws which were easily the size of steak knives. Upstairs, the cabin was trashed. One of the walls had completely collapsed into a jigsaw of logs. The roof looked like it was going to go next. He got Ruby up and they both stood for a moment, staring at the dead beast.

It was bloody and blasted, but it was still easy enough to see the sort of killing machine it was. Its jaws were open, a web of bloody vomit having been regurgitated in its death throes. Nothing remotely like this had stalked the earth in many eons. With its near-exposed skull, it looked prehistoric (something accentuated by the bony spines rising out of its back). With its long, shaggy hair pushed away from its belly, he could see something like polyps—seemingly dozens of them—attached to its lower abdomen. But they weren't polyps; they were *ticks.* Swollen gray ticks the size of large strawberries.

Christ.

"It looks alien," Ruby said. "It doesn't look like something from this planet at all."

Which, Frank figured, summed things up concisely.

Together, they stepped out into the misting rain. It seemed refreshing after the stench of the beast and its grisly death. He could see the Cane River in the distance.

"We need to get across it," he said.

"Any ideas?" Ruby asked.

But he was fresh out. The idea of being stuck in these goddamn woods another night was almost more than his seriously strained mind could handle, but he didn't see a choice.

"I suppose," he said, sighing, "the best thing to do would be to scout around the water's edge and hope we spot a cabin or a cottage or something. One of them might have a boat. And either way, we'll need somewhere to get some rest."

Ruby was exhausted, but she didn't give in. "Eventually, we have to find something," she said.

*Or something has to find us,* he thought.

"What about Mick and Maribel?"

He swallowed. "I suppose we should do something."

Now that the threat of the beast had passed, the grief settled in and with it, of course, came the guilt. *Maybe if I hadn't gone down to the cabin, they'd still be here. Maybe if I'd stayed with them we could have fought off those shitkickers with the guns.* But it was pointless to be thinking like that and he knew it. Sometimes things were just the way they were and you couldn't fight the fucked up finger of fate.

"It's probably too muddy to dig a grave," he told Ruby, "but maybe we can cover them with some brush or something."

Together, they started up the hillside.

## 83

When they got up there, they nearly overlooked Mick. Where they had left him was a profuse growth of things like spreading white ferns and pale tubers. He was right in the center of the budding mass.

"Oh God," Ruby said, turning away, disgusted.

He was covered in a shroud of emerald green mildew that seemed to have grown up from the puddles and muddy earth around him, snaring him in a sheer web. White rootlets anchored him to the ground like wood rot. There were button-shaped, corpse-white toadstools growing from his mouth and eyes, colorless greasy petals erupting from his nostrils.

Frank swallowed down his revulsion.

He stepped forward and pressed the barrel of the .30-06 to Mick's chest. It gave as if there were no bones in it. He pushed down harder. Mick had gone spongy and loose like the fruiting body of a fungus.

And that fast.

It was The Food. It was mutating every living creature into things nature had never envisioned. Appalled, he pushed through the chokecherry until he found Maribel. She was in no better shape. Yellow threads of morbid fungi had nearly enveloped her, flowering things bursting from her eyes. There were puffballs rising from her gunshot wounds.

"Can we just go?" Ruby said. "I can't look at this anymore."

He nodded, feeling weak inside. They'd been good people, real good people. They hadn't deserved to be gunned down and then have something like this happen to their remains. Just before he turned away, Maribel's lips opened with a sticky sound and a white bulb pushed from her mouth. It opened its petals like a funeral lily.

He took Ruby by the hand, leading her away.

## 84

As the sun—or what they could see of it—sank further in the western sky, they followed the edge of the Cane River floodlands as the rain fell heavier and then heavier still. It came down in sheets that the wind whipped into a fierce spray that felt like needles against their faces. If they thought they had been sodden before, now they were drenched. They were sponges inundated with water. Heavy, slogging things that pushed through wet brush and ducked under dripping tree limbs, forever stumbling through ankle-deep mud and running water.

It had reached the point now where they could not actually remember what it was like to be dry. As Frank moved ever forward, always casting an eye behind him to make sure that Ruby was still with him, he thought, *dry, dryness.* But these words were abstract concepts. He could not adequately picture them or even seem to recall what it was like to have warm, dry skin.

Finally, he pulled Ruby beneath a tree. Both of them were clammy and shivering. She looked worn out and he knew that she was. The constant rain had bleached her skin. The olive hue to it was gone.

"We have to find some place," he said to her. "I don't give a damn what it is. I'd settle for a fucking outhouse right now as long as it was dry."

She nodded. "My skin hurts from being wet. What sense does that make?"

"Maybe it makes too much sense."

They walked side-by-side now, holding hands, drenched, drowning, sinking into the mud, but stronger for the physical connection.

It was full dark by then.

They fought up a hillside that ran with water, stumbling and falling, feet skidding out from beneath them on greasy clay.

At the top, they pushed through the forest, and Frank began to gauge the chances of getting a fire going. He figured they were about nil. Nothing was dry. *Nothing.*

Then—

"Look!" Ruby cried.

Overhead, the moon was a hazy orb in a sky studded with black clouds. But it still lit the world, and in its light, Frank saw a house sitting atop a ridge in the distance.

"Thank God," he said.

They marched towards it with renewed determination. The rain came down that much harder as if trying to stop them. The wind whipped it into a lashing, cutting spray, but they pushed on. It stripped leaves from trees and pummeled the ground and created rushing streams where none had been before.

Frank and Ruby went right through it.

## 85

Later, he realized what a fool he'd been. What fools they'd both been. The rain had made them crazy and the exhaustion tapped their common sense. They practiced no stealth approaching the house. They took no precautions. Anything might have happened. They could have been shot down or attacked in any number of ways, but in their current state they didn't seem to care. They needed to get inside that house. They needed its dryness and protection. There seemed to be nothing else.

They lucked out.

The door was open and nobody pulled a trigger on them. And it was dry in there. Gloriously, deliciously dry. He had never known it could feel so wonderful to exist without the rain tap-tap-tapping on his head. He had never imagined it could feel like this. Both of them dropped their raincoats and just stood there for a moment, feeling it, swimming in the dryness, letting it seep in through their pores and begin to evaporate the wetness from their faces.

"WE'RE STRANGERS OUT OF THE RAIN! WE JUST NEED SHELTER! WE'RE NOT LOOTERS OR ANYTHING! WE JUST NEED TO DRY OFF!" Frank called out, his once husky voice shrill and squeaky. Like the rest of him, it had been broken by the rain, the rain, the rain.

By flashlight, they found candles and dry matches. Once they were lit and they could see the light and feel its heat, Frank went over to the flagstone hearth. A generous supply of firewood had been left. The wood was dry and the kindling caught right away. Oh, the heat! He could feel the flames drying the water off of him. My God, it was nearly an erotic thing. Ruby and he crouched before it for some time, breathing the heat and dryness and sucking in the warmth.

"I'll find us some blankets so we can get out of these things," she finally said.

The house was very well cared for. It was clean and smelled of pine sap. It had an open concept. The bottom floor was just one big airy room, the living room giving onto the kitchen and dining room which led out to a big deck that had once overlooked the river but now overlooked the Cane River floodplain. The floors were hardwood, not laminate, the walls and ceiling high above tongue-and-groove. An open staircase led to lofts above. There was a mounted deer head over the fireplace along with a lot of snapshots, many quite old, of family and friends.

Ruby returned with blankets.

"There's a cedar chest full of them," she said. "I don't know who owns this place, but bless 'em."

She talked non-stop, practically giddy from the dryness (if such a thing were possible). Regardless, as she talked, she forgot completely about her vanity and started stripping right in front of him. She pulled off her wet shirt and threw it almost angrily to the floor. Her shorts and socks and underthings went next.

"I don't have anything you haven't seen before," she said by way of explanation, wrapping herself in a blanket. "Now get out of those things before you get pneumonia."

He did. He wasn't used to undressing before women he barely knew, but he did not hesitate. And Ruby gave him no privacy. She watched him, then wrapped him in a blanket. Whatever had made her strip in front of him, he felt it, too. The almost manic need to get out of those wet things and the sheer physical and spiritual joy of feeling the dry air against his skin.

Then they sat before the fire, toweling their hair, reveling in the sheer perfection of it.

Maybe in the back of Frank's mind, there were sexual fantasies brewing, but nothing happened. They were both tired and the fire was more than enough.

## 86

They set their shoes by the fire and draped their clothes over an ottoman nearby to dry. Then by candlelight, they feasted. They ate canned spaghetti, tinned Vienna sausages, and Chicken in a Biskit crackers. They washed it down with a bottle of warm Merlot. For dessert, they had canned peaches. It was wonderful. Maybe a nice thick Porterhouse steak and all the fixings would have been his meal of choice, but Frank couldn't remember the last time he'd had a meal he enjoyed so much.

They slept in front of the fire, toasting themselves like marshmallows. Outside, the rain continued to fall and the world drowned. But inside, it was warm and dry. And they were both content.

The wine gave them a good buzz, the food made them feel mellow, and the fire made them feel human. They chatted, made plans, thought out loud, questioned everything including themselves...then they drifted off. Maybe an hour later, he felt Ruby slide under the blanket with him. Her mouth was hot against his own, her tongue like fire. When he entered her, she moaned and trembled. It didn't last long. Neither of them were totally awake and both were beyond tired. But it was wonderful. Really wonderful.

"I think for the first time in days, I'm warm," she said, her head on his chest, her shiny black hair spread out over his belly. "Really warm."

"Me, too."

She felt good and he felt good. And that's all there was to it.

## 87

He came awake several hours later to the sound of rain falling and something else, something he could not be sure of. He laid there, Ruby wrapped around him, listening. There had been something...unless it was just the wind. That was always a good one. He remembered telling Jasmine that when the tree branch outside her window scraped against the siding. She was certain it was a spook. The memory of that made his heart ache.

There it was again.

What was it?

Not the rain. Surely not the rain. A sort of...scraping sound. He swallowed. Waited. Swallowed again. Ruby slept on. He heard the scraping again. Carefully, he untangled himself from Ruby so as not to wake her.

He pulled himself out from under the blanket and stood there by the dying fire, listening, feeling. He felt scared. From head to toe, he was bristling. He breathed in and out, not daring to move. And there it was again: the scraping. It was coming from the sliding glass doors that gave out onto the deck. They had locked all the doors and windows so they could sleep in peace. And now someone was trying to get in.

Someone.

Something.

He went over to the chair and grabbed his .45 and the flashlight. Maybe it was some fool out in the rain as they had been. It was possible.

He just didn't believe it.

The rain tapped against the windows, the wind moaned along the eaves. It sounded like every ghost story he'd read as a kid. This did not make him feel any better.

He crossed to the kitchen and stood there by island, his elbow on the granite top. He had not turned on the flashlight yet, and he wouldn't until he got a good sense of things. He moved quietly into the dining room. Every inch of him felt tense. If somebody had tapped him on the shoulder, he was certain he would have jumped three feet.

He heard the scraping again.

Only it wasn't a scraping exactly, more of a jiggling. He could just make out a shadow against the vertical blinds.

Somebody was out there and they were trying to get in.

Frank sucked in a deep breath. Did he wake Ruby? Did he tell her they had visitors? No, he would leave her alone. The latch out there jiggled a couple more times. He moved towards the doors, feeling vulnerable because he was naked. Even the gun did not help with that. His knees felt weak. His heart pounded. He reached out with the flashlight, parting the blinds and turning on the light.

He saw a slumped over, vague gray shape retreating down the steps and into the curtain of rain. He only caught a momentary glimpse of it, but it was enough to make the skin at his spine crawl. There was something wrong about it. Something he didn't like.

But it was gone.

*That's all that matters,* he thought. *Whatever it was, you either scared it off or it's moved on.*

He tried to take comfort from that but found that he couldn't. He was still breathing fast. A droplet of sweat ran down one temple. He turned back towards the living room and Ruby. He had the oddest, most disturbing feeling that it was not a good idea to leave her alone. He padded across the floor.

Then he heard it again.

It was at the front door this time.

Over the rain, he could hear a sort of pawing sound out there. Now a jiggling as someone tried the doorknob. He went over there, though he wanted to do anything but. He could see the knob moving from side to side.

The terror he felt at that moment made his scalp crawl like dozens of spiders were in his hair, their tiny legs skittering against his skull.

The doorknob moved from side to side. Not frantically, but very slowly as if whoever was out there was infinitely patient and could wait all night if they had to. And that sort of inhuman patience alarmed him.

He smelled something.

What the hell?

It was more than dampness and mildew and the horrendous things that blossomed in the night, this was a hot, foul yeast-like odor that reminded him of mushrooms growing in the dark dampness beneath rotting logs.

It grew stronger, sharp and vinegary.

He got as close to the door as he dared and from the other side, he heard something like a voice, but bubbling and gelatinous and perfectly horrible. It made the blood drain from his head, leaving him woozy.

The doorknob jiggled.

The stench increased, as if what was out there was aware of his presence and wanted *him* to be aware of it. He could almost feel the clamminess of it seeping through the door.

He couldn't take it anymore.

He reached down and unlocked the door which was either the wisest thing he had ever done or the stupidest. He backed away, his heart drumming. It felt like it was in his throat, like it might fill his mouth at any moment with its throbbing bloodiness.

The doorknob jiggled, then it turned.

The door swung open and the night came sweeping in. Rain, wind, a few stray leaves scattered at his feet. What he saw was a monstrous, nodding gray shape. It was Maribel. She was dead, and yet she was standing there, somehow resurrected on that dark, wet night. Rain dripped off her, it ran in rivers from her hair. Her face was pallid as a toadstool and stretched, bent, pulled out of shape by what was beneath her skin. She stared at him with one eye that was fibrous and yellow like the guts of a puffball.

She made another perfectly awful attempt at speech.

Frank let out a cry and drilled three rounds into her. He saw them punch through the fish belly-whiteness of her flesh. No blood came out, just a sort of watery black discharge. Whatever she had been in life she was no more. She was a swollen human mushroom, a grotesque horror that had been birthed in the sodden black soil, invaded by some sort of fungus which itself was horribly mutated by The Food. Strands of it grew out of her mouth in ropy bunches, grew like creepers up from between her legs. Her throat was gilled with fluttering vertical slits and her hair was replaced by twitching yellow strings. She was porcine, bloated, and greasy, her flesh smooth as the button of a shitake.

She reached out hands to him, but they were no longer hands as such…just living rubber gloves, the fingers distended and pulpous. Where the nails should have been there were oily rootlets twisting in the air. But the most disturbing part was that there was something inside her chest that was throbbing with a constant pulpy noise like a rotten tomato squeezed in a fist. It was no heart surely, but maybe a fruiting body, the core of the thing she now was. It made her entire body quiver like pudding.

What happened then, happened in a blur.

Frank heard Ruby cry out behind him. As Maribel closed in on him, perhaps to absorb him into her mass, he swung the flashlight, actually burying the shaft of it into the morbid softness of her head. He swung it and kept swinging it, breaking pieces off of her. She began to come apart, her fingers writhing on him like worms.

And then he was tearing at her out of sheer panic, ripping out moist cobs of flesh.

When she hit the ground, the dropped flashlight—which was inches away—revealed her wreckage. She was split and severed, torn and squashed. Her eye looked around, rotating in its socket. Black goo gushed out of her and the throbbing fruiting body in her chest was revealed, a horrendous black-red mass seamed with yellow. It pulsed and pulsed.

Frank staggered back and Ruby charged in, shouting. She had a length of birch in her hand, and she smashed the offending pulsating body into sauce that quivered and spluttered out fluid, then died.

After that, the thing that had been Maribel no longer moved.

And neither did they for some time.

They found that they couldn't.

## 88

After that, they both felt dirty. They felt soiled and fouled in ways they could not adequately understand. They went out on the deck and stood in the rain and let it wash their naked bodies clean. Then they came back inside, toweled off, and sat by the fire. They fed sticks of pine into it until it blazed high and crackled with sap.

They had not spoken since it happened. Frank broke the silence by saying, "Thanks for doing that. I don't think...I don't think I had the guts to smash that *thing.*"

Ruby nodded. She blinked a few times, the orange light of the fire reflected in her face. "I'm losing my mind," she said.

"No, you're not."

"Yes, I am."

He made to put an arm around her, but she flinched. "If you're losing your mind, then I'm losing mine, too."

She stared into the embers. "Maribel was dead. I know she was dead."

"That wasn't Maribel. It was something twisted up, reengineered by The Food. A fungus. Like a mushroom. It appropriated her body. It must have absorbed her and...I don't know...made her like it."

"But she came after us."

"Yes, it must have used her memories."

Ruby licked her lips. "I can deal with nature running wild. It's crazy, but I can deal with it. But the dead walking…that's insane."

"Yes, it is."

She came into his arms and he held her. She trembled and chattered her teeth. She sobbed low in her throat as if she did not want him to hear it. But he heard it. After a long time, she cleared her throat and said, "If something happens to me, I want you to burn my body or cut it into pieces. I don't care what. Just don't leave me whole. I don't want to be like that. I don't want to become a thing like that."

"Nothing'll happen. I won't let it."

"I keep thinking, wondering…what if, what if there really is such a thing as a soul? We go to church and they teach us that there is, but who really believes it? I mean, down deep? We live in a physical world. We reject paranormal things like ghosts and all that. None of us *really* believe in the supernatural. I was raised a Catholic, but I don't really think I'm going to some sort of paradise when I die. I'd love to see my mom and dad again, but I know I won't. But it's nice to tell yourself that you will. It's comforting. We all, on some level, want to believe it even if our common sense tells us it's bullshit. We're afraid to admit it, though. We're all superstitious at our core and we're afraid we'll piss off God or something."

Frank sighed. "What brings all this on?"

"Maribel. What if her soul was trapped in that thing? And if not her soul, what about her mind?"

"I don't know about any of that. I'm a farmer. I work the land. Dead is dead. I've seen a lot of it and dead is just always dead. There's nothing more to it. What happened to Maribel's corpse was no supernatural Stephen King shit—it was a process of parasitism that's beyond anything we can imagine. But it's explainable by biology and natural science. Don't read too much into it or you *will* lose your mind."

"I guess that's the way to think," she said.

"There is no other way. The earth is real. The soil is real. Nature is real. The rest is delusion. It only exists in our minds."

### 89

All through that long, strange night, neither of them slept. They rested, but they did not sleep. They listened, always ready for something terrible to happen. They heard frightening shrieks and cries, the roaring of beasts that sounded positively prehistoric. Whistling sounds and croaking and chirruping. And once, they thought they heard something very much like a human scream. It didn't come again and for that they were grateful. Frank listened for footsteps on the deck and the sound of someone trying to get in. He heard neither. An hour or so before dawn, it got very quiet out there. They managed to sleep for an hour or two. When they woke, it was light out. The rain was still falling and the day was gray and hazy, but it was day. The light almost made them believe that what had happened during the night might not have happened at all.

### 90

Their clothes were dry as were the rucksacks. They had a quick breakfast of Spam and powdered eggs and then they went back out into it again. There were several sheds and a pole building behind the house tucked away in the trees.

They checked both sheds and got lucky: they found a canoe and paddles. It wasn't that surprising given the cabin's proximity to the river, but it was still good. And right then, they needed good.

### 91

The rain, which had been more of a wet mist than anything, started falling for real by the time they got the canoe down to the water's edge. The Cane River looked more like a lake surrounded by flooded bottomlands now. It seemed to stretch on endlessly like some tropical swamp, misty and haunted.

Frank looked out across it. "About two miles on the other side of that is the highway. That'll lead us to Montpalk."

Ruby let out a long, low sigh. "Then, *finally,* we'll be getting somewhere. I feel like some kind of explorer finally coming out of the jungle."

Montpalk to him meant not just civilization of sorts and the National Guard, maybe some decent food and a decent bed, but

Jerrod and Jasmine. *God, if you exist, let them be there. Let all of this nightmare mean something in the end. I'll crawl through Hell to get to them as long as I know they're there.* He couldn't think of anything in his life he had ever needed so badly.

"Smells funny," Ruby said.

Frank had noticed. River bottomlands often smelled a bit rank in the summer, but this was worse than that…it was a stench of carrion and rotting vegetation, of green vapors rising from miasmic swamps. In the back of his mind, it was what he expected some primordial backwash of the Amazon to smell like. *Or the late Mesozoic,* he thought. The waters were green-slimed, mire-black, and steaming. Now and again, a few bubbles broke the surface. He knew it was from trees and vegetable matter rotting below, still…*still* he wondered if some nameless horror was lying on the bottom, waiting for food to swim by.

"I don't know what we might run into out there," he admitted. "But I'd rather take our chances on it than spending another day in these fucking woods."

"You don't hear me arguing."

"Let's do it then."

## 92

Once they had their gear loaded, Ruby climbed in and Frank pushed them off. As they paddled out into the smelling, stagnant waters, he said, "We're like a couple young lovebirds rowing away the day."

"Romance just ain't what it used to be," Ruby joked.

Frank decided he wasn't going to think of all the terrible things that could go wrong because they were many. In his mind, he saw only the other shore. That was his goal. Nothing else existed or could exist within the frame of his mind.

"When we get across," he said, not sure if he was speaking to her or just thinking out loud, "we'll beg, borrow, or steal a vehicle and get into Montpalk. Then we'll start looking."

Ruby didn't say anything, but he knew damn well what she was thinking—*and if your kids aren't there, what then? What then, Frank?* He was only glad that she didn't put it into words. He

156

shook it from his head. Right now, they had to reach the other shore.

The rain was falling lightly. A light breeze blew. The day was warm, fingers of steam rising from the black waters. Insects buzzed past them now and again, and they both heard strange cries in the distance, splashings and bellowing noises.

It was like crossing some primordial swamp. The tops of trees breaking the surface of the water only enhanced the idea that they were traversing some tropical reed bog. The smell of green rot and stagnation was nauseating. It had a marked subterranean stench to it, as if they were crawling through a drainage pipe. There was something terribly suffocating about being out there in those black waters, nameless creatures crying out, clumps of brush and dead things floating past them.

Frank figured it would take them about thirty minutes to cross, if things went well. They were already a third of the way there. *Keep rowing, keep rowing, get this done with.* Neither of them were speaking. Maybe that was because there was nothing to say, and maybe it was because they were too tense at the idea of what might be in the water with them.

Ten minutes passed in silence.

Then fifteen.

They were out in the middle now, and he didn't even want to contemplate how deep the water beneath them might be. The mist was heavy and he could see little but vague shapes in it. They were encountering quite a few floating trees and entire bushes. The flooding must have eroded hillsides and all that was rooted to them. They bumped against the bow and slid along the canoe's length. A dead dog, maybe a husky, drifted past them. Frank wasn't sure if Ruby saw it or not, and he wasn't about to draw her attention to it because it looked as if something had taken a very large bite out of it.

*I wonder how many people will be dead when—and if—this is all wrapped up?* he wondered. *How many hundreds or thousands will never be accounted for?*

But that was grim, defeatist thinking and he refused to go any farther with it.

"Did you hear that?" Ruby asked.

The sound of her voice startled him. He swallowed down his unease. "What?"

"I don't know. I think something bumped into the side of the canoe."

"Probably a branch or something."

"No," she said with some conviction, "I don't think so."

He heard it now, too. A sort of bumping sound from below. They had both paused rowing, waiting for he knew not what. Maybe for it to just go away or to get worse. *Bump, bump, bump.* He didn't like it at all. It was not an accidental sound; no, it sounded very much on purpose.

He started rowing and Ruby followed suit.

They were both rowing as hard as they could, pushing the canoe ever forward. It was moving fast and the speed made them both feel better. Then whatever was down there bumped again. And not just in one place, but five or six locations right down the length of the keel. *Thump-thump, thud, thud, thud.* Whatever it was, it was hitting them with a vengeance now, coming from beneath and to both sides. The impacts were jarring, making the canoe bob and sway.

Now there was a splashing to both sides.

"They're jumping out of the water!" Ruby said.

"Row," Frank told her. "Row as hard as you can."

But even then he knew it wouldn't be enough. He wasn't even sure that if they had a motor they could have gotten away. Whatever it was—fish or something infinitely worse—were really pouring it on now, hitting the canoe from every side. They were leaping and splashing. They moved so quickly, it was hard to say what they were. Dark shapes, big like pickerel or pike. The water was roiling, the canoe shaking.

And then Ruby let out a scream.

One of them leaped over the bow and another bounced off her arm and landed in the canoe. Maybe Frank had been thinking, *Asian Carp, maybe it's some of those damn Asian Carp,* but when he got a look at their guest flopping at his feet, he knew better. It was hard to say exactly what it was, a sort of a serpentine shape that writhed in the bottom of the canoe, slapping its tail wildly. They both pulled their feet away from it as more of them thudded into the keel, bounced off the sides, and leaped over the bow and stern.

"It's a pollywog," Ruby said. "It's a goddamn tadpole."

Of course, Frank's first reaction was, *that's ridiculous,* but it didn't last because that thing sure looked like a pollywog. It had a bulbous head and a sinuous body. The only problem was that it was nearly three feet long. He tried to push it away with the oar, but it was wild and squirmy, jumping and flopping about as if it were being electrocuted.

Another one leaped in a perfect arc right over the canoe, narrowly missing the tip of his nose by a scant three inches. Then another jumped in, slapping against Ruby's arm (and eliciting a scream from her) and landing on the seat next to her. It was smaller than the other one, but its movements were equally as frenzied. She threw herself clear and the canoe nearly capsized.

"Jesus Christ!" Frank said. "Watch it!"

"WELL, DO SOMETHING!" she shouted at him. "KILL THEM OR SOMETHING!"

Of course, the idea of the guns passed through Frank's mind, but he wasn't too keen on the idea of drilling holes through the canoe which was being viciously battered from all sides as it was. The big one in the bottom was getting more sluggish. He cracked it in the head with his oar two, then three times until it shuddered and some kind of brown fluid like molasses flowed from it, mixing with the water at his feet.

Another jumped in and this one cracked him in the side of the head, nearly knocking him over. It was the biggest yet. It landed on his leg and slid down, rasping against his jeans as it went as if it had nubby teeth on its underside. He gave it a whack, too, but it was surprisingly resilient.

Several hits and none of the fight had gone out of it. It wriggled and jumped. He hit it again. Instead of trying to curl up defensively as the other had, it vaulted forward and seized the steel toe of his work boot. If he wondered if it had teeth, now he knew. It clung to the tip of his boot, its body corkscrewing as if it were trying to shake the boot to death. It was definitely some type of bastard pollywog—he could even see the leg buds on it.

*Christ, what kind of frog does it become?* a voice in the back of his head wondered, imaging some titan from a Japanese kaiju film.

Frank kicked out and smashed it against one of the seats.

But another jumped into the boat.

Frank raised the oar and prepared to smash it, when he realized it was looking at him. It wasn't flapping around like the others. Its green-black body was sort of coiled as if it was about to spring, huge gelid black eyes staring up at him. Then it moved. Its legs were nearly formed, and it clawed over the bottom of the canoe to get at him right before he brained it with everything he had. It rolled over, its mouth gulping and he could see its teeth—nubby but sharp as drill bits.

Meanwhile, Ruby, worked into a real frenzy, smashed another to pulp with her oar and batted away others that leaped out of the water. Frank did the same. After a few moments, there was no more activity.

"Row," Frank said. "Your ass off."

They both went at it, the canoe slicing through the waters. One more of the pollywogs thudded into the boat and then that was it. The canoe was either out of range by then or the creatures had lost interest in it.

The shore was getting closer now.

They rowed towards it, seeing nothing else.

### 93

After about five minutes with no more activity, they began to relax. They rowed at a less frenetic rate. The shore was about three hundred feet from them and they could feel it getting closer. It seemed to be reaching out to them even as they reached out to it. The rain fell and a dirty mist rose from the water in a veil. The only sounds were the oars chopping into the water.

Frank was lost in thought, thinking about what was ahead. Woods. Fields. Farms. Then the highway and at the end of that black ribbon there was Montpalk which had begun to take on fantastical proportions in his mind like Oz or Whoville. It was a magical place where all dreams came true and all tales had a happy ending.

*If only,* he thought. *If only...*

It was about that time that they both became aware that amongst the debris floating in the water—branches, logs, clumps of grass, a few stray dead animals—there were clots of white goop. There was only one thing it could be.

"That's the stuff," Ruby said. "The Food."

It had to be. It looked like globs of white bread dough. Little islands and strings of the stuff passed by.

"Don't touch it," Frank heard himself say.

"Now why in the heck would I do that?" Ruby asked him.

"Just saying."

Yes, he was just saying. The way he would have said it to Jasmine or Jerrod. Stupid, but he couldn't help himself. It was hard to get out of the habit. He watched the clumps of The Food, wondering as he had so many times what it really was and from where, far below, it had come. By then, he was seeing a lot of it which made him think that there was a wellspring of the stuff beneath the water.

"Stop," Ruby said.

"What?"

"Stop rowing."

"Why?"

Then he saw and something in his chest dropped into his belly. About fifty feet from the raft, or at the point where the rising mist obscured everything, there was something under the surface, something immense. *Is that...is that a tree?* But he nixed that right away because if it was a tree, then it would have had to have been the size of a redwood. As the canoe drifted closer, he could see that whatever it was, it just broke the surface. It looked pale green and lumpy with circular rings. If he had to compare it to anything, it would have been the trunk of an elephant.

Both of them had their oars in the water by this point to break the forward momentum of the canoe.

Frank had no idea what it was, but he was pretty sure that he didn't like it. It was gigantic and unnatural and filled him with the worst sense of foreboding.

"Let's try and row around it," he whispered.

They pulled on the oars, bringing the canoe back fifty feet or so and then they pushed off to the right, moving parallel to the object, trying to find its end. After an easy hundred feet, they still hadn't. That's when Frank began to wonder if it wasn't some sort of geological formation, a sort of a hilltop just breaking the surface.

But it sure as hell did not look like a hilltop.

*It looks like something guarding the shoreline,* he thought then. *Like a living rampart.*

Of course, that was highly speculative, because he didn't really know that it was alive. It looked like it could have been, but there was nothing to suggest the same. Only his instinct. A gut-sense that told him, *Here be monsters,* like something on an old sea chart. A year ago, he would have laughed at the idea, but he was not laughing now. There was something very unfunny about that long cylindrical mass. He saw that it was not perfectly straight but serpentine. But that was about all he could see in the haze.

"It's moving," Ruby said, not bothering to conceal the horror she felt.

Frank wanted to tell her she was wrong, but it *was* moving. Very, very slowly, it was moving towards them, sort of drifting in their general direction.

"Row," he said. "Let's try and get around it."

The very idea seemed ludicrous, but it was something. It was better than just sitting there, waiting for the fucking thing. They rowed steadily and then, after about five minutes to their amazement, it was gone. They had reached its end or it had submerged and didn't really matter either way because it was gone.

But would it be that easy?

That's what Frank was wondering because whenever was it that easy these days? He thought of Claw-Face that had wrecked the truck and the kites attacking the convenience store, what waited in Ray Trawley's farmhouse and the thing that had gotten David that night when he met Ruby and the others.

It was never easy.

It was always fucking hard.

So even when they rowed their asses off towards the shore and it was something like twenty or thirty feet away, he still did not believe it. And when there was a colossal eruption of water like a freaking tidal wave that simultaneously swamped and flipped the canoe over, he was not at all surprised.

He heard Ruby cry out just before she went under and then he was dunked, too. The water was freakishly warm. Dirty. Slimy. And deep. He did not touch bottom. He came back up, splashing, looking frantically around for Ruby, but she wasn't there. The water was roiling madly like that in a steaming pot. He felt a great rushing motion beneath him that nearly sucked him under. It pulled at him, dragging him out further.

"RUBY!" he screamed. *"RUBY!"*

But there was nothing but the water thrashing around him, spraying up in gouts, conflicting waves battering into him. She was gone. She was just...gone. He fought through the water, reaching around, trying to find her, trying to get a hold of her but there was nothing. Another wave smashed into him, propelling him towards shore.

Then: "Frank!"

He saw her. She was out farther. He swam to her as she swam to him. Then he had his hands on her and was swimming in with her. When his feet finally found bottom, he pushed them towards the shore. He looked behind them and saw something like a tower rising fifty or sixty feet from the water. In the haze, he could not see it well, but he knew it was a living thing; it was the creature. It kept rising up and up. It had to be easily thirty feet or more in girth, its vermiform body wrinkled and pebbly, a sickly yellow green in color. That's what he saw. It was an enormous worm-like nightmare with dozens of thick, blunt-ended tentacles spoking out from it.

Then it crashed down.

Ruby and he scrambled onto the shore as the thunder of the creature sent another huge wave at them that flattened them. Drenched and nearly incapacitated with fear, they climbed up a grassy hillside and crawled through a thicket of saplings that led to another hillside. It was here that they paused, gasping for breath.

Pulling himself up with the help of a shattered fence line, Frank looked out and saw the waves crashing into the hillside below them. There was a great spinning vortex where the creature had gone down.

"Let's get the hell out of here," he said.

## 94

They didn't talk about what they had seen, because what was the point? Where would it really get them in the end? Instead, they did not look back; they marched straightaway into the scrub forest before them. They'd lost their rucksacks and weapons. No food. No water. Frank had the .45 and knife on his belt, but that was it. Still, despite the adversity, they did not relent. They had a goal, and they would see it through because there really was no choice in the matter.

The country was hills and hollows, hills and hollows. Up one and down another. They came to the apex of a high bald knob, and the countryside spread out to all sides like a carpet. Frank could see that in the distance, the land flattened out and there were farms. He could just make out the rising cylinders of silos over the treetops.

"Looks like there was a fire over there," Ruby said.

He could see a blackened swath that moved steadily to the south. He didn't think fire had done it. It was a dead forest. What had gotten to it was the same thing that had wasted that other forest he had seen that was crumbling to ash. And it was the same thing that had gotten to Carl Shinneman and his farmhouse. Something that sucked the life out of things along with every drop of moisture. Whatever it was, it was still active.

## 95

An hour later, they had to rest. They were both hungry and both thirsty. He worried about the dehydration. It would tap them a lot faster than hunger.

"I really have to rest," Ruby finally said.

"Yeah, I hear you."

They sat on a log while a gentle mist of rain fell from the sky. It had rained on and off all morning, mostly off which was a good thing. Still, the world was wet. Even sitting on the log, they could feel the dampness seeping into them. Frank stretched his legs and worked the kinks out of his back. He noticed, with some unease, how thick and green was the undergrowth. The ferns looked tropical, flowers blooming. Moss that was unpleasantly verdant grew on the boles of trees. Weird pale rootlets grew from the soil.

"I never liked beef," Ruby said.

Frank just looked at her. "What?"

"I was thinking about food. I'm starving," she explained. "I never liked beef. Right now, though, I could go for a steak."

"Me, too."

"You were a beef-eater?"

"Oh, hell yes. I used to get a couple sirloins or ribeyes two inches thick and I'd marinate them for two days before I grilled them up. Lots of onions and mushrooms. Baked potatoes on the sides. Sour cream, real butter. A nice salad and some bread."

"God, that sounds good. Were you a hunter?"

"Deer and that, you mean? Sure. Deer, partridge. Never cared for bear meat or rabbit, though. I never killed anything unless it was threatening me or for meat. My old man taught me that. If it leaves you alone, leave it alone. Never kill just to kill. Only assholes do that."

"That's wise. I was against hunting. I was against exploiting nature."

He shrugged. "We have to hunt deer. We fucked with the natural order of things. We eliminated their natural predators, the wolves. They're coming back now. But still, the deer breed like crazy. If they're not harvested, they'll starve to death. That's a bad end for any living thing."

"I wonder if all this is because we screwed up the natural order," she said. "I wonder if The Food is nature's way of evening the odds."

"Maybe it is. If it goes on and on, the human race will have a tough time surviving."

"The Food will get to us, too. We'll start changing. We'll become something else."

But that was the very thing he did not want to be thinking about. "Let's get going. We should make those farms in an hour. Then we can have a drink and something to eat."

Holding hands, they started out again.

96

Finally, they came out of the woods and there was a meandering dirt road ahead of them. And beyond it, a field of yellow grasses that were so bright they were nearly a hallucinogenic chromium yellow. Beyond that, the first of the farms. Frank could see an apple orchard that looked gray and sickly and a few withered hayfields, a couple working barns and outbuildings, a silo and a big farmhouse. There was a tall, old-fashioned windpump set high on a steel tower. Its fan blades were spinning slowly.

He did not see any people about.

And the way things were going, that could either be a curse or a blessing. Together, they started down towards the farm, crossing the field of bizarre yellow grasses and not speaking. Frank had his eye on the pickup. That's what they needed. They needed water badly and food to a lesser degree, but the truck was the thing. They had to have it.

"We'll go into the farmhouse and see what we can find. We need the keys to that truck."

If there was no one down there, it would be an easy thing. A little water—bottled, of course, because he trusted nothing that came from the ground now—and food and they'd drive off. But what if there was someone down there and they weren't so eager to give up the pickup? That was the gray area in his thinking. He was very desperate now, and he'd been through a terrible amount of shit. He wasn't sure what he'd do if he was refused what he needed. In fact, he was scared of what he might do.

The apple orchard stank of rot. The trees were gnarled and flaky, oddly scaly in appearance. The fruit they bore was grapefruit-sized, but not remotely healthy. It was soft and dripping, a dirty moist gray, ribbons of slime dangling from it. The grasses underfoot were wiry. They scraped against their shoes. Had they been barefoot, Frank figured, the grass would have cut them open.

But everything was like that at the farm, smelling and rotten and unnatural, strange pod-like growths poking out of the muddy soil. Creepers and vines hanging from the outbuildings. He thought more than once that he saw them move.

As they crossed the apple orchard, he heard a sort of rumbling. At first, he thought he'd imagined it, but when Ruby stopped, he stopped. They both stood there, listening.

"What the heck is that?" she said.

It grew louder and louder still. It was coming from beyond the farmhouse. Whatever it was, it was trouble, and it would be on them in seconds. He looked around. They'd never get to the farmhouse in time or the barn for that matter. There was only one thing to do.

"C'mon!" he shouted above the rumbling.

Taking Ruby by the hand, he ran with her over to the latticed steel tower of the windpump. There was a ladder that reached up to the mechanism high above. It would get them off the ground. He sent Ruby up first and then he followed. He climbed until he was twenty feet off the ground, and by then, he saw exactly what it was.

Hogs, is what he thought, but these weren't hogs of the domesticated variety, but boars, wild boars. They were tusked and deadly and there were dozens and dozens of them. They weren't native to the area, he knew, but had been brought here by idiots looking for something new to hunt. Russian boars. Very aggressive, very dangerous. They had escaped private hunting preserves and set up breeding populations in the woods. Before The Food, the wildlife people had been having a hell of a time getting them under control…and now, they had become something else.

That they were eating The Food was obvious.

Not that he was surprised. The boars were omnivorous, absolute gluttons that would stuff themselves with anything available. The Food had been too tantalizing. Now they were much larger than they had been before, no longer dark but white and puffy and pink-eyed, like things that lived in caves. Their bristles looked like needles.

Frank knew that if Ruby and he had stayed on the ground, they would have been trampled to death or gored.

"Is it safe now?" she asked after they passed.

"Yes, I think so."

They climbed down and saw the boars enter the treeline in the distance. Another tragedy averted.

## 97

The way Frank was figuring things, the sooner they got away from the farm and out onto the road the better. First, the farmhouse. That would be the best bet for the truck keys. They passed the pickup (no keys in it) and the combine and stood before the porch.

"I don't know, Frank," Ruby said. "It might not be such a good idea to go in there. It doesn't look right."

And it didn't.

It was a typical Midwestern farmhouse in all respects, save that it just looked wrong. Something had gotten to it. It was slouched and gray, the boards split open to reveal yellow pustules and a furry red fungus. The entire structure looked not so much like it was falling apart, but going soft with rot. Even the windows were crooked, the roofline drooping.

"Wait out here. I'll be quick."

Ruby just nodded. Of course, she was thinking the same thing he was: about the other cabin that had not been a cabin really but a sort of fungi that *looked* like a cabin. Sucking in a slow breath, he climbed the steps to the porch. They did not give out beneath him or anything. Nor did they crack open. No, they just felt sort of elastic, bending under his weight and then springing back into shape with a sort of rubbery pliancy.

Weird.

The porch itself was much the same. The railing shivered like it was made of Jell-O. He prodded the door with the barrel of the .45. It, too, was not right. It was too soft. Swallowing, he gripped the doorknob. It was brass. Tarnished, but still metal. Whatever had gotten to the wood could not touch it. He pushed the door open, brushing chalky stains from his fingertips, and a warm, nauseous wave of stink blew into his face. It smelled at first rather like rising dough, then gradually worsened until it embodied the foulness of an open, infected wound.

*You're taking big chances,* a voice in Frank's head informed him. *This house is no longer a house—it's a fucking organism and you know it.*

But if he could just find the keys.

He moved down a hallway whose walls were covered in strange rising blisters, as if there were air bubbles beneath the paint. There was a sort of glistening slime on the ceiling. It looked as if it wanted to drip. He ducked under it and found the kitchen. The appliances, of course, were untouched, but again, the walls were bubbly, the windows covered in a dark fuzz. Some sort of black rot was devouring the kitchen chairs and table. The floor was buckling, a festering purple crud oozing out of jagged cracks. Like the porch, it was not firm in the least but sort of springy. Just walking on it was unpleasant as if it would let go at any moment.

The keys, the keys.

He wasn't there for a fucking survey. He gazed around. He moved past the cupboards which were coated in gray mold. There. The pegboard. Keys. There was only one set. As he reached for them, something dropped from the ceiling, a sort of slop of gray ooze that splattered at his feet. The cupboards seemed to shiver with a slow, rolling undulation. There was a gassy expulsion from the wall opposite that filled the air with spinning yellow spores.

Frank grabbed the keys with such violence that he tore the ring out of the pegboard. It split open like a scab, a purple-red fluid gushing out. More of the slop dripped from the ceiling. He felt the floor quiver beneath him. It made him unsteady, dizzy.

The entire house was moving.

It was fluid and alive. Maybe it had been sort of dormant a few moments ago, but now he'd injured it, and it was waking up all around him. The floor quivered again. He fell back against the refrigerator which was now leaning forward like a bad tooth. The walls seemed to be crawling, the ceiling made of something like gray pudding. The floor buckled upwards, spilling him over and opened in a dark, fusty gash. He trembled on the edge of it, staring down into a convulsive pit of yellow and pink tendrils that reached up towards him.

He scampered away from it, finding his feet as the house became a fleshy, roiling thing, walls melting into floors, the ceiling dripping, great globular forms that might have been furniture once creeping in his direction.

As he reached for the door, something in his head exploded in great vibrant sunbursts that blinded him, filling his eyes with burning sulfur as he saw distorted, grotesque images of things being born from other things that split open and then open again.

He was on the floor, pulling himself along like a worm as the floor became a mire of fungi that he began to sink into. He moved faster and faster as the house writhed and went soft as putty around him. The walls sprouted pink tentacles that coiled over him, not hurting but forever caressing. It was a great colonial animal, and he was crawling through its guts as pulpous tendrils touched him like inquisitive fingers and the floor tried to drown him.

There was the door.

He saw the door.

"LET ME OUT!" he heard his own voice scream. "JESUS CHRIST, LET ME OUT OF HERE!"

The house seemed to react to his voice or his thoughts, milking the impressions from his mind and he was sucked into a narrow duct-like chamber whose walls were flexing quilts of muscle that pressed against him, squeezing him, and he couldn't breathe, there was no goddamn air…and then there was a rushing velocity and he was ejected out into the yard, vomited out, regurgitated like bad meat, an indigestible nugget.

"Frank!" Ruby said, taking hold of him and dragging him free. Rain was in his face. It was chilly and cruel. He was haunted by the warmth and tenderness of the house.

Ruby helped him up and he half-ran and half-stumbled with her towards the truck.

It was only then that he dared look behind him.

What he saw—no, he couldn't be seeing it, he was tripping his brains out—was impossible, but its reality did not waver. Looking upon it, he didn't know whether to laugh or scream or perhaps to do both at the same time. He had the sensation that his mind was ripping wide open like a seam.

The house looked as if it had curdled. There were no hard lines or edges, everything was soft and gelid and shivering. It oozed and gurgled and threw out yellow-orange tendrils and mushroom-shaped caps that sprouted wiry red hairs that fluttered in the rain.

And then it happened.

The house pulled itself off its foundation with a sound much like tree roots torn from the ground. It quivered and pulsated there a moment like some immense, gelatinous amoeba. Then it began to move. Its locomotion was convulsive and watery. It bulged and dilated, shrank down to a rubbery sack then inflated itself like a great yellow-pink-green striated balloon, extending a pseudopod, then pulling itself forward, repeating the process.

It was moving in their direction.

Frank and Ruby didn't wait to see what it was doing. They jumped into the truck and, Thank God, it turned over. Then they were wheeling down the drive, finally in motion.

## 98

Ruby drove and Frank sat there, his eyes glazed and body feeling sort of loose and ultra-relaxed. He felt like he'd been shot up with Demerol or something. The feeling was fading bit by bit. Both windows were open, scooping air into the cab along with a certain amount of wet mist.

When he finally felt like he was in charge of his mind again, he said, "Did I really fucking see that? Did I honestly see a house get up and walk?"

"Yes," Ruby said, but would say no more on the subject regardless of how much he coaxed her.

They drove and he sat there, clearing his mind. They were on their way. They were finally on their way to the highway that would lead them to Montpalk. *The Yellow Brick Road,* Frank thought as watched the rainy countryside sweep by. *Where all journeys must end and all things are possible.* The idea of that made him giggle, but he didn't dare. Ruby would think he was still under the effect of the spores and he would probably scare himself.

They both closed the windows now that the rain was really pouring down. Ruby had to slow down. Once, she had to come to a complete stop because the road was cracked open, The Food hanging out of the crevice like the stuffing from a chair. As they cut into a field and moved around it, Frank saw bubbles of the stuff rise up and float away.

Then they were on their way again.

"You feeling better?" Ruby asked him.

"Yeah. I'm okay now."

"You took a really stupid chance, you know."

He sighed. "I know. But we needed this truck."

At that moment, he was close to loving her. He liked her a great deal, but love did not come easy to him. It took him time. It had taken him a long time with Janet, too, but when he loved her, her loved her completely and without question. He watched Ruby drive. He studied her long black hair, her face with its high cheekbones and dark, brooding eyes. She was attractive, yes, but he was feeling more than simple lust or a simple crush. He was starting to feel very deeply about her and he could not decide if that was a good thing or a bad thing.

"Why are you staring at me?" she finally said.

"Was I staring?"

"Yes."

"I was thinking how great you are. Coming along with me. Putting up with all this shit so you can help me find my kids. There's not a lot of people who would have done it. Not many at all."

"I'm a teacher. I love kids."

"There's more to it than that."

She smiled and her whole face lit up. The play of her dimples, her wide mouth and sparkling white teeth set against her olive skin. It was practically magical. "I guess there is."

The rain poured down, striking the truck in sheets. It was something he was beginning to worry a great deal about. All that water. That and the abundance of The Food. It was not a good combination.

Ruby slowed down even more, rolling to a stop. The wipers were whipping back and forth and she was leaning forward, peering out at something he could not see.

"What is it?"

She shook her head. "Nothing I guess. Must be my eyes. I thought there was something out there, a truck or something parked in the middle of the road."

"You want me to drive for awhile?"

"No, I'm good."

She got the truck moving again, easing forward slowly, still peering out there. He knew she was certain she saw something and that made him nervous. The rain was coming down too hard. It was difficult to see anything. Finally, she relaxed and got them rolling again as fast as she dared. She began asking him questions about Jerrod and Jasmine and he was only too happy to answer them. Talking about them made him feel good. It was as if he were opening a valve in his mind and letting off steam or pressure.

"We're going to find them," he said, believing it, really believing it. "You'll like them and they'll like you."

"I have no doubt of it," she said.

Frank turned from her and suddenly something was coming out of the storm at them. Ruby cried out, hitting the brakes and swerving at the very last moment around a stalled tanker truck. She had barely got around that when there was a minivan and then a bus. She hit the brakes, but the tires skidded over the wet surface and they crashed into a parked car.

## 99

"Ruby! Ruby!" Frank said, fighting with his seatbelt. "Are you all right?"

"Yeah...I'm okay."

The engine of the truck had died from the impact. They had hit a little British Cooper, pushing it into the side of a UPS truck where it crumpled into a mangled mass of metal. The hood on the truck was popped open. In the rain, he could see cars and trucks everywhere, most of them just vague gray shapes. There must have some kind of pileup.

"You sure you're all right?" Frank asked.

"Yeah...just stunned. I'll survive."

If they hadn't had seatbelts on, both of them would have gone right through the windshield. There was no doubt of that. They were on foot again; there was no way around that, but least they weren't hurt. That was the important part.

Ruby popped her seatbelt catch, and as she did so, Frank saw a massive shape lurch out of the rain, bearing down on the truck. He saw it, then something black and whip-like came lashing out of the haze, smashing the windshield into a sheet of spider-webbed glass that fell onto the dash and slid into their laps. Rain blew in.

It all happened very fast.

And what happened next happened even faster.

That same monstrous black appendage came out of the rain again, tapping along the buckled hood of the truck.

"Get out!" Frank said.

They both did, just as it came through the missing window, scraping along the dash in search of something that could only be them. Frank got out, but just barely. He was drenched almost immediately. The impact had crunched his door so it only opened a few feet. He slid out and ran around the back to Ruby. She came running towards him and then something hit her.

It came sweeping out of the rain.

Something long and tentacle-like and horribly mottled.

It hit her.

It grabbed her.

It yanked her up into the air.

Frank ran for her, crying out, knowing the worst had just happened and that he was pretty much powerless to do anything about it. Ruby screamed as she was yanked away. He ran in the direction she disappeared, trying to see as sheets of chill rain splashed against him. He heard Ruby shriek one more time with a wet, gurgling sort of sound. Then there was a crunching noise which he knew were her bones. Then something—a *lot* of something—hot and wet hit him in the face. It must have been blood, but the rain washed it away instantly.

Suddenly, he was alone.

### 100

He was standing there in the rain, not sure what direction to go in. Panicked, broken, great anguish pouring out of him, he ran in the direction she disappeared. There were wrecked vehicles everywhere and he threaded his way amongst them. It was like some great auto graveyard. There was glass and broken bits of metal underfoot, sometimes entire bumpers or tires.

He pushed on, feeling hot and cold and completely out of his mind. He saw something white on the hood of a black Subaru wagon. He knew what it was even before he got close—Ruby's hand. It was palm-down on the hood, fingers splayed as if it had been trying to break her fall. From the long delicate fingers, he knew it belonged to her. It could have belonged to no one else.

"RUBY!" he screamed into the storm. *"RUBY!"*

There was no reply, of course, just the sound of the rain falling and sweeping about him. And then...from somewhere out there, a high, keening sort of chirruping as if in answer. It was like the world's largest cricket had called out to him, but loud, incredibly loud, and filled with a sort of primeval fury.

Frank stood there.

He was just beside himself. His common sense told him to run, but he did not run. He started walking in the direction of the cry. There were battered vehicles everywhere, some smashed into one another and others flipped over in the ditch. He began to see bodies—a flayed man hanging out of the window of a dump truck, a woman who had been cut in half like she was snipped with a giant pair of scissors. He saw the body of a toddler that was headless. A man whose legs were missing. It went on and on, seemingly without end.

He heard the cry again and now it was much closer. It was piercing and unearthly and absolutely unsettling.

He would see the thing.

At any moment, he would see the horror that took Ruby.

He pulled out the .45 and made ready to face it. He smelled a weird sweetish stink that was positively sickening. Then something low and coarse like rotting vegetables, potatoes black with slime.

The cry.

God, it was deafening.

"OVER HERE!" Frank shouted at it, totally throwing caution to the wind now. He couldn't help himself. He was filled with hate and anger and the need for vengeance. "COME AND GET ME!"

He saw a vague shape, an immense shape, climbing over a wrecked minivan. He couldn't see what it was exactly, only that it appeared to have more legs than any earthly creature he could imagine.

He fired three times at its silhouette with no apparent effect. It was still coming. It was coming for him. Instinct kicked in and he evaded. He climbed over the hood of a pickup truck and ducked behind an SUV whose windows were splattered inside with old blood.

The thing was still coming.

He could hear it picking its way in his direction.

He ran in a zig-zag course, trying to throw it off, but it did no good. It seemed to know where he was. There was no way it could have seen him in the rain which meant it was either smelling him or sensing his body heat.

He had to do something.

Hiding in a vehicle wouldn't work. The thing would tear it apart until it reached the soft gooey center which was him. He ran down the shoulder, listening to the creature chirruping and making a sort of fluttering noise as it hunted him down.

In the distance, he could just make out some buildings. It was his only chance. He splashed through the drainage ditch at the side of the road and pulled himself up into the grass. Then he ran. He ran flat out, moving faster and faster, the speed giving him confidence. He turned once and, yes, the creature was coming. Now that it was out of the junkyard of vehicles, it was moving faster, too. Very fast.

The buildings were close now.

Frank saw a crushed gravel lot and a series of sheet metal pre-fab buildings. He saw graders and front-end loaders, a big CAT excavator. There were hills of gravel and dirt behind the buildings.

It was the county road commission garage.

The doors to one of the big garages were open. He could see heavy equipment in there that was being worked on. It gave him an idea. He ran through the puddles and into the garage. There was a bulldozer and a scraper, a couple dump trucks. Then...yes...another dump truck, this one a massive yellow Mack diesel with a snow blower attachment hooked to the front. The boys must have been getting the equipment ready for the coming winter.

Frank saw the creature.

It was pushing through the field, looking, in the rain, like some kind of gigantic spider. One thing was for sure, it was not going to stop coming for him. It would keep coming until he killed it or it got him.

Soaking wet, tired, angry, grieving...too many things to catalog, Frank climbed up into the cab of the dump truck. The keys were in it. He started it up and discovered it had a full tank.

"All right then," he said under his breath. "Let's play a game."

He threw the truck in gear and started it rolling just as the monstrosity crossed the parking lot. When it was twenty feet away from the truck, it paused, as if considering the folly of what it was about to do or formulating a new plan of attack.

Frank waited for it.

Just the sight of it sickened him. It was beyond anything he could have imagined. It was about twelve feet tall, maybe twenty in width, a writhing, pulsating mass of flesh and limbs and coiling appendages, some of which were boneless like those of an octopus and others segmented like the legs of crickets. It was no one thing, but a boiling, seething biological proliferation of life forms and unrelated parts welded into a throbbing whole and seemingly held in stasis by a web-like mesh of tissue. It was raw and dripping, oozing slime and puddles of pink discharge.

"Jesus Christ," Frank uttered.

It waited.

He waited.

It faced the truck with spurred limbs like those of an ant, long black whip-like appendages coiling and snapping before it. It had dozens of legs. Some of them were those of animals and some were human and some were neither. He saw dozens of faces rising from its central mass like bubbles, rising then sinking away as if they were drowning in jelly and gore. Human arms reached out from it as did the paws of beasts. Several human torsos dangled from its underside along with dozens of wormy red tentacles. He saw Ruby. She was fused to its biology, hanging from its side. Her mouth opened and closed like that of a carp dying on a beach, her body greasy with gelatinous secretions.

Frank shook with rage.

Center of the thing, there was a mouth that was easily as big around as a manhole cover. It had no teeth that he could see but was surround by a fluttering, squirming ring of blunt tentacles that looked rubbery and transparent. He had the worst feeling that they did the job of teeth, only more so.

Frank engaged the auger of the snow blower.

The entire truck shook with the unleashed power of it. He put the truck in drive and rolled it right at the monstrosity. It reacted in kind. Too stupid and arrogant to realize the threat the whirring snow blower blades presented, it let out one of its chirruping cries that was high and harsh and pissed-off.

Then it charged.

Skittering, scampering, slithering, and gliding. Frank drove the truck right at it. The creature attacked. It hit the blades with fury and was pulled in, chopped, split, mulched, and ejected from the shoot in a shower of gore that sprayed over the gravel.

It was surely one of the most disgusting things Frank had ever witnessed. It let out an ear-piercing shriek like a thousand forks scraped on a thousand blackboards as the blades cycled it through. The truck jerked and rocked on its springs. Blood and mucilage splashed over the hood and spattered the windshield. He gritted his teeth as the crunching/sawing/tearing/wet ripping noises went up his spine and over his scalp.

Then it was over, and something like a ton of raw hamburger was spread over the parking lot, chunks and shanks and nameless oddities floating in the puddles.

He slumped behind the wheel, feeling very old and used-up, emotionally damaged and physically beaten. He kept seeing Ruby's face and hearing her voice and feeling her touch. It all kept running through the reels of his brain until he let out a resounding scream.

*This is a nightmare.*

*I'm living a fucking nightmare.*

*I've lost my kids. I've lost a wonderful girl who was probably the best friend I've had since Janet passed.*

*Jesus H. Christ, where does it all end?*

If it hadn't have been for the kids, he would have slid down in the street and descended into depression for hours and hours, but he couldn't allow it. Jerrod and Jasmine were out there and they needed him. That was what had kept him going this far. He couldn't give up now.

He killed the auger and drove across the lot. He figured he could roam through the fields and get around the traffic jam of wrecked cars. It took about ten minutes, but finally, there was the open road. He got the truck out on it, staring forlornly into the rearview mirror at the wreckage fading in the rain and distance.

"I'm sorry, Ruby," he said, choking back the tears. "I'm so sorry."

### 101

He drove and kept driving, avoiding wrecked cars that dotted the highway from time to time. The rain stopped for an hour or so and then came cascading down again, sinking the world. The countryside was flooded, farmyards had become lakes and ball fields were bogs. Everything was steaming and misty. Little towns set down in hollows were completely inundated, rooftops, trees, and flagpoles rising like the masts of sunken ships. The foliage was lush and green, sometimes pale and sprouting, tangled and tropical-looking. Much of it, he had never seen before.

He passed houses that were soft, furry mounds of fungus, connected to other houses by ropy strands of mycelium like the ratlines of brigs and barks. Windows were shuttered by creeping hyphae. He saw grotesque corpse-white growths like puffballs or toadstools. Streets covered in living carpets of brilliant red fuzz. And he saw that which fed the fungi, great mats of The Food erupting from the ground upon which immense, mutant birds picked and pecked.

Once, he saw some gigantic creature far in the distance disappearing into the haze. It was slumped and shapeless, like some immense creeping slime mold.

The closer he got to Montpalk, the more he saw wreckage and sprawled corpses sprouting yellow, flowery growths. Flocks of winged titans crossed the sky. Furry mammoths crossed the road in front of him. What they were, he honestly couldn't say.

Everything had gone crazy.

If The Food was allowed to proliferate unchecked, within five years, the world would be unrecognizable as such. A darkness would fall and life forms that were known would cease to exist, replaced by primeval things from the Earth's distant past or by things that had never existed before and could not under any sane circumstances.

In addition to the biological oddities, he began seeing signs that indicated to him the collapse of rational thought—pagan-looking altars at crossroads, huge crosses erected in empty fields, biblical verses and other crazy shit scrawled on highway signs. It was a short drop for the human mind from modern rationality to medieval superstition.

And Frank understood that all too well.

## 102

Finally, he had to park the dump truck.

There was simply nowhere else to go. The highway and surrounding fields were jammed with vehicles. There was no way through. He saw people mulling around. Some gathered in groups. Some of which were unruly. Some shouting and preaching. Staring at it all, he decided this is what it looked like when the machine broke down.

People wandered by, gray and faceless, stumbling through the rain. Dirty, ragged, blank-eyed. They'd been through it, they'd all seen things they would never get past. And they'd all suffered.

Lacking anything better to do and with no constructive plan in mind, he began asking people about Jasmine and Jerrod and Candy. Describing them. Describing her. Telling them anything he could think of that might stir a memory. Most people ignored him. Some heard him out, then shook their heads. Others tried to get him to join their group. Those who seemed sane warned him about going any farther. That the town was infested by things they would not put a name to. That the Army or National Guard or both were going to burn it flat.

Frank, feeling more dismal, disenfranchised, and hopeless as the minutes passed, finally leaned against a car and began to sob. No one paid him any mind. He got it out of himself, but even clear-headed, he still had no plan other than to walk right into the town and begin searching block by block by block.

And then a voice said, "So who are you looking for?"

## 103

He turned and there was a man in a dirty overcoat standing there. He had a gray beard and long gray hair. He looked like some kind of half-assed street corner prophet or a hippy who'd been down the long hard road.

"My kids," Frank said. "How'd you figure?"

"Everyone here is looking for someone and those that ain't are looking for something inside themselves."

"I bet they are."

"So tell me."

Frank figured he had nothing to lose, so he sketched it out for gray beard in some detail. "I guess they're either dead...or they're in Montpalk somewhere or gone to Volk Field."

"It's possible."

Frank swallowed, wiping rain from his face. "But not likely?"

The man smiled. His teeth were yellow, but there was compassion and understanding in his eyes. "Not saying that. I hope they're down at Volk, I really do. If there in the city...well, they're in the heart of it. The heart of the trouble."

He explained that there were known to be three enclaves of survivors. The Army had cleared out the others. But the last three were under siege by nature run wild (as he put it). The Army was not letting anyone get in. They had lost three platoons trying to get the others out and still were no closer to making it happen.

"They're waiting for reinforcements. When they go in, they're going in in force. Until that happens, they're staying put. And they ain't letting anyone else go in either."

"A guy back there said they're going to burn the town."

"That's rumor, but maybe. The Air National Guard has been using a lot of napalm on The Food and things created by it. They're not fucking around."

"Who are the people in these enclaves?"

Gray beard shrugged. "People from the city. People who wandered in looking for shelter. Stragglers. Maybe that woman and your kids."

Frank was silent for a moment. "I need to get in there."

"Army won't let you."

"Gotta be a way."

"Well, how determined are you?"

Frank just looked at him. "My kids. They're all I fucking got. If I lose them, I lose myself. They're all that matters."

Gray beard studied him very intently for some time, perhaps looking for chinks in his armor. "All right, if you're that set on it," he said. "Then you better come with me."

### 104

Gray beard's name was Ernie LaPalm but everyone called him "Seed," which was an odd sort of name until he admitted to Frank that up to four months ago, he'd been a pot baron of legendary proportions.

"It started for me in 'Nam," he admitted while they dried off in the back of a bus. "See, I was this straight-laced little nerd. I didn't drink. I didn't smoke. I saluted the flag and read my fucking bible. I never even got laid before the war, man. Then...things changed. I was with the 2/9 at Long An chasing the VC and doing my bit. That's where I first got high. After that, well, I was never the same again."

Seed said he became a trafficker when he got back from the war, a real cowboy in the 1970s and '80s, working in conjunction with various outlaw motorcycle gangs who distributed what he grew. Then in 1993, he got busted moving dope over the state line and did four years Federal time. They busted him again in 2008, but sprung him in 2010 and made him a job offer.

"Medical marijuana laws changed and they needed people to grow it. People with the proper know-how, if you can dig that."

Seed had gathered together eight other people who had friends or family in Montpalk. They were planning a midnight excursion into the city. He introduced Frank to them and he asked them about Jerrod and Jasmine. None of them had seen the kids. At least, that they knew of. Questions went back and forth.

"I think tonight would be a good night," Seed said.

Everyone agreed. They'd already tried two other times but had been driven back by the soldiers. Seed had a new plan on how to infiltrate themselves in.

"And what's that?"

"You'll see, my brother. You'll see. We're gonna go in, lay low until first light. Then we'll start looking. First, at the Twelfth Avenue civic center, then St. Matthews on Brand, and finally at the Salvation Army Mission uptown. That's our three enclaves. If our people are anywhere, that's where they'll be. Trapped right in the fucking dead zone."

He wouldn't go into specifics on that and Frank didn't ask him to. There was one last person Seed wanted Frank to meet and that was a guy named Jimbo. He was going to be their scout. He was a native, and he knew the quickest ways to each of the enclaves.

"We'd find this real hard without him, man," Seed admitted. "In 'Nam, we had these ex-VC dudes we called Kit Carson scouts. They helped us locate the enemy because they knew where they enemy hid and how they thought. Jimbo is our Kit Carson scout. When Jimbo came in out of the city, he told the Army where thirty-seven people were holed up. He not only told them, but he told them their names. He's got one of those memories. He can remember anything. Only thing is, he don't speak. Something bad happened and he don't speak. He wrote down every name for the Army and they got all those people out by chopper. Ain't that something?"

It was. It really was, Frank had to admit. He didn't know if any of this was going to lead anywhere or just end in disaster, but he felt good. He felt positive. He felt like they were finally moving in the right direction. That was something.

*If they're there, Janet,* Frank thought. *I'll find 'em, swear to God I will.*

Seed took him over to a Greyhound bus to introduce him to Jimbo who sat in the back. He was a big black dude, fierce-looking. He just sat there and stared into space.

"We're going in tonight, Jimbo," Seed said. "You okay with that?"

Jimbo nodded.

"Jimbo don't ever say anything, Frank, but he's always listening and he's always watching. Ain't that so, Jimbo?"

Jimbo nodded.

Frank realized he'd never asked Seed who he had in the city.

Seed laughed. "Got a brother named Raymond. He's like me before the war. Real patriotic and all that. Flags all over the fucking place. He won't have anything to do with me. Won't even let me meet my nieces and nephews. He's real uptight, man. But— get this—every year he sends me a card on Veteran's Day to thank me for serving in 'Nam. You dig that? Asshole hangs up when I call him, but he thanks me for serving. What a fucking guy. Anyway, I want to find him if I can. Don't ask me why, but I just feel I have to." Seed shook his head and sighed. "The shit we do for family, eh, Jimbo?"

Jimbo nodded.

"Frank here thinks his kids are at one of our enclaves and they just might be. We gotta find 'em. Kids always come first."

Jimbo nodded.

"What were your kids' names again?"

Frank said, "Jerrod and Jasmine."

"That's right."

Jimbo nodded.

Seed smiled. "Well, tonight it's on. You cool with that?"

Jimbo nodded again.

As Seed and Frank prepared to leave, Jimbo grabbed the sleeve of Frank's coat. He pulled him in close like he wanted to kiss him. Then, to Seed's surprise, he spoke one word: "Pennywise."

### 105

It was pointless to try and get anything more out of him, when Frank badgered him with questions, he just took out his notebook and wrote *Pennywise* again and again.

"Mean something?" Seed asked.

"Pennywise is a punk band," Frank said, barely able to control his excitement. "That woman my kids are with, she has a Pennywise logo on the back of her hand."

Seed sat next to Jimbo. "Jimbo, you seen a woman with a tattoo like that?"

Jimbo nodded.

"She have kids with her?"

Jimbo nodded.

Frank couldn't wait for dark. Things were starting to fall in place.

## 106

The Magnificent Eight.

That's what Seed called his posse that went into Montpalk. It was comprised of himself, Frank, Jimbo, a couple whiteboy traffickers named Skeeve and Ritz, an ex-cop named Mosk, and two sisters who looked like they might have been gangbangers once upon a time, Louise and Hep. They were looking for their aunt. Mosk was looking for his wife. Skeeve and Ritz were old friends and business associates of Seed's. They just liked shooting things.

So that was the band that lit out that night after the sun set.

Jimbo led them in. He led them within a block of the Army lines and then they waited while he scouted ahead. The soldiers were not terribly motivated and that was a good thing. Scattered groups of them huddled around fires in barrels, leaned against armored vehicles and smoked, ducked in and out of tents and trailers.

Jimbo came back after about ten minutes.

It was cool, according to Seed. Jimbo had found a way, and if everyone followed him and kept their mouths shut, they'd be inside the city in fifteen or twenty minutes. A light rain was falling, a chill hung in the air. They followed Jimbo through a maze of alleys, then into a warehouse where they navigated by flashlight. Down a set of cellar steps, through a basement crowded with rotting junk, and then up a set of steps to the street above.

Everybody stayed put as Jimbo scoped it out.

Finally, Seed whispered, "Okay. Now real quiet."

Frank was the last in line. When he crossed the street with the others, hugging buildings on the other side, he saw that the fires and lights of the soldiers were about a block behind them now. Getting in was easy…if you knew how like Jimbo did. They walked another two blocks, then gathered in a little park.

"It's cool now," Seed said, speaking in a regular voice. "Jimbo's going to lead us to the civic center now. Keep your eyes open because the shit can come from any direction. You all digging that?"

Jimbo led the way out. He was carrying .357 Magnum. Skeeve and Ritz were behind him with twelve-gauge riot guns. Everyone else had an assortment of weapons, from little .38s Louise and Hep carried to Mosk and his purloined Army M4 carbine.

Ahead, Frank heard the cries of night things screeching and howling. It was amazing. Montpalk was the same old Montpalk he'd seen a hundred times before…but yet it wasn't. Yes, the streetlights still burned and there were cars parked at the curbs and in driveways, but it had changed. Other than some wild outgrowths of fungi on the houses and some sort of yellow-green mold clogging sewer gratings, it looked the same. But it wasn't. It felt different. It wasn't the rainwater in the streets or the flowering vines draped over light poles and street signs, it was something deeper, a psychic or spiritual thing that Frank could feel right down into his core.

The city felt dirty, contaminated and infested.

### 107

Fifteen minutes later, an Army chopper passed high above, panning the streets with searchlights. Seed said it was a gunship so they darted into a little house to hide out for a few minutes.

"You think they'd shoot us?" Frank asked.

"Damn right they would," Mosk said. "They'll attack any target of opportunity. It's their job."

Skeeve and Ritz grunted at the very idea.

"It's all about oppression," Hep said. "Put people down and keep 'em there."

"There's got to be order," Mosk said. "Without order you have chaos."

"Chaos," Skeeve and Ritz said at the same time. It made them giggle. Mosk just shook his head.

As Seed watched the streets, Hep stepped over to Frank. She was small, Latin, and pissy-looking. She had long black hair and bad teeth. "You leave your kids here?"

"No…I didn't leave 'em. Let's just say somebody took 'em here to protect 'em, but it didn't work out that way. It's a long story. Complicated."

She just eyed him up. "Yeah, I know the shit. What my old lady did to us was long and complicated, too. I think about it every day. She weren't dead, I'd kill her. That's what I'd do."

Frank had the feeling that he was being indirectly threatened. "It's not like that…"

"I bet it's not."

"Listen, you don't know what you're talking about."

Louise came over and led Hep away. "It's all right," she said, but whether it was to Hep or him or both of them he didn't know.

*You don't have to like these people,* Frank reminded himself. *You don't have to be pals with them. You're all together because you want to get the same job done.*

Ritz and Skeeve were busy searching the house by flashlight. They were going through drawers and closets, looking for things to steal. Frank was pretty sure that Seed had invited them for muscle, not for their ethical or moral standards.

Frank was kind of offended by what they were doing, but then he relaxed. What did it matter? If he had to deal with this to get to his kids, what did it really matter?

"Shit!" they heard Skeeve cry from down the hallway. "There's a lady in here."

They all went down there and sure enough, there was. In the flashlight beams, they saw a woman sitting in the corner up against the wall. She was naked and infested.

"She's all fucked up," Hep said.

Which was a massive understatement. She looked like she was made of elastic, her trunk bent almost completely in a U, head nearly touching the floor. Her neck and chest had split right open and something like tubers and pale purple orchids were growing out of her. The worst part, beyond the rank stink of rotting grass clippings that wafted off of her, was the fact that the flowers or whatever in the hell they were, were moving. Sort of fluttering as if there was a breeze. But there was no breeze. Rootlets moved beneath her skin which was an unhealthy cinnamon shade.

Jimbo took one look, made a pained sound in his throat, and left the room.

"What should we do with her?" Ritz asked.

He and Skeeve both had their shotguns on her.

"Waste her," Mosk said. "That's all you can do with 'em when they get like this, waste 'em."

Frank didn't see the point—she was like some vegetative mass. He had no sooner thought that, than she sat up, bringing her head close to where it belonged in relation to the rest of her body. As the growths spilling out of her fluttered and seemed to pulse, she grinned at them with rotten black teeth and opened a single eye that looked very much like a moist yellow star fruit. Some sort of crawling threads came out of her other eye socket. They looked like worms, long slender white worms.

She began to pull herself up as if she were attempting to stand. Frank saw that the vulva between her legs was swollen like a massive tumor and just as blue as topaz. She continued to smile at them and now her face split from lips to forehead in some hideous black chasm. It was filled with the wormlike growths. They looked bean sprouts, hundreds of tangled glistening bean sprouts.

"Fucking waste her!" Hep said. "Cap the bitch!"

Skeeve and Ritz opened up with their riot guns, shattering the human-vegetable chimera into pieces that were quite lively, writhing on the floor. No blood came out of the carcass, just a transparent fluid.

That was enough.

Everyone got out of there and joined Jimbo in the living room. Together, they went out into the streets.

"Don't worry about that shit," Louise said to Frank. "We're gonna see a whole lot more of that, trust me."

## 108

"Way I'm seeing this play out," Seed told them about ten minutes later as they hid between two buildings, "is that we get to the civic center tonight. Then, maybe, at first light we can reach the church. That sound about right, Jimbo?"

Jimbo nodded.

"Aunt Rena will be at the civic center," Louise said. "If she's anywhere, that's where she's got to be."

Hep nodded. "I can't wait to see her."

"Me, too."

"About how far to the civic center? Two blocks?" Seed asked Jimbo.

Jimbo shrugged, thought it over, then nodded.

"Let's do this then."

Jimbo led the way out again and right away they heard action in the distance: the sound of gunfire, explosions, and choppers.

"They're still looking for those missing platoons," Mosk said.

"And since they can't find 'em, they're blowing the shit out of anything that moves," Skeeve said. He almost sounded jealous.

"Got to keep order, ain't that right?" Hep said to Mosk.

He, wisely, ignored her.

They moved down the center of the street because it seemed the safest way to go. There were too many shadows in too many yards and too many soft, shapeless things wriggling in them.

Jimbo led them across a park and he stopped about halfway and the others gathered. Frank saw what had him spooked—though initially, he wasn't sure what he was looking at. Was it a plant? An animal? He just couldn't be sure and the closer he looked, the more confused he became.

All flashlights were on it. It stood about fifteen feet tall, like some freakish gourd set on end, supported by a clutch of fibrous roots growing from its lower extremity. They were thick and tangled, the pale anemic white of boiled spaghetti. Above this, it was bulbous and spiky like the seedpod of a chestnut, only more oblong. The flesh was pebbled, scaly, almost reptilian in appearance, gray-green in color. From the top of the pod, there was a wrinkled, elongated trunk-like structure that terminated in a bell or a spout, and from it, there dangled four yellow-green appendages that were maybe five feet long, ribbed or segmented, an elliptical bulb growing from the end of each.

Frank didn't think they were bulbs, however, because they were puckered like toothless mouths.

As he looked closer—but not too close, because there was something unbearably grotesque about it—he realized that its outer skin was almost like a shell, a thick outer shell like that of a mollusk. If it *was* a plant, then the stem or fruit would be beneath...he supposed.

He had never seen anything like it.

He'd gone to agricultural college and had two years of botany under his belt. This was either an exotic species or it was something completely new. He opted for the latter.

"What the hell is it?" he asked.

Seed circled around it, fascinated, it seemed. Jimbo was nervous, real nervous and skittish. Same went for Hep and Louise. Skeeve and Ritz kept their distance, their riot guns trained on it.

"Nobody knows what they are," Mosk said. "They've been showing up everywhere lately. They grow like crazy. It's an invasive species, but one like we've never seen before."

Frank had a pretty good idea that he wasn't being told everything. He had a feeling that Louise and Hep and certainly Seed knew something more about this thing. It was clear that the girls were afraid of it and so was Jimbo. That in itself was amazing. The guy was a walking mountain...how could a plant scare him?

Yet, as Frank looked on it, drinking it in, he found that he was scared himself. There was something horrendously unnatural about it. Something that made him cold right to his bones.

But maybe it was the rain.

At least, that's what he told himself.

"Let's go," Seed finally said.

They moved across the park, Jimbo stepping very lightly, stopping a lot and scoping out what was ahead before moving on. *He's spooked,* Frank thought. *Something has him spooked.* With the way things were, there could have been a lot of reasons for that, but Frank was certain it was the plants because they were seeing an awful lot of them. Some were small, two or three feet in height, others were tall as a man, still others towering fifteen or twenty feet in height. In the distance, he thought he could see the silhouettes of others much larger than that.

Twice, Jimbo changed direction because there were veritable forests of the things. And wherever that was the case, Frank noticed, everything else was dead around them—the grasses were gray, the trees leafless, shrubs and bushes withered as if they'd been in a drought. Wherever they grew, they leeched the soil and killed off everything else. They were in the park, of course, but also infesting yards and empty lots, some so large they knocked over fences as they grew. He even saw some huge individuals rising from cracks in the pavement.

"They must grow really fast," he said.

No one answered him.

Finally, they came to another forest of the things. Seed chatted away with Jimbo in their peculiar fashion and it didn't sound like it was going well. Finally, he turned to the others.

"Okay, we've got a decision to make here," he said. "These goddamn things are everywhere. If we try to go around, it'll add another hour or more to our walk. I vote for cutting straight through. It's night. These things aren't usually very active at night."

"Active?" Frank asked. "What are you talking about?"

"Man, don't you know nothing?" Hep said. "These fucking things kill people. They suck the skin right off you."

Frank looked to Seed for clarification. He didn't get that, but he didn't get denial either. There was something very deadly about these plants.

Everyone voted to cut through the plants. It was obvious that they didn't like the idea, but they wanted to move on, to get where they needed to go.

"Be careful of the taproots," Seed said. "We don't want to wake 'em up."

They moved forward single file, the plants rising all around them. They had to squeeze between some and circle around others whose exposed root systems were splayed out like tentacles. A curious sweet smell came off of them. It was not offensive really, just unbearably sweet like candy.

"Sap's running," he heard Mosk say.

They moved on, deeper into the forest and then Ritz tripped over a root, bounced off one of the plants that was eight or nine feet tall and everyone froze. The plant was trembling. Its roots were vibrating. Frank could have sworn the sap was running copiously because the sweet smell—like some weird and fragrant combination of honeysuckle, candied apples, and wisteria—was stronger than ever. So strong, it made him feel almost giddy. He could hear activity from within the plant. Under its shell, there was a moist, fluid sound like berries in a press.

And if that was crazy in of itself, then it got a little crazier.

The plant kept vibrating from root to apex, and then it made a noise, a sort of thrumming that became a scraping rasp that itself rose up higher and higher until it became a purring, a shrill and humming *deet-deet-deet* sound like the electric buzzing of a cicada. The noise was repeated throughout the stand of plants again and again.

*They're communicating,* Frank thought, though the idea was absurd. Because if they were communicating, that meant they were intelligent to a degree. *To a degree, yes. Just remember that bees and ants communicate, too. It doesn't make them smart.*

The sounds faded away and the grove became silent. They started moving again for about five minutes. Five minutes in which everyone was nearly coming out their skin and then Jimbo stopped again. There was a large plant right in front of him. It was moving, vibrating like the other one but with a much more frenzied rustling sound.

Frank heard Louise whisper, *"Skin-Sucker...got something in it."*

The rustling built and then the shell opened. With a moist cracking sound, it opened lengthwise like some huge mouth or the insect-catcher of a Venus Fly-trap (something which was applicable because the shell halves were viciously spiked, as if they were made to seize prey and hold on) and the stem was exposed. It was a great husk, swollen and stout, a spongy, juicy pink and chambered like a seed case, encircled by a wiry network of fine tubers that looked much like the sprouts of a potato, but very fine and wiry like hair.

This is what he saw in the flashlight beam.

And then he saw more.

There was a crackling sound and the pink bulging stem split open lengthwise with a hairy sort of crevice. The plant made a low murmuring sound and then a quantity of slime and oily discharge erupted from the crevice, spilling out something like eggs. It sounded like an orange being juiced. The eggs were a pale yellow in color and about the size of footballs, connected to the birth canal by sinewy fibers.

As Frank watched, as they all watched, the ovum cleft open one after the other with a flux of liquicious tissue, sounding like popping bubbles, and a fetal horror was born from each. They were curled up inside, each of them about two feet in length, looking like bony, hairless weasels with long rat-like tales that squirmed and corkscrewed. They were blind, but hardly helpless. They crawled free of their birth sacs, each gnawing away the cords that connected them. Though they were clearly some sort of obscene animals, they rose up on their stubby hind legs, standing uneasily like toddlers, and unfurling bony arms that had been webbed to their sides. At the end of the arms were not paws exactly, but something more along the line of rudimentary hands, four-fingered, tipped with curling gray claws.

Frank just kept shaking his head from side to side. *Plants...fucking plants don't have eggs, they have seeds, and even if they did, they could not give birth to animals...they could not give birth to animals.* It all whirled around and around in his head until he thought he would pitch right over.

The newborn creatures lifted pink, glossy heads into the air and let out the most hideous, squalling cries. They were strident and sharp and eerie.

Then they went at each other.

Whatever biochemical mechanism keeps newborn animals from attacking each other for food, they lacked it. They went at each other with hinged jaws and rows of needle-like teeth. There were three of them, and they both attacked their weaker sibling, tearing it open and feeding on its entrails while it squealed and fought.

It was horrible.

It was Louise and Hep and Mosk that started shooting this time. They blew the two attacking creatures into pieces and then the injured one as it began to crawl in their direction hungrily, gnashing its teeth and dragging bloody viscera behind it.

The plant, its duty done, tucked its appendages away and closed its shell back up. It made no more sounds. Frank and the others stood there in shocked, uneasy silence for maybe a minute and then Seed got them moving. It had to be done. If one plant could give birth to horrors like that, then the others were surely capable of birthing even worse nightmares.

## 109

They managed to get out of the zone of the plants—*Skin-Suckers,* Frank thought, *how wonderfully descriptive*—but when they did, they found that the fungi proliferated astonishingly. Fuzzy blankets of fungus grew up the walls of houses and some were so soft with rot, they were collapsing into themselves like Halloween pumpkins. Fences and rooftops and telephone poles were encrusted with gray-white mounds of mold. Mutant toadstools, five and six feet high, colored in hallucinogenic shades of crimson, indigo, and neon yellow had taken over yards and playgrounds. A baseball field was home to gigantic outcroppings of mushrooms with spherical caps that must have been twelve or fifteen feet in circumference.

When a reconnaissance chopper zipped high overhead, they ducked into a yard, dangerously close to some of the weird growths, and Louise cried out because there was something growing from a fungoid mound on the side of a house. Something which reached out to her with arms carpeted in mold. They had to double back once when the street was blocked by several immense toadstools.

That's when they began to see people.

They weren't people any more than the woman in the house was a woman. They were fungal things wearing sweaters of mold, scarves of it wrapped around their necks and growing like beards from their faces. Some were slightly tainted with the malignance while others were shambling monstrosities with nodes for heads and stalks for arms. Skeeve blew away a sexless, shambling form, and its head exploded like a puffball, sending a cloud of dusty yellow spores airborne. The power lines overhead were draped with vine-like fungi, trees sprouting multi-colored bulbs like mushroom caps.

There were worse things, of course.

There were always worse things.

Seed drew their attention to several spherical mounds of creeping mold. There were three of them and they were quite large. Hep claimed they were houses, or had been houses. Nobody doubted her. As they passed a residential district, they noticed an empty gap in the middle of a row of houses. The cellar holes were there, but not what had been built upon them.

Frank tried not to speculate on such things, but his mind, that ever-cycling machine, told him, *If you're not totally fucking crazy yet, it's coming. God yes, it's coming.*

But as disturbing as all that was, what was even worse was The Food they saw. It gurgled from the mouths of sewers and crept sluggishly in gutters and bubbled up from cracks in the roads. They saw dozens and dozens of people squatted over it, shoving handfuls of the creamy white goo into their mouths. With them were dogs and rats and clouds of insects.

Everything was drawn to it.

It would own the world, given time.

## 110

The civic center.

It was deadly silent as they approached, guns raised. If there were survivors in there, they might be aiming weapons at them right now. In the dim moonlight, it would be hard to tell one creeping form from another. They stood there waiting as a light rain fell and water ran in the streets.

Frank could barely contain himself.

This might be it.

This might be what he was waiting for.

But why was it so damn dark? If there were indeed survivors in there, wouldn't they have a few lights lit? Then again, maybe they had blacked out the windows.

He was beside himself.

*Kids, if you're not in there, please be somewhere else and be safe.*

Jimbo and Seed led the way with Mosk and Frank behind them followed by Hep and Louise. Skeeve and Ritz watched the back door. The first thing they saw in the beams of their lights was broken glass. The front doors of the civic center were shattered. They saw not only glass but spent shell casings and stains that must have been blood. But not new blood, but old.

Frank's heart began to sink.

Then they found bodies. There were three of them. What had happened to them was anyone's guess because there really wasn't much left of them. They were basically lattices of bone that looked like they were sprayed down with wet scarlet paint. What flesh remained—sinew, tendon, and ligament mostly—looked as if it had been chewed or nibbled into strings. It clung to the skeletons and dangled from their shattered bones which were scattered for many feet in all directions. The floor was a muddy sea of blood magma drying into a sticky film. It was on the walls, the ceiling, and splattered on the windows along with bits of tissue.

It was sickening, but Frank and Seed stepped through it, over the carpet of finger bones and femurs, rib bones and spinal vertebrae scattered like dice.

"Look," Seed said.

Frank saw it, too. There was equipment tossed about, most of it spattered with blood. He saw helmets, web belts that looked shredded, a few scattered boots, rifles and packs lying around. He examined one of the boots. It looked like it had been punctured repeatedly by something like a leather punch. It was split right open.

"Soldiers," Seed said. "They must have come here looking for survivors."

"And something found them," Mosk said.

Hep and Louise said nothing. They just stared at the carnage, then turned away as if they couldn't take any more of it. Skeeve and Ritz were looting around, looking for things to steal that weren't covered in blood.

"Maybe the Skin-Suckers did this," Hep suggested.

"No way," Skeeve said. "Look at this mess...looks like they were fed through a wood chipper."

He had his light on the wall and there was no blood there but bits of tissue.

"Let's go look around," Seed suggested.

## 111

Nobody really wanted to, but that's why they had come. They found more bodies in a large conference room. Mostly skeletons, but there were also body parts. There was a head still in a helmet, its face locked in a scream. Part of a leg. An arm that must have belonged to a child. A woman who was nearly whole, her face gnawed into flowers of sushi. A little boy who had been split open, then apparently eaten from the inside out. Same for somebody's pet Collie; it looked as if its asshole had been cored with an auger and everything inside yanked out and reduced to scraps of red meat.

"It must have happened fast," Seed said.

Frank figured he was right. *Real* fast. So fast that these people never had a chance to even think of mounting a defense. Although most of the others turned away, Frank did not. It was grisly work, but he searched through the remains because he had to. He had to know that his kids weren't there. As far as he could tell, they weren't. He guessed maybe fifteen people had been in the room. As to whether the soldiers had been here when it happened was unknown. They may have happened upon the slaughter later and met the same fate.

Swallowing down his disgust, Frank just stood there, not knowing what to think. A voice in his head whispered, *you're reaching a point where you might have to accept some terrible things. You might have to accept that Jasmine and Jerrod are dead. Are you strong enough to do that?* But he wasn't. He knew he wasn't. He would keep clinging to hope and pretending that he would find them even when, deep inside, he knew better. He'd be like old Mrs. Caspian who'd lived down the way from him when he was a kid. When her bulldog, Rickles, had vanished one night, she spent years thinking he would come home as mysteriously as he had disappeared. She saw him everywhere—in town, in the country, running down sidewalks, playing with kids in a park. She'd once seen him on the six o'clock news, she claimed, casually padding past a newswoman who was interviewing a city selectman in the street.

They found more bodies in the gymnasium, dozens and dozens of them, an absolute litter pile of corpses and skeletons, soldiers and civilians. There was gore everywhere. Bits of flesh stuck to Frank's boots like bubblegum. There was just no way to go through it all. It would have taken a major mortuary team days and days to make sense of it. If his kids were there, there really was no way to know. It was as if a blood bomb had gone off, anatomy and bones strewn in every direction. Like a cauldron of human remains had been liberally ladled out and splashed around.

Even Skeeve and Ritz wouldn't go in there. They hung back with Louise and Hep as Frank, Seed, and Mosk sorted around. Jimbo just shook his head and walked off. The only good thing that came of it were weapons. The three of them strapped on flamethrowers, took carbines and gas masks.

Hep lit a cigarette and stared off into the night. Louise stood by her. They were both bugged by the idea that everyone was dead because that meant that their aunt was dead, too, unless she wasn't there at all.

Frank thought of saying something to them, then he decided it probably wasn't a good idea. He didn't really know them, and he had a pretty good feeling that they did not want to be known. Whatever they were feeling, it was not for him.

"Enough," Seed finally said. "Let's go."

### 112

"Why didn't they use the flamethrowers?" Skeeve wondered out loud as they moved down the street.

"Probably afraid to. With all those people around, it was too risky," Mosk said.

Jimbo was leading them on in the direction of St. Matthew's. Once they got there, they'd hole up for the night. See what things looked like when day broke. The original plan, of course, was to wait until morning to reach the church. But as things stood, they didn't like the idea of waiting. Montpalk by spotty moonlight was an endless graveyard. The houses and buildings were silent monoliths, cars and trucks parked at curbs or stalled out in the roads.

They passed through about two blocks where there really was no sign that anything had happened. Everything looked fairly normal other than the two inches of water in the streets from the backed-up rainwater drains. Leaves and sticks and garbage floated about, but that was about it.

Then they entered yet another zone of fungus infection where everything was rotting and smelling, soft and oozing and moldered. There was a high, repulsive smell of decomposition that reminded Frank of cellars with damp rot. That and a pungent, sweet smell of fermentation like over-ripened carrion dissolving into pulp. He brushed against a white picket fence that was threaded with veins of black mold. It was flaccid under his touch. It wiggled when he bumped it.

He heard things moving around them, splashing and skittering, but whatever they were, he never saw. It was little things like that that he was grateful for. He saw what he first took to be downed power lines dangling from the roofs of houses, but they were in fact tendrils of fungi that netted one soft structure after another together.

The rain started to pour down again, and he began to feel just as miserable as he had when he slogged through it with Mick and Maribel and…Ruby. He was trying hard not to think about her, but as the rain pattered against his face, running down his nose and filling his eyes and flooding down the back of his coat, she was there beside him, drenched and beautiful, her eyes huge and dark, her wet hair tossed over one shoulder in a black mane. He ached inside. He ached to touch her again and hear her voice and feel her head on his shoulder—

"Frank!" Seed called out. "Get the fuck out of the street!"

The others had taken refuge beneath an awning outside a furniture store, pressing together in the dark doorway. But why? Then he knew. It was a rumbling he could feel through his boots. A rumbling that was not a rumbling exactly, but more along the lines of a steady, measured thumping that made plate glass windows rattle in their frames.

*Boom, boom, boom.*

He joined the others in the doorway, glad to be out of the rain, but terrified at the idea of what was coming in their direction. They held onto each other as something gigantic came out of the gray rain and gathering darkness. They could only see parts of it— immense spurred legs like chitinous pillars, wavering appendages like threshing hooks, and the image of a gigantic wormlike body that towered above the buildings. If anything, it looked like a titanic shaggy insect that boiled with steam.

Then it passed by and was gone.

It left triangular gouges in the road and that was all. What it might have been or what The Food might have mutated it from was anyone's guess.

Hearts beating again, they pushed on.

### 113

Ten minutes later, they were moving at a good clip. They weren't seeing much of anything. Then again, you couldn't see much in the rain. It came down with savage force and Seed's company of merry men—and women—were forced to take refuge under the overhang of a bank until the worst of it passed. Which it did eventually, leaving flooded streets in its wake and eight shivering, miserable people who were all probably wondering just why the hell they had agreed to any of this in the first place.

One of them, however, had no qualms and that was Frank because he was not going to stop until he knew about his kids. He'd been through too much and was certain he would soon be wading into much more, but he was driven.

If the others lost their heart, he would not.

They could turn back, but such a choice was unthinkable to him. He had to find his babies. There was nothing else.

When the rain lessened to an annoying chill sprinkle, they stepped out onto the walks again and Jimbo got the mule train moving. Frank wondered (and not for the first time) what drove him. According to Seed, he'd left no family or friends in the city, yet he was willing to lead the others in there at great risk to himself.

But why?

*Sometimes there is no why,* Frank told himself. *Sometimes you just do what you have to do because it's the right thing and to not do it is beneath consideration.*

He figured that's how it was for guys in wars. They took crazy chances and suicidal risks, and if they came out of it in one piece, they were heroes; if they didn't, they ended up in body bags. But they did what they did because somebody had to and it was the right thing. It wasn't really about patriotism or flag-waving or any saccharine Hollywood bullshit, it was about doing the right thing as a human being. Sometimes that was enough.

They heard rumbling again.

It stopped everyone dead in the street. Had the monster returned? Had he brought Godzilla and Ghidrah the Three-Headed monster with him this time? But, no, this was different. This was a smaller sound, but busier, much busier.

Lights came splashing down the street. Jimbo looked very concerned.

"Armored vehicles," Seed said. "The Army's sweeping through. Get to cover!"

They turned on their heels, following Jimbo into an alleyway that cut between two buildings. They had barely made it fifteen feet when lights hit them, dazzling, blinding lights, and a voice shouted over a bullhorn. "STOP RIGHT THERE! NOBODY MOVE!"

A half-dozen soldiers in full battle rattle moved towards them. They weren't screwing around. Their weapons were raised and sighted in killing mode.

"Just take it easy!" Seed called out to them. "We're just—"

"SHUT THE FUCK UP!" the voice told them.

Seed and the others allowed themselves to be marched back out into the street at gunpoint. Frank tried several times to explain the situation, but the guy with the bullhorn—a sergeant so hard-assed he was practically a walking cliché—didn't want to hear about it. So they stood out in the street as the vehicles rolled up, stopping about thirty feet away which, Frank figured, gave them a good kill zone should they need it.

There were two trucks, a Hummer, and what looked to be a Bradley Fighting Vehicle, a freaking tank. Frank had a really bad feeling that they were about to be escorted back to their point of origin.

A guy on the Bradley, apparently an officer, said, "What are you people doing out here?"

Seed tried to explain the matter, though Frank had a suspicion that it wasn't going to do a bit of good.

"You're making your way to St. Matthews?" the officer said. He clearly wasn't buying it. "This city is under martial law. I can have you shot right now for violating that. And you expect me to believe you're on a mission of mercy? C'mon, mister, how fucking stupid do I look?"

Frank had to bite his tongue so he didn't answer that one.

"Looters," the hard-ass sergeant said. "Goddamn looters, that's what."

They hadn't been told to drop their guns yet, but that was coming. They were in a very bad situation. They were carrying Army-issue equipment. If the soldiers looked in Skeeve or Ritz's pack and saw the things they had stolen, it would be hard for Seed's people to convince anyone they weren't criminals.

"Shit," Frank said under his breath.

The hard-ass sergeant was circling around them. "Nice stuff. Flamethrowers. M4s. Not only are you assholes looting, you're in possession of government-issue."

Where any of it would have led and what their chances of survival would have been (particularly after it was learned that they had swiped the weapons off dead soldiers) was anyone's guess.

But it never came to that.

Something else happened.

114

As the sergeant reamed them out about being looters and the officer considered their fate and the others watched them with narrowed eyes and fingers on triggers, there was an intervention.

Frank was one of the first to see it…or them.

In the sky, just above the buildings, reflected in the lights of the vehicles and limned by moonlight, there were objects drifting about. Large objects. He couldn't see them clearly enough to be sure what they were, only that there appeared to be hundreds.

As the sergeant gave them hell and the officer nodded appreciatively, a couple of the grunts with rifles started swatting at something, pulling at something on their uniforms as if there were long, offending hairs on their fatigues.

*What...what in the hell is this?*

A couple of the soldiers cried out. They panicked and started firing up into the sky. The sergeant started shouting and the officer joined him. All around them, it seemed, fine white strands like tendrils of mist drifted about.

Except it wasn't mist, it was...*webs.* Long gossamer fibers of drifting web. Spider web. And by then, everyone was looking up and everyone saw it at the same time. And not a one of them didn't shrink back with atavistic horror.

There were spiders in the air.

Dozens and dozens and dozens of them. They were drifting downward on what looked like gauzy balloons of silk the way spiderlings sometimes do...but these were no spiderlings. Maybe they weren't exactly B-movie sized monsters, but they were big. At least as big as tarantulas, if not quite a bit bigger. They began dropping everywhere, but mostly right on top of the soldiers and their vehicles. As soon as one of them made contact with the ground (or a soldier), its balloon deflated and collapsed, looking much like some sort of afterbirth it was dragging.

Soon enough, the street around the vehicles was alive with hundreds of skittering, creeping forms. It became a crawling river.

"GET THE HELL OUT OF HERE!" Frank cried out.

Which was something Jimbo was already endeavoring to do. He shoved Louise and Hep towards a flower shop. There was an iron ladder set into the side of the building that led to the flat-topped roof high above. Hep scrambled up it followed by Louise, then Ritz and Skeeve, the Jimbo himself and Seed. Frank tailed behind with Mosk, blowing away spiders with their M4s until there were just too many of them. They climbed up the ladder, too, hands helping them up onto the roof.

Frank saw more spider balloons drifting down on them. Everyone started firing, bursting them before they got within fifteen feet of touchdown, the air wet with a mist of spider blood and spider parts.

One of them made it down, landing not five feet from Frank. He saw its balloon deflate and it turned towards him. It was pasty-white like The Food itself, a skeletal-looking thing with sharp spurs on its legs. He couldn't tell if it had any eyes, but it did have a mouth, a truly horrible chasm of fangs that seemed to retract and extend as it breathed.

It made a hissing sound and he blew it away.

Down in the streets was where the real action was. The soldiers were dying horribly, covered in an undulating carpet of spiders. Maybe a couple of them had run off, scared right out of their minds, but most of them were dying below. The spiders had driven them down by sheer numbers, and as they lay there, tangled in webs, screaming pathetically, the spiders went after them like buzz saws. There seemed to be thousands of them. So many, you couldn't see the soldiers, just that creeping white carpet of monstrous arachnids. The skittering legs. The wet cries of the soldiers.

"Watch it!" Seed cried out.

A dozen more spider balloons were coming down. They knocked six of them out of the sky, but the others landed. Louis and Hep killed two of them, Mosk wasted a third. Then the other two came right at him with amazing speed. He opened his mouth, maybe to cry out, and they hit him, hit him hard. The air whooshed out of his lungs as if he'd been tackled by a three-hundred-pound lineman. He went down and the spiders went to work on him.

No one knew what to do in those first few dangerous moments. They couldn't shoot. They didn't dare use the flamethrowers. Jimbo kicked one that was riding Mosk's chest. It made a squeaking sound, but that was about it.

Frank, as stunned as the others and equally horrified and repulsed, pulled out his knife and brought the blade down on the back of the spider that Jimbo had kicked. Its body was remarkably, sickeningly soft—it was like stabbing a fat, over-ripened tomato. Brown goo squirted from the entry wound, splashing up Frank's arm. He fell back with a cry. The spider squealed with a high, unpleasant mewing sound like a stepped-on kitten. It abandoned

Mosk right away, spinning in circles, Frank's knife still stuck in its abdomen. It thumped into the four-foot lip of the roof, then crawled up it uneasily, dragging two of its legs. It reared up for a moment, hissing, then Skeeve blew it in half with his riot gun. Below, Frank heard his knife clang to the street along with a splattering like rotting fruit.

Skeeve and Ritz used their rifle butts to knock the other spider from Mosk. It reared up, too, and spat something from its mouth that, thankfully, hit no one. It didn't get a second chance—it took ten rounds at close range.

Mosk was dead.

There was no doubt of it. He was hideously swollen purple and black, his eyes bulging from their sockets, his tongue pressed out between his lips.

"They must have been poisonous as hell," Seed said.

It took about fifteen minutes before the spider pack abandoned the soldiers and moved on, rushing away into the night.

After about ten more minutes more, Frank and the others went down there. What they saw was an atrocity. The still-running vehicles were spattered with blood and meat. The soldiers looked like they'd been atomized, reduced to flakes and scraps and liquid. There was little left but bones and these were scarlet and dripping, badly worried. Their uniforms were shredded, dead spiders lying about, some crushed or mangled or blown into fragments.

Frank figured he now knew what had gotten everyone at the civic center.

"We could take one of those vehicles," Ritz said. "Beat the shit out of walking."

"That's an idea," Skeeve said.

Seed led everyone over there. There was blood everywhere, torn up bodies sprawled over the seats. Everywhere they looked, there was gore.

"Anybody up for this?" Seed asked them.

But nobody was.

"Can we just get out of here?" Louise said.

"We can do that," Seed told her and led his people away into the night.

## 115

Hep and Louise were pretty adamant that they did not like the idea walking around out in the open with the spiders. Everything in the city was bad enough, but the spiders made it all that much worse. They began checking parked cars for keys and it wasn't long before they found one.

"What do you think?" Louise asked everyone.

Seed shrugged. "I guess I'm cool with it. Just understand that if one of those helicopters sights us, we're probably going to get blown away."

Everyone was willing to take the chance.

"Jimbo?" Seed asked.

Jimbo nodded.

The vehicle the girls had chosen was a cargo van. There were only seats in the front. The rest was storage. According to the lettering on the door, it had belonged to a dry cleaning outfit which explained the racks of coat hangers in the back.

"We only got three, four blocks to go," Hep said. "We only got to get that far."

Frank couldn't make up his mind whether he liked the idea or not. If his kids were at that church, he wanted to get there in one piece. But the majority ruled. Jimbo got behind the wheel and off they went. The first block went fine, there was no trouble at all. Frank felt himself relax a bit. He hadn't realized up until that moment how tense he was. The others seemed to relax a bit, too. Seed sat up front with Jimbo. Frank and the others sat cross-legged in the back.

Ritz and Skeeve were openly bragging about all the things they'd stolen while Hep bitched about personal freedom and martial law. Louise asked Frank about his kids, and when he told her things, practically gushing about them, she said they were lucky to have him. It was a nice moment, but it didn't last.

"Things are moving out there," Seed said up front.

"What sort of things?" Skeeve asked.

"Not exactly sure…big things. See 'em moving around the edges of the headlights. There, then they're gone. Maybe it's my eyes. Maybe I been staring out there too long."

But nobody was buying that; they knew Seed too well.

"Better slow it down a little," he said to Jimbo.

Now the light talk had all but evaporated. Frank and the others sat in the back in a guarded, apprehensive silence.Frank sat there, feeling like he was part of the group and leagues separated from it. In the front, Jimbo moved the van forward slowly. Beads of sweat stood out on his face like pimples. Seed peered out of the windshield, sensing something, waiting for it to show itself as he must have waited for the enemy in nameless jungles of Indochina nearly fifty years before.

Hep fumbled a cigarette into her mouth, nearly dropping it three times. Skeeve lit it for her.

"Why the hell are we going so slow, man?" she asked. "Shouldn't we speed up and get outta here?"

It made perfect sense, but Seed shook his head. "There's shit out there, my girl, that can break this van in half or crush it flat. I'm trying not to advertise. Which is another reason I didn't want us in a vehicle—it draws the wrong kind of attention."

He got no argument.

Which was something that Frank had noticed more than once. The others might spit and claw amongst themselves like alley cats, but they never argued with Seed. There was always respect in their eyes when they addressed him. It was as if he were some sort of sage to them, a paragon. Maybe, in his own way, he was all the things they were not and could never be. Whatever it was, it was solid. Frank had the feeling that Seed had done something, something important, for each and every one of them, and there was nothing they wouldn't do for him.

Seed watched, Jimbo drove, and everyone else waited.

They didn't wait long.


## 116

Something thudded into the side of the van. Louise let out a low, muted cry. It could have been anything. It sounded very much like somebody had rapped the quarter panel with their knuckles. *Hard.* Maybe it was a stone kicked up by one of the wheels.

Frank's mind offered him any number of safe, mundane explanations, but none of them stuck. They were all too slippery because his instincts sensed something bad and they could not be talked out of it.

Something hit the back door.

Something large enough to make the van rock on its springs.

"Headlights might be attracting some of the local wildlife," Seed said. "You okay driving in the dark, Jimbo?"

Jimbo nodded.

"All right. Kill the lights then."

Jimbo did. He piloted them down the dark streets.

In the back, it made things even worse. Now they didn't even have the dash lights to chase away the shadows. There was only the glow of Hep's cigarette and that was no comfort at all.

It was like being in a cave, Frank decided. Rolling deeper and deeper into the darkness, wondering when you were going to hit a wall or roll right over the edge.

Something hit the other side of the van. Then something else, something heavy, landed on the roof. Now all eyes were staring upwards. They knew that whatever it was, it was still up there.

Then it moved.

It slid over the roof with a slow, sliding sort of noise. Frank was imagining a python up there, a very large python, gliding bonelessly. Then it slid free. It was gone just that fast.

"What the fuck was that?" Hep asked.

That's when something hit the windshield. It slapped against it, an enormous black shape that covered it.

Jimbo slammed on the brakes.

Then he turned on the lights.

The shape moved with a fluid, sinuous locomotion. It was no snake. Frank was sure of that. What he saw in the dash lights was something black and shining, not reptilian but more eel-like, slick and vaguely evil. It was very bony. Its skin was stretched tightly between bone slats like the canopy of an umbrella. He was nearly certain that although it was several feet in width, it was no thicker than a padded envelope.

The van shook again and it slithered away, leaving a gooey, mucus-like emulsion over the glass. In the headlights, there was only the wet, deserted streets now.

Seed cleared his throat. "Drive, Jimbo. Get us the hell out of here."

Jimbo got the van rolling and there was something encouraging and sedative in its very motion. There was practically a concurrent psychic sighing from every mind in the back. Frank sensed it. He breathed in, then out. His muscles relaxed.

"That's enough of that bullshit," Ritz said.

Skeeve laughed. Louise chuckled.

Then the van swerved, as if to avoid some obstacle. Everyone in the back was thrown into one another. There were cries and shouts.

"Something there," Seed said, almost gasping. "Something fucking...*big.*"

The van was hit again.

It squealed on its tires. Then the windows of the delivery doors in back shattered as some unseen force battered them.

Skeeve was the one who lost it.

He brought his riot gun up practically before anyone had recovered and fired at the windows, blowing one of them out into the night. The noise in the confined space of the van was like a fucking grenade going off.

"WHAT THE FUCK ARE YOU SHOOTING AT?" Hep cried out with some volume.

But Skeeve didn't bother answering her question. He didn't have to. The delivery doors were hit again and again with enough force to dent them in. They looked they like were buckling in their frames. Frank noticed this a second or two before he saw a mammoth black head bash in the other shattered window.

Somebody screamed.

What Frank saw was a huge, gulping mouth trying to chew its way into the van. It was as black and shiny as the tail had been, smooth like rubber. It chomped and bit and bashed at the doors. It had teeth that were triangular. The inside of its gaping maw was just as pink as cotton candy.

And it kept coming and coming.

Jimbo stomped on the accelerator and got the van really racing, but they couldn't outrun it. It hovered there, biting at the doors, and Frank was reminded of Pac-Man's endlessly chomping mouth. It bashed the doors one last time and then it was gone.

They had no idea what it was.

No ideas what it could have been.

They were just thankful it had business elsewhere. Frank was leaning farther and farther in Seed's direction. They needed to get out of the van; it was most definitely drawing the wrong kind of attention. He brought the matter up and got silence from Skeeve and Ritz. Louise said nothing, but Hep snarled at him how she wasn't about to become fucking spider bait.

"I don't even know why I'm doing this," she said. "I mean, what's in it for me now? My aunt's dead. I should just turn back. Why should I go to the church? For you? For your kids?"

Frank felt himself boil momentarily, but he didn't say anything. What was the point? He told himself she was hurting and scared. That's all it was.

"You're doing it because it's the right thing to do," Seed told her in his mellow, easy grandfatherly tone. "There's no pay off for doing the right thing, dear. You do it because it's simply the right thing to do."

That quieted her. There were tears in her eyes, but she wiped them away before anyone could notice. Everyone was feeling the way she did, Frank knew. The others were just better at concealing it.

There was a loud *thump!* as something dropped on top of the van. Something heavy. Something very heavy.

"They're back," Skeeve said.

But Seed shook his head, nervously eyeing the roof. "No, I don't think so."

Whatever it was, they could hear it up there, making tapping and scraping sounds as if it was trying to find a way in. This was followed by a fierce buzzing noise. It was like that of a fly, but cranked through a guitar amplifier until the entire van reverberated with it. *Loud*, didn't begin to describe it.

*"DRIVE!"* Hep screamed, hands over her ears. *"GET THIS FUCKING THING OUT OF HERE!"*

Which is exactly what Jimbo was trying to do. He slammed on the brakes, pitching everyone in the back to the floor, and pulled a U-turn, squealing away down the street. But it did no good; their rider was still on top of the van. If anything, the tapping up there was even louder and that scraping/rasping sound was nearly constant now. It sounded like it was working the top of the van with the world's largest saw-tooth file. Then the buzzing came again, maybe even with more volume this time. And as it did so, the entire van rocked.

Nobody said a thing.

Now there was more buzzing, only it seemed to be coming not just from what clung to the roof, but from every direction. Jimbo had the hi-beams on, and they all saw what came swooping out of the sky at them—insects, immense black insects on dragonfly wings. They hit the van from all sides and several more settled onto the roof. The buzzing was incessant now. So deafening that people began to cry out. And worse than that, the power of those many wings nearly lifted the van from the road again and again. In the end, Jimbo couldn't control it. The downdraft of the wings was creating a wild, sucking tempest that jerked the van this way and that.

"Hang on!" Seed said.

The van jumped a curb and smashed into a STOP sign, snapping it right off. This did nothing but infuriate the bugs.

One of them began to crawl down the window. Frank saw immense forelegs that were spurred, followed by a narrow, streamlined, skeletal-looking body that had to have been five or six feet long.

Louise was shaking. "They're gonna get in," she said in a high, panicked voice. "They're going to get in...*I gotta get out of here! I have to get the hell out of here!*"

Hep took hold of her and then so did Skeeve and Ritz. She was nearly hysterical, fighting and squealing with terror.

Frank understood perfectly—it was like being in a can and praying that what was out there didn't figure out how to use a can opener.

Jimbo and Seed had retreated into the back with the others. One of the insects began crawling up the hood again, then it backed down. It scraped the glass with its forelegs which were long and hinged like those of a praying mantis. The undersides were set with spines like knitting needles. They looked not only sharp but deadly. Once it seized its prey, they would never escape. Now it was looking through the window. It was like seeing the head of an ant magnified a hundred times. It had ruby-red compound eyes and scissoring mandibles that were bony and jagged, fine hairs jutting from its heavy skull. Its whip-like antennae twitched and vibrated. It cocked its head this way, then that.

*Like a mutant flying ant,* Frank thought. *And look at those eyes...no intelligence, just appetite and a cold hatred for other living things.*

The creatures crawled over the van, scratching and scraping it with a sound like knives. They tapped it. Thumped it. Then, apparently bored, the wings buzzed in a cacophony of thundering noise and they flew off.

After a few minutes, everyone relaxed.

"Let's get the hell out of here," Frank suggested.

The side doors were buckled in their frames and they wouldn't open. Everyone had to file out the front passenger-side door. Louise's legs were so weak, they would barely support her. She leaned against her sister as they dragged her off into the shadows.

And not a moment too soon.

The buzzing came again. A single insect settled onto the roof. Frank could see it easily in the moonlight. It was about six feet long with a glossy black carapace that was mottled gray. Its body was plated, heavier forward and narrowing at the tail where it became a stinger. Its head was large, set forward on a chitinous neck. Immense transparent wings fluttered, ready for takeoff. As Frank watched, its body arched and tried to plant its stinger into the van. This was the tapping noise they had heard. Its mandibles and forelegs scratched away at the roof, as if hoping to reveal a tender spot for stinging.

After a few moments of this, it made a sort of whistling/clicking noise, then flew off into the night.

It did not come back.

"Jesus H. Christ," Seed said. "This keeps up, we're gonna need ourselves a real big can of Raid."


117

In a perfect world (something Montpalk surely wasn't), they would have been granted a breather to calm down and work the kinks out of their nerves, but it was not to be. Fate or God or Providence or lopsided Destiny had their number. It had them on the rack, and now that it had shown them the red-hot pincers, it was going to let them feel molten iron against soft, yielding flesh. It had inserted a screw in their backs and now it would turn it.

The fungus infestations became decidedly worse.

Gray-white blankets of mold covered the sidewalks and a pulpous red-purple fungi grew up out of the sewers, inundating the streets. It was like a spoiled pudding beneath their feet. Each time they stepped down, their boots sank two or three inches in the slop, releasing a horrendous odor of putrefaction. The moldering excrescence grew up the sides of houses and buildings, hanging in ropes from withered trees like Spanish moss. Fences and walls were crumbling with dry rot or going soft and gelid. Shapeless, mottled forms netted in orange fuzz crept all around them.

Seed fired on one with his newly acquired M4, and it let out a horrible dry squeaking, green sap dripping from bullets holes in its spongy hide.

There were lots of them. Things that might have been human once but were human no more. Some were like mutant puffballs, great wooly sacks that inched about like slugs, apparently feeding on the abundant fungi, seams of The Food that bubbled up from below, and often each other. Frank saw walking spherical toadstools that were pulpy white, creeping slime molds, and human mushrooms that were palpitant and yeasty, nodular growths and cap-like heads nodding as he passed. Still others were great masses of corruption, bulging and sporing, crepitant things that peered about with eyestalks and breathed with great rubbery external bladders. Many of them were leaking sticky fluids and exhaling clouds of spores. He saw two doughy-faced individuals that were absolutely gelatinous, dissolving into one another, bubbling and fizzing.

It was insane, all perfectly insane.

Yet, for all that, none of the creatures seemed particularly interested in Frank and the others. They made rasping noises or phlegmy sounds, but that was about it. Most were perfectly happy, it seemed, in the fungal oblivion of their netherworld.

The further Seed's people went, the worse it got.

Everything was covered in growths. Houses were mounds of mold, telephone poles and fences melting into the communal fungoid sludge. As the Magnificent *Seven* trudged ever forward, the slop rose above their ankles to their calves. The streets were webbed in vines of mold that had to be chopped through. Glops of foul-smelling secretions dropped onto their faces and into their hair, sliding down the backs of their necks like cold slime.

And then, when it seemed that they would need machetes to chop through the tangled, snarled ropes and ribbons of the stuff, the fungus began to peter out and before them was a dry and dead quarter.

"The dead zone," Seed said. "Now things'll get interesting."

## 118

Frank had seen it before.

It was just like the dead forest he'd investigated the night they escaped from the farm. Everything was dead. Not only dead, but dry and crumbling and going to dust. Houses were collapsed, trees leafless, shrubs and bushes shriveled to sticks. There were flakes drifting in the air. Everything crunching underfoot. As they walked, trees fell over and shattered like glass. Houses fell into themselves. Everything was creaking and crackling. There were abundant human skeletons littering the streets. And even these, they found, crumbled to ash when they were touched.

Yes, just like the forest, the life, the moisture, had been leeched from anything that was alive or had once been alive. It was a zone of death that would spread out and engulf the entire city sooner or later, sucking it dry. But unlike the forest, the cause of it was very apparent.

The plants.

The Skin-Suckers were everywhere.

They were draining the life out of everything to feed themselves, to propagate their numbers which were alarming to say the least. They were everywhere. There were hundreds of them spread out in every direction. Some were little more than saplings, a few feet in height. Others eight and ten and twenty feet tall. Some real monsters grew in the distance and they were twice that in size.

"We don't have a choice now," Seed said. "If we want to reach the church, we're going to have to go straight through this forest."

There was no other way, and that's how the trouble started.

## 119

Jimbo led the way once again, and the others fell in uneasily behind him in single file. The plants were silent, no noises, no anything.

"Taproots," Seed said, directing it at Ritz.

They were in a congested forest of them that was much worse than the thicket they'd been in before. They couldn't have any accidents. As they followed Jimbo, they stepped very carefully, avoiding not only the exposed root systems but the large plants that grew to either side and the saplings underfoot. They had no way of knowing what might set them off, so they were very cautious.

They began to find remains.

In whole and in part. Human and animal. Most were wasted right down to bones, but a few still had meat on them, though not much of it. This is what Hep had meant by "Skin-Suckers." The plants were carnivorous, and they meticulously fed on flesh and blood. Yet, they were also draining the life from the grass and trees, so maybe omnivorous was more applicable.

Regardless, it was a real horror show—the results of their meals were everywhere. Frank noticed that some of their human victims had been soldiers which meant that the Army had indeed made it this far, but apparently no further.

The roots were the real problem, of course. They were splayed all over the ground, thick and almost muscular-looking, coiled and looped like snares. Avoiding them was nearly impossible. It was like trying to tiptoe through a snake pit. At the very top of each pod, at the apex of the bell from which the long appendages grew, there were reedy strands of some very fine material that floated in the breeze like the gauzy webs of spiders.

"What the hell is that stuff?" Louise finally asked.

"I don't know, but don't touch it," Seed instructed her.

She gave him a look that seemed to say, *Now why the fuck would I do that?*

The rain was light, very light, little more than a sprinkle. The moonlight was thin and patchy. Knife-edged shadows created by the flashlight beams danced around them.

Then—

There was a rustling from one of the large plants. It seemed to come from inside it, as if rats were nesting within. Then it began to come from quite a few of the plants along with low slithery sort of sounds.

Frank didn't like it.

They were all closed up as yet, but that didn't mean anything. He knew how quickly they could open. There was a sudden rising sweet smell in the air. They all knew what that meant: the sap was running. It was much stronger than before, sickening in its intensity.

"But nobody stepped on the roots," Hep said, clearly frustrated by what was happening or about to happen. "Nobody touched them!"

Seed looked around at the dour faces in the line of march, gray and wizened and very afraid. "Our footsteps might be enough. Now shut up and move!"

The plants were vibrating now like the tails of rattlesnakes. And that's how it sounded. *Like children's rattles,* Frank thought as he stepped lightly, trying to go as fast as he could. Yes, they were all vibrating, and he could feel it right through the soles of his muddy boots. It was getting louder as the sweet smell grew stronger.

They were waking up.

There was no doubt of it.

And then he heard it, over the vibrating/rattling sounds and the constant rustling which sounded like a high wind in a cornfield, he heard it quite clearly: *Deet-deet-deet-deet.* That same high-pitched droning he'd heard earlier. Now it came from dozens of dozens of different locations. Even the saplings underfoot were making a sort of trilling noise. It was a buzzing that reminded him of telephone lines when he was a kid which, when you stood beneath them, hummed like plucked violin strings. It rose up to a feverish, intense pitch, higher and higher: *deet-deet-deet-DEET-DEET-DEET*...and the plants came alive. Their bulbous forms shivered and quaked, the bells at their apexes pulsating. The long greenish

216

appendages that grew from them were not hanging limp now, no, they were wavering up in the air like vipers, sweeping back and forth as if they were casting for scent. The bulbs at their ends were quivering.

Frank noticed with some anxiety that the fine silk strands that had been blowing in the breeze like cobweb strands only moments before, were now sticking straight up like spines. They grew from the bells like hairs and something had them agitated.

*It's us,* he thought. *They're some sort of sensory mechanism like exposed nerves and they sensed us. It wasn't our footsteps, but these fibers.*

It was at that moment that Skeeve let out a wild, agonized scream.

He was maybe seven or eight feet in front of Frank. All lights were on him and what they revealed was a horror. One of the green appendages from a fifteen-foot plant near to him shot out like the tentacle of a squid, its bulb opening into something like a suction cup or a mouth. It suctioned itself to his face. There was a slurping, sucking kind of noise and the appendage—which had been big around as a wrist—suddenly inflated to the thickness of a weightlifter's thigh, going from a dirty gray-green to a brilliant scarlet red as it literally sucked the flesh from him. His head seemed to cave-in like a beer can crushed in a fist.

The pod's three other appendages went into action, vacuuming the meat and blood out of him in the same fashion at the very same time. They made a horrendous wet suckling sound...and he folded up beneath them, shriveling and decompressing like one of those garment bags you see on TV where they suck the air out with a vacuum to save space.

He was a big guy, and in a matter of what seemed seconds, it looked as if you could have stuffed what was left in a grocery bag. Even his bones as they dropped away appeared shrunken.

The others started shooting.

Not Seed and Jimbo, but Louise and Hep and Ritz. They were popping away at the plants in every direction, making a bad situation even worse. Frank dropped to one knee because there were rounds zinging in every direction. That's when the weight of the flamethrower seemed to make sense to him.

"WATCH IT!" he called out.

He held the gun in his hands, unlocking the safety catch just as Seed had showed him, and aimed the igniter spout at the Skin-Sucker that had devoured Skeeve. He pressed the firing trigger and a stream of burning fuel engulfed the plant and two others that pressed in from either side.

They went absolutely crazy as they burned.

Emitting high whistling noises like hot teakettles, they spun in circles like flame-licked dervishes. They crackled and popped like corncobs in a fire, scattering blackened bits of themselves in every direction.

Then they quite literally fell apart.

Their death cries got the others all worked up.

They started closing in on the intruders, and it was the most shocking thing Frank had ever seen. *Walking plants,* a voice in the back of his mind said. *Walking fucking plants.* It was mind-boggling. Maybe that term was shopworn, but nothing else seemed to apply.

Suddenly, the grotesque appendages from a dozen Skin-Suckers were whipping through the air. Seed dodged several, sprayed a wall of fire at an approaching mob of plants, driving them back. Hep and Louise and Ritz laid down an impressive field of fire, but the plants were unfazed for the most part from bullets.

Frank saw Hep firing away with her .38 and then one of the appendages snaked out and ripped the gun from her fingers. She stood there wide-eyed and three other appendages found her. One attached its suction mouth to her throat, another to her thigh, the third to her belly. The fourth still had the .38 in its cup, and it was waving it wildly back and forth, as if it could not decide what to do with it.

Hep let out a scream that was short and quick. By the time anyone moved, she was reduced to little more than a skeleton.

Louise went berserk. "HEP!" she cried out. *"HEP!"*

She charged in, emptying her .38 and then going at the nearest plant with her bare hands out of rage. That lasted about two or three seconds before she was snared by its appendages, letting out a manic screeching that was part hate and part pain. Even though the thing had her, she fought. God, how she fought. She clawed and tore at the creature, digging out green clots of its woody flesh and tearing ruts in its hide.

She thrashed.

She jumped.

And the plant responded. As the flaring suction cups held her, its shell opened and she was pulled in, pressed against the spongy pink husk. Immediately, it secreted a sticky fluid that stank like acetone and Louise was quickly trapped in it like a fly in amber. She was glued to the Skin-Sucker.

She almost broke away several times, but the viscous discharge would not let her go. Each time, there was less of her. She let out a final wet scream that sounded like, *"Shhh...shhh...shhh..."* and Frank wondered if she was trying to say *shit.* Her face was a flayed red mask by that point, one arm seemingly stripped down to tendon and bones. She was dissolving. Whether the secretion was a digestive enzyme or a self-defense mechanism, it was highly corrosive by nature, and Louise seemed to melt into it until her flesh had gone liquid and there were only bones.

The bones dropped away, of course, in snotty tangles, but the liquefied remains of Louise were sucked into the thing, absorbed into the seedcase-like chambers of its stem.

Frank and Seed kept pouring out the fire and carving themselves a path through the plants that got out of its way as fast as they could, moving with their ordinary mode of locomotion— they would extend several roots like pseudopods and then the others roots would follow. It was weird, but functional. It made them teeter from side-to-side as they came on.

"RUN! NOW! GO! GO!" Seed shouted and Frank stormed after him.

Ritz almost made it, but a weave of appendages found him. Frank turned back and saw the blood pumping out of him as he was laid raw. Then the plants closed in and he was lost from sight.

Frank and Seed poured on the speed, following Jimbo until they broke free of the forest. Seed turned and emptied the rest of his flamethrower's fuel behind them, cutting off any advance by the plants. Then he tossed the tanks and stumbled on with Frank. They pushed through the dead zone of crumbling trees and grass gone to gray ash, through the bones and husks and blackened, mummified debris of animals that were unrecognizable or were generated by The Food and had never been named. Flakes of dehydrated, dead things fell like snow.

"There," Seed said, gasping.

Frank saw. The church. There was the fucking church. There was St. Matthews, tall and imposing. While the neighborhoods had disintegrated around it, the church, made of blocks of gray stone, still stood high and proud. That was a great thing to see. What was even better is that there were lights on.

This was truly sanctuary.

Frank and Seed climbed the steps together, gasping, out of breath, coughing and wiping grit from their faces. They pounded on the door again and again. Finally, it was opened.

## 120

When the door opened—and, ho, Jesus, it was a big-ass monolithic sort of door—Seed, Jimbo, and Frank fell inside. Into a place of warmth and smooth yellow light that sometimes guttered orange against the walls. Then hands were on them and faces pushing in and people asking questions and it took all the strength they had to let them know that they were the last survivors of a party that came to liberate them and, no, they were not with the Army.

Frank, weary far beyond his years, looked around for a sign of his children and did not see any. There were lots of people, men, women, and children, crowded into the church, but he did not see the ones he loved best.

And the knowledge of that made something inside him sink even lower...if that was even possible. Seed talked non-stop, answering questions and asking quite a few of his own. Frank had to admire him, really admire him. Guy was seventy at least and he had the energy level of a twenty year old. Nothing seemed to stop him or slow him down. There was no friction in his world, only free flight.

Frank sat there while a voice in his head tormented him by saying, *They're not here and you know they're not here. Why don't you quit with your fantasy-land optimism? They're lost to you and will never be found. You let them down. You let yourself down. And you let Janet down. And what do you think of that?* He thought little of it in fact. He just sat there on the floor, too tired to cry and too beaten to lift his head. When hot tea was offered him, he declined.

There was nothing he wanted now.

Nothing at all.

And then a voice said, "It sure as hell took you long enough."

He looked up and Candy was standing there, only he didn't believe it. It was a hallucination or his imagination running away with him. But he could not blink the image of her away. She was there. Big, grinning, the Pennywise tattoo on the back of her hand.

He reached up and gripped it. "The kids...where are the kids?"

Then he heard something that melted all the ice inside him, filling him with warmth and comfort and all the possibility that the world could hold: "IT'S PAPA! IT'S PAPA! IT'S PAPA! IT'S PAPA! IT'S PAPA!"

And then Jasmine was in his arms and he felt the familiar, comforting weight of her and the sweet scent of her and his face was in her hair as tears rolled down his cheeks.

She saw and kissed him again and again, brushing the tears away with a touch that was so much like Janet's that he wept inside and his heart glowed like a hot coal.

"Oh, now!" Jasmine said. "It's not that bad, is it?"

And he laughed. From somewhere deep inside, something held tight in him for so long cracked open like a bird from an egg and emerged, filling him. He laughed and laughed and Candy laughed with him. Jasmine laughed, too, with that look on her face that said, *What's so funny?*

Then she was on his lap and Jerrod was there. Frank reached out for him and Jerrod shook his hand. "We knew you'd come, Dad. We just knew you would." Then he went down to his knees and Frank held him while he shook. There. That was it. This was all Frank ever needed and could ever want and here it was, handed to him. He was happy. He was incredibly happy.

"I bet you have a story to tell," he said to Candy.

"Oh, I've got one...but by the looks of you, I think yours might be just a little bit more interesting."

She went down on her knees and hugged them all at once and Frank kissed her. "Thank you," he said. "Thank you for all you've done."

"I took care of them the way I would have taken care my own," was all she would say about it.

And what more could you ask for?

## 121

"You went down to the farm," Candy began by saying an hour later when the kids were sleeping and they were alone. "We waited up in the woods for hours...but you never came back. Jerrod wanted to go down there. Nothing I could say would stop him. Then some kind of militia was prowling around. Shitkickers with guns. I got the kids out of there."

Which is pretty much what Frank had originally thought might have happened. It was the wise thing to do.

"We found a group of people that were coming here. The National Guard were setting up safe zones in the city. That's how we ended up in this place. They brought us here. People just kept coming. We figured you would, too, if you were, you know, alive."

It was only a few days later that the plants started popping up out of the ground. The Guard was busy transporting people down to Volk Field, but the plants seemed to double in size everyday and it became a madhouse.

"We heard the Army trying to get to us...we heard them dying out there," she explained. "People tried to get out, but none of them ever made it. If the plants didn't get 'em, other things did."

They talked for awhile and he sketched out for her some of the shit he'd been through and what the situation was with the Army, how they had lost quite a few and were waiting for reinforcements.

"Well, let's hope they won't forget about us," she said.

"They won't."

She shrugged. "I don't want to piss on your parade, Frank, but we've been here quite awhile...I'm not sure if they give a shit."

That was something that worried him. According to Candy, they had food and water because there had been a grocery store down the way. It was gone now. It had been torn apart when a wellspring of The Food erupted beneath it. Luckily, they had stocked up beforehand. But, even so, there were only enough canned goods and water for maybe three or four days. Then, there would be nothing left but to try and get out on foot or in cars.

Frank didn't like that idea. On foot was too dangerous, and as far as cars went, everything out there was destroyed. What cars he had seen were wrecked or flipped over or trapped in neighborhoods whose roads no longer had any egress.

"Who's running this place?"

"Tavares, Bill Tavares. He's a pretty good guy. We had a priest here, too, but he went out on an expedition to get through the plants. He never came back." She sighed. "There's about thirty of us now, Frank, and a good number of them are women with their kids. We gotta get these people out of here."

After that, he tracked down Seed and explained the situation, but Seed already knew it. He'd been chatting with Tavares.

He grabbed the olive drab canvas bag he'd brought in with them from behind Army lines. Together, they went up to the belfry. In the fading moonlight, they could see the ravaged city lying to all sides. It was flooded, shattered, infested by fungi and the ever-present Skin-Suckers. The zone of death seemed to go on forever.

"They're not coming in any closer, not yet," Tavares said.

"Even if they do, they can't get in," Seed said.

But Frank wasn't quite so sure.

About a hundred yards from the church, the Skin-Suckers had set-up what almost looked like a defensive perimeter. They were ringed right around the church in a crowded forest, as if they knew there was prey inside and that it might try to escape. They were all of the ten- and fifteen-foot variety, huge and menacing things. Their appendages slithered in the air as if searching for something to latch onto.

There were hundreds of them out there now, and the chorus of noise rose and rose until it filled the world and echoed in their skulls.

"Rain has stopped," Seed said. "Now, we take advantage of the fact."

He opened the sack and brought out a military flare gun that was wrapped in plastic. He had ten rounds for it.

"There's no way they can ignore this," he said. "We'll fire off two or three a night until they come for us."

"What if they don't?"

Seed shook his head. "They will. Trust me, they will. You know, man, after what I've been through in my life, I'm the last guy that would trust people in positions of power or authority, that's why I took precautions."

Frank just stared at him. "What sort of precautions?"

"I got people watching out for us, man. They're going to be putting the pressure on the Army back at the camp to come and get us. They'll be watching for the flares," he said. "But just to be on the safe side, I got a guy whose cousin is a major in the Air National Guard. If the Army doesn't get off their ass, the Air Force will motivate them."

With that, he broke open the flare gun, inserted a cartridge, and hung out of the side of the belfry. He aimed the pistol into the sky and fired the gun. The flare went straight up, several hundred feet above them and went off with a blazing red fireball that drifted off over the ruined city for some time before falling to earth and going out.

"Operation Get-the-Fuck-Outta-Here begins," he said.

Frank smiled. Ever since he found the kids, he was filled with optimism. This would work. It had to work.

### 122

They fired two more flares off before dawn. If anyone had seen them, there was no indication of the same. By that afternoon, a development of a much grimmer variety had taken place. Frank was up in the belfry with Seed, Tavares, and another guy named McKey, who'd been some kind of soldier once. They were searching the ravaged landscape and even the sky, looking for signs that a rescue of some sort was coming.

They saw nothing.

About the time they were going to call it quits, something did happen.

The earth around the church began to rumble. Tremors passed through it that shook everyone off their feet. They came in seismic waves, each worse than the last until it seemed like the building was going to break free of its foundation. They could hear people crying out below, shouting and screaming. Things crashed and shattered. The building groaned and squealed with fatigue. The belfry seemed to sway back and forth. The whole damn church was coming apart, it seemed. The earth under them began to rumble. Tremors shook the world.

It had been no freak earthquake but something of a much darker variety. About half a mile from the church, the ground was split right open in a jagged abyss that must have easily been hundreds of yards across.

"Look!" he said. *"Look!"*

From the belfry, they could see north, south, east, and west. And what they saw was that the chasm extended completely around the church. It was a deep, ragged gash without surcease. The church was literally sitting on an island now. There was not so much as a finger of land connecting it to the rest of Montpalk or an earthen bridge of any sort. They were trapped. Completely trapped. Unless the Army got off their dead asses and choppered them out of there, there literally was no escape. The church and the land it sat on was their fortress now, their fortification, their redoubt.

The church shook again as tremors rolled over the island. Not as violently as before, but in Frank's mind, this is how it would end—the ground would fall away bit by bit, shelf by shelf, until the church itself was swallowed up in the subterranean darkness of the chasm.

But the land wasn't falling away.

No, not at all. Something was happening in the crevice, something was rising with force and power and kinetic energy. The Food. It bubbled up out of the chasm in a great frothing, doughy white sea that burst its banks and flooded inward several hundred feet. It slopped and quivered like Jell-O in a bowl. It was alive, quivering and undulant, ready to feed the world and change it into something perfectly horrible and perfectly blasphemous.

"If anyone has ideas about what the fuck we should do," Seed said, "I'm all ears."

But no one spoke.

No one said anything. It was as if Armageddon were approaching and they had front row seats to it. The only hopeful development was that The Food had risen no more. The idea of it flooding the church, of being drowned and entombed in that vile stuff was unthinkable.

But that didn't seem to be a danger.

At least, not yet.

### 123

The good thing is that no one was hurt in the tremor. Physically, they were in good shape, but psychologically they were shaky. Very shaky. Frank had to admit that Tavares was doing a good job of holding things together. He was a born leader. Like Seed, he had a calming effect on those under his watch. But his glue was weakening. They had been trapped at the church for weeks now, and anytime somebody tried to make a breakout, they didn't get very far. These people needed something to cling to besides hope because that was beginning to run real thin now that The Food had hemmed them in.

"This is getting bad," Candy said to him. "I'm not one to give in but, shit, if they don't pluck us out of here pretty damn soon, we're going to drown in that stuff."

"Something's gonna break here," he told her. "I feel it."

And that wasn't bullshit, because he *did* feel something. But whether that was good or bad, he really couldn't say. Only that it was building.

### 124

By late afternoon, nothing had happened, and Frank began to wonder if he was just imagining things. God knew, his nerves were frayed and his mental gears were nearly stripped, so sensing something that wasn't really there would not have been a great surprise.

Up in the belfry with Seed, he watched as the rain fell in a relentless dismal curtain, flooding the world, turning it gray and hazy. A dirty mist rose from the ground, obscuring the wreckage of the city in the distance. What sunlight made it through was dirty and dull as if filtered through a dusty windowpane.

*Wait...what's that?*

Squinting, Frank caught sight of something moving beyond the crowded forest of Skin-Suckers, something unbelievably gigantic. It was like a great dark mountain moving ever forward. But something that size...was he really seeing it or were his eyes playing tricks?

No, there was definitely something there.

*It's real enough,* he told himself, *and it's coming in this direction. And not by accident. If you believe nothing, you better believe that.*

He tried to swallow down his unease, but it was lodged in his throat like a lump of tar. "Seed," he said, hoping his voice didn't betray the raw terror that was expanding in his chest, "out there...am I really seeing that?"

He knew he was, yet he needed to downplay it and not just for Seed but for himself. Especially for himself.

Seed was looking now, too, leaning out of the belfry tower, squinting like a sailor staring off across an angry sea into vast distances at unknown horizons.

"Shit," he said, swallowing repeatedly. Beneath his long gray beard, the Adam's apple in his sinewy throat bobbed up and down. "Look...look at the size of it."

Frank was seeing more of it now, but not enough to even remotely identify what it might be, but enough so that its gargantuan dimensions began to fill his mind with the most awful sense of rising anxiety. As it came on, he thought of the weapons they had—handguns and carbines, rifles and one flamethrower—and he nearly laughed with cold, clammy fear at the futility of it all. Trying to take down that moving edifice with what they had would have been like trying to slay Goliath not with a sling but with spitballs and a pea-shooter.

The plants became visibly agitated as the thing bore down on them. They were practically shrieking, moving about ponderously, trying to get out of its way. Whatever the creature was, it paid no more mind to them than a man does to the ants he steps on as he strolls down a sidewalk.

Then, out of the haze and driving rain, Frank saw it.

Seed saw it, too. He gasped.

It was a titanic creeping mass that he at first thought was an amoeba inflated to cosmic proportions, a creeping, oozing, fluidic nightmare.

But that wasn't quite it.

It was a mammoth, undulant mound of creeping horror that seemed to glide ever forward with a slithery sort of noise. It was taller than a two-story building and many hundreds of feet across. Much like the plants themselves, it was armored in a beaded yellow-green shell or carapace that was formed of hundreds of rubbery interlocking plates. It was bifurcated down the center into two pulsing hemispheres like a human brain. It had no eyes, no discernible face or recognizable anatomy, only a dozen boneless tentacular limbs that were a drab, warty yellow, rising from it like massive serpents. They terminated in enormous bell-shaped suckers that were like crusty brown lips outside and a striated juicy pink within.

Frank did not think he was exaggerating when he told himself that each of the writhing, vermiform limbs were easily several hundred feet in length or that the suckers at their ends were big around as the mouths of train tunnels.

It rolled right over the tops of the plants, grinding them to mulch beneath it. As Seed and Frank watched, riveted to the floor with a numb, mindless terror, they saw it bridge the crevice of The Food like a child stepping over a curb.

It crawled.

It slithered.

It secreted a gushing wave of jelly before it that it slid forward on like a slug with its attendant slime.

It made a strange warbling sort of din that echoed with disturbing continual sucking/pulsating noises that sounded as if they were reverberating through a subterranean tunnel.

Whatever it was, it went right up Frank's spine. It didn't seem like any sound a living creature could create.

He thought he was going mad.

He had seen horrendous, repulsive things in those many weeks since fleeing the farm, but nothing like this, nothing so utterly grotesque, alien, or aberrant as this mountainous, squirming monstrosity.

It was coming for them.

It was coming to feed on the survivors in the church.

And there was nothing that could stop it.

## 125

Frank and Seed came bounding down the stairs into the church to sound the alarm, but it had already been raised. A crowd of people were peering through the huge oaken doors as that palpitating mound sped towards St. Matthew's. Tavares was busy herding people towards the altar and the rectory beyond. He was telling them to close the doors.

Jasmine and Jerrod were calling out to Frank as Candy pushed them past the altar to the rectory door.

"Go! Go!" he cried above the din of voices shouting and whimpering. He raced towards the front of the church. "CLOSE THOSE FUCKING DOORS!"

They were finally shut and bolted, the vestibule doors as well. The church was shaking as the creature approached. Frank followed Seed towards the altar, the others lagging considerably behind. The seriousness and dread peril of the situation was like a switch thrown—they were bounding down the nave now, knocking others aside and going right over the top of those that had fallen. Some were leapfrogging the pews.

Panic had set in and it was a stampede.

At the rectory door, Frank shouted, "HURRY! FOR GODSAKE, HURRY!"

Then the creature hit the church.

The entire structure trembled, seismic waves knocking people right off their feet. The group that had been watching the creature's approach were down.

And Frank knew they weren't going to make it.

He started back for them and Seed yanked him away.

"It's too late!" he said in a high hysterical voice. "It's too damn late for them!"

And it was.

## 126

The high, arched stained glass windows to either side of the church exploded inwards in a glittering, multi-colored barrage of flying glass.

The colossal suckers came sliding in, the mouths opening and closing with a horrible slobbering sound. Their pink insides had no teeth, but were gilled like the undersides of mushrooms. The vestibule doors blew off their hinges and another snaking limb slid down the nave, its sucker throbbing.

What happened then was almost unbelievable.

The squeaking/pulsating noise of the creature was so loud it was nearly incapacitating. The bell suckers began to open and close with frightening rapidity, and the result of that was a shrieking tempest of wind that rushed through the church, creating a storm of glass shards and prayer books, water bottles and cardboard boxes and blankets and all manner of spinning debris. People were sucked off their feet and sucked off the floor, flipping end over end as that tornadic suctioning force took hold of them, drawing them towards the hungry bell-mouths.

Frank saw a woman and a man pulled into the sucker that came down the nave. A split-second before they would have been ingested, they broke apart like dry clay, atomizing into a mist of blood and bone and flesh that was sucked away.

A dozen people were taken that way.

Frank had to brace himself in the rectory doorframe so he wasn't caught in the vortex. Even then, Seed had to hang onto him as he was being likewise held by Jimbo. Frank reached out for a screaming woman who was crawling towards him with great exertion.

He clutched her hand.

He held it firmly in his grip.

Then her body went airborne as if gravity had suddenly been canceled out. Frank couldn't hold her. There was just no way. He felt her slipping away as the cycling fury claimed her. He saw the stark look of animal fright in her eyes and heard her voice screaming, *"HELP ME! DEAR GOD, HELP ME!"* and then she was yanked away into the cyclone. She was sucked into one of the bell-mouths, breaking apart like cigarette ash.

Then Jimbo dragged both Frank and Seed through the doorway and the door slammed shut. Beyond it, it sounded like a hurricane was rushing through the church.

### 127

"Thanks, Jimbo," Frank managed to say as they filed down the cellar stairs from the rectory.

Jimbo, of course, nodded.

Then, to everyone's surprise, he muttered, "Pennywise."

Frank knew what he meant. It translated out roughly as, *Get your ass over to your kids. They need you.* If it hadn't have been for Jimbo's impressive strength, Frank doubted whether he or Seed would have made it.

The basement of the church consisted of a long community room that was used for funeral lunches, wedding buffets, and church social groups. At the far end was the kitchen and a storeroom beyond. It was in these areas that everyone was packed (quite literally like sardines in a can).

Frank scooped Jasmine and Jerrod into his arms, holding their shivering bodies as Candy held onto him and countless other bodies pressed in from all sides. People were sobbing and praying out loud in high, damaged voices. Others were nearly hysterical with fear while still others tried to calm them.

St. Matthew's was shaking and shifting as if it were riding out an earthquake. It groaned and creaked. Timbers squealed and split, things cracking open inside the walls. Ceiling tiles fell. Plaster dust puffed into the air in great clouds. Above, up in the church itself, things were falling, crashing and shattering. It was coming apart. The survivors were going to be buried alive in its rubble. The cellar would become a mass tomb.

A few lanterns taken from above still burned, but their light was dusty and dim. The basement windows, far too small for the bell-suckers to fit through, were black from the bulk of the creature pressing up against them. It had engulfed St. Matthew's like an antibody engulfing a disease germ.

"Papa, Papa, Papa," Jasmine sobbed. "Please make it go away...oh, please..."

"It will," he lied. "It will."

And then, miraculously, it did.

## 128

Silence.

Other than a few things creaking and falling above, there was nothing. The old church was groaning with fatigue, but it was still standing. That was something. Hell, it was everything.

Nobody made a sound.

They were like frightened deer in the woods, afraid that the slightest movement or sound would alert a nearby predator. Frank waited with the others. He held his children and could feel them drawing shallow breaths, feel the beat of their hearts. He couldn't imagine anything in this world that could please him more.

After about ten minutes, Seed said, "Well, painful as it might be, somebody's got to go up there and have a look. Any takers?"

"I'll go," Frank said.

Jimbo nodded.

"It's the three of us then," Seed said.

"I'll come with," Jerrod said.

"No, you won't!" Jasmine told him, ever the little mother.

"Son," Frank said. "Let us go up first. If it's safe, I'll give you a holler. If that thing's still out there, the less people the better."

Frank couldn't see Jerrod's face, but he knew he wasn't happy with the decision. He accepted it, but he didn't like it. A month ago, he would have complained about it, but not now. His tenure with Candy had done him some good.

"Papa..." Jasmine started.

He kissed her. "It's okay, Duck. We're just going to look."

She didn't care for the idea either, but like her brother, she accepted it. Frank did not like being separated from them, but this had to be done. He followed Seed and Jimbo out of the kitchen and across the community room. They opened the basement door and listened.

Nothing.

They went halfway up the steps and paused there, too.

Still nothing.

They repeated the process at the door at the top. Nothing concerned them. Same thing in the rectory hall. They went to the door leading out into the church. It was still closed, though somewhat buckled in its frame. With considerable effort, Jimbo got it open. They stepped out into the church into a deathly silence punctuated only by the subtle creaking of the building itself.

The church was a mess.

Pews were torn up and cast about, split open and shattered. There was refuse everywhere. The stained glass windows were gone. There were two great holes punched in the roof high above. The walls were cracked with jagged rents. The altar was smashed. There was drying blood sprayed about.

They moved down the nave, sidestepping the wreckage. Frank saw an arm and a couple scattered bones. There were copious amounts of a clear, dripping slime everywhere. The smell was gassy and foul.

The vestibule doors were torn off. The huge outer doors were hanging by their hinges just barely.

"Let's go see," Seed said.

They crept up to the mangled outer doors and looked out into the world. The creature had indeed withdrawn, leaving a trail of jelly two or three feet deep in its wake. It was still there. It had retreated across the crevice to where the plants had been but were no more.

"Hell's it doing?" Frank asked.

Seed just shook his head. It didn't seem to be doing anything. One noticeable thing was that its color was no longer a yellow-green but a sickly blue like decaying flesh set with white bubbly bands. Another was that its limbs were drooping like heat-parched flowers. Even the suckers looked wilted.

"What do you make of that?" Seed said.

"Either it's dying or it's gone dormant," Frank told him. "Take your pick."

Then it began to move. It began to quiver minutely, then to shake. The limbs dropped to the ground like dead snakes. The mound itself trembled with spasms. And was it Frank's imagination or did it appear to be inflating like a helium balloon, swelling, distending, stretching with an unpleasant rubbery sound? They all clearly heard a hissing coming from it. Plumes of steam issued from seams in its carapace.

Then they heard a screaming, shrieking sort of noise.

But it wasn't coming from the creature; it was coming from the sky overhead. Four jets passed high above like hunting wasps, zipping through the haze with great speed and agility, and Frank had no doubt that they were zeroing in on the creature or what it was now becoming.

"That's the Air Guard, I'll bet," Seed said. "Didn't I tell you my people would come through for us?"

Frank was as excited by the prospect as he was disturbed by what was happening to the creature. Its shell was making a squealing, straining sound...and then it split wide open from the fissure that ran down its center. The entire thing seemed to be breaking apart, cracking open like an egg and that was appropriate because something was being born from it.

Frank saw it happen.

So did Seed and Jimbo.

If they hadn't been with him, he would have thought he was losing his mind. The shell, the casing, the outer plating of the creature—whatever it really was—fractured wetly with a horrendous noise like breaking ice, revealing a soft inner core that looked as juicy as the pulp of a grapefruit. This, too, split open and sloughed free with a mountainous slime-wave gushing of noxious pale green afterbirth that sloshed and coagulated like mint jelly. There was a mucid membranous envelope just beneath that was webbed or sutured like a skull in intricate patterns. This sheared as well.

There was something in it.

Something that had been coming to term.

And now it was being born.

They saw it emerge with a slopping wet sound like entrails emptied from a bucket. It pushed itself out, netted with strands of stringy afterbirth. It was a gigantic thing that seemed to grow larger as it climbed free, a flabby and maggoty fetal monstrosity of pulpous white meat. It was some obscene, repellent travesty of a human embryo, pulsing and black-veined, wrinkled and convoluted, its swollen belly set with bloated suckers as big around as wagon wheels. Its immense head seemed to droop forward from its own weight, bulbous and gleaming, the flesh fungoid and oozing. It had two immense eyes like black shiny glass and a jagged mouth of gnarled yellow teeth that was stretched across the seamed face like a trench.

It wormed its way free, reaching out with one flaccid three-fingered hand. The other arm was a shriveled stump. It had no legs, just a broad, spade-shaped tail like that of a tadpole.

Though it was vaguely semi-human in appearance, it was certainly not human any more than it was necessarily mammalian or reptilian. If anything, it was a wriggling invertebrate fetal horror blown up to epic proportions and quite possibly, the progenitor of a chimeric, loathsome species that, given time, may well have exterminated the human race.

But it wasn't given that time.

The Air Guard jets zoomed down at it and it seemed to see them coming, letting out a bawling, whining squeal of pure undiluted hate as they released their payload of cluster bombs on it. They were incendiaries. They went off in rapid succession, WHUMP, WHUMP, *WHUMP-WHUMP-WHUMP!*, releasing an incinerating fire-storm that completely engulfed the nightmare spawn, rolling clouds of burning phosphorus rising up eighty feet. The spawn screeched with agony and deranged wrath as it sizzled and cooked and was cremated right down to whatever bones it might have had. It struggled vainly, shrieking and shrilling, then finally sinking into the lake of fire, sputtering and popping and cracking open, everything inside going to steam.

"GET DOWN!" Seed cried out as more bombs fell.

He and Frank and Jimbo hit the floor, and a searing heat wave hit the church, igniting withered bushes forty feet away. The heat was so intense that Frank thought it would burn the hair off his head and suck his eyeballs right out of their sockets. Then it passed and there was a sickening blowback from the cremated spawn that stank of scalded flesh and burnt hair.

They pulled themselves up and stood there, shakily, watching the spawn blaze like a bonfire, a blackened and twisted form that was barely visible through the consuming wall of flames.

But it wasn't just the spawn that was affected, but the crevice filled with The Food. It burned, too, boiling to steam and flaking away into the air.

By then, everyone was rushing up from below and Frank heard Jerrod shout, "Dad! Dad! Are you all right?"

Frank put his arm around him. "Son, I'm better than I have been in a long time."

Then Jasmine was clinging to him and the world seemed right. Everyone was staring out at the massive bonfire in the distance. Neither Frank nor Seed tried to put any of it into words. What they had seen was something they would never forget and probably never speak of for the rest of their lives.

Frank could feel the optimism and camaraderie of the survivors returning. It was real, nearly palpable, and infectious. They all stood there for some time as the flames burned, purifying their world. Nobody spoke for about ten minutes, and that was when they heard the choppers coming in to pull them out of there.

"Candy said she'd like to come back to the farm with us," Jerrod said. Apparently, there was a bond between them now.

"Can she?" Jasmine asked.

"Kids, if we had a farm to go back to, she'd certainly be welcome," he told them. "But wherever we end up, she's invited."

Then the choppers were touching down and soldiers were racing around, securing the area, as others began to lead the survivors to the waiting birds. It was time to go. It was finally time to go. Medics came, checking people out, attending to the wounded, the sick, and the elderly.

"You ready for a helicopter ride?" Frank asked Jasmine who beamed up at him.

"Sure, but I need to pee first!" she exclaimed.

"Good God, girl, you've a bladder like a thimble."

"I do not!"

He followed her back inside as Seed and Jimbo led the others to the waiting choppers. It had been a long, ugly pull, but Frank had the feeling that it was coming to an end. Clutching his daughter's delicate hand in his own, he was certain of it.

—The End—

# CHECK OUT OTHER GREAT KAIJU NOVELS

## KAIJU WINTER
by **Jake Bible**

The Yellowstone super volcano has begun to erupt, sending North America into chaos and the rest of the world into panic. People are dangerous and desperate to escape the oncoming mega-eruption, knowing it will plunge the continent, and the world, into a perpetual ashen winter. But no matter how ready humanity is, nothing can prepare them for what comes out of the ash: Kaiju!

## RAIJU
by **K.H. Koehler**

His home destroyed by a rampaging kaiju, Kevin Takahashi and his father relocate to New York City where Kevin hopes the nightmare is over. Soon after his arrival in the Big Apple, a new kaiju emerges. Qilin is so powerful that even the U.S. Military may be unable to contain or destroy the monster. But Kevin is more than a ragged refugee from the now defunct city of San Francisco. He's also a Keeper who can summon ancient, demonic god-beasts to do battle for him, and his creature to call is Raiju, the oldest of the ancient Kami. Kevin has only a short time to save the city of New York. Because Raiju and Qilin are about to clash, and after the dust settles, there may be no home left for any of them!

# CHECK OUT OTHER GREAT
# KAIJU NOVELS

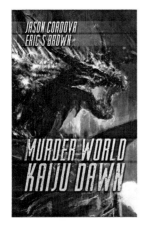

## MURDER WORLD I KAIJU DAWN
## by Jason Cordova
## & Eric S Brown

Captain Vincente Huerta and the crew of the Fancy have been hired to retrieve a valuable item from a downed research vessel at the edge of the enemy's space.
It was going to be an easy payday.
But what Captain Huerta and the men, women and alien under his command didn't know was that they were being sent to the most dangerous planet in the galaxy.
Something large, ancient and most assuredly evil resides on the planet of Gorgon IV. Something so terrifying that man could barely fathom it with his puny mind. Captain Huerta must use every trick in the book, and possibly write an entirely new one, if he wants to escape Murder World

## KAIJU ARMAGEDDON
## by Eric S. Brown

The attacks began without warning. Civilian and Military vessels alike simply vanished upon the waves. Crypto-zoologist Jerry Bryson found himself swept up into the chaos as the world discovered that the legendary beasts known as Kaiju are very real. Armies of the great beasts arose from the oceans and burrowed their way free of the Earth to declare war upon mankind. Now Dr. Bryson may be the human race's last hope in stopping the Kaiju from bringing civilization to its knees.
This is not some far distant future. This is not some alien world. This is the Earth, here and now, as we know it today, faced with the greatest threat its ever known. The Kaiju Armageddon has begun.

# CHECK OUT OTHER GREAT KAIJU NOVELS

## KAIJU SPAWN
## by David Robbins
## & Eric S Brown

Wally didn't believe it was really the end of the world until he saw the Kaiju with his own eyes. The great beasts rose from the Earth's oceans, laying waste to civilization. Now Wally must fight his way across the Kaiju ravaged wasteland of modern day America in search of his daughter. He is the only hope she has left . . . and the clock is ticking.

From authors David Robbins (Endworld) and Eric S Brown (Kaiju Apocalypse), Kaiju Spawn is an action packed, horror tale of desperate determination and the battle to overcome impossible odds.

## KUA MAU
## by Mark Onspaugh

The Spider Islands. A mysterious ship has completed a treacherous journey to this hidden island chain. Their mission: to capture the legendary monster, Kua'Mau. Thinking they are successful, they sail back to the United States, where the terrifying creature will be displayed at a new luxury casino in Las Vegas. But the crew has made a horrible mistake - they did not trap Kua'Mau, they took her offspring. Now hot on their heels comes a living nightmare, a two hundred foot, one hundred ton tentacled horror, Kua'Mau, Kaiju Mother of Wrath, who will stop at nothing to safeguard her young. As she tears across California heading towards Vegas, she leaves a monumental body-count in her wake, and not even the U.S. military or private black ops can stop this city-crushing, havoc-wreaking monstrous mother of all Kaiju as she seeks her revenge.

CPSIA information can be obtained
at www.ICGtesting.com
Printed in the USA
LVOW07s0806060817
543996LV00001B/48/P